She glanced up to find Jensen Crawley watching her, closely, his expression blank.

Had she overstepped? Just because she didn't buy into the whole generations-old Briscoe-Crawley feud didn't mean he didn't. It's not like the two of them had ever talked about it. *Not that we've had all that many conversations, period.* For all she knew, he could think like his father did now: the Briscoes were the enemy. "Is this okay?" She nodded at Samantha and Harvey for clarification.

"It's more than okay." He smiled as he turned his attention to his daughter and the dog. "Samantha's usually very wary around animals. This is...nice."

Oh, that smile. That hadn't changed. Not one bit.

A sharp whistle reached them, announcing the arrival of her brothers. The sudden tension in the air told Mabel all she needed to know. People might grow and change, but the grudge between their two families wouldn't.

Dear Reader,

Welcome back to Garrison, Texas. The little town, nestled in the Hill Country, is bustling with activity as its citizens rally to save erste Baum, a community landmark, from developers. The old tree is the heart of the region—with many a wedding, birthday and festival taking place in the shade of its huge branches.

That's why Mabel Briscoe has come home. She has never been one to back away from a cause, and she's not going to start now. Collecting signatures and supporting the Save the Tree movement has her out and about, falling in love with her hometown all over again—and the people who live there. People like Jensen Crawley and his adorable little girl, Samantha.

Too bad the Briscoes and Crawleys have been rivals for generations, and making friends with Samantha, or Jensen, is out of the question. Even though she and Jensen seem drawn to one another, Mabel knows the truth. Saving erste Baum will take work, but it's doable. Healing the Briscoe-Crawley feud, however, is all but impossible—no matter what her heart might want. I hope you enjoy your stay in Garrison and make plans to visit again real soon.

Happy reading,

Sasha Summers

HEARTWARMING

The Wrong Cowboy

—

Sasha Summers

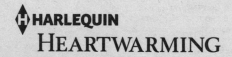

HARLEQUIN®
HEARTWARMING™

ISBN-13: 978-1-335-42654-3

The Wrong Cowboy

Copyright © 2021 by Sasha Best

Recycling programs
for this product may
not exist in your area.

This edition published by arrangement with Harlequin Books S.A.

For questions and comments about the quality of this book, please contact us at CustomerService@Harlequin.com.

Harlequin Enterprises ULC
22 Adelaide St. West, 40th Floor
Toronto, Ontario M5H 4E3, Canada
www.Harlequin.com

Printed in U.S.A.

Sasha Summers grew up surrounded by books. Her passions have always been storytelling, romance and travel—passions she's used to write more than twenty romance novels and novellas. Now a bestselling and award-winning author, Sasha continues to fall a little in love with each hero she writes. From easy-on-the-eyes cowboys, sexy alpha-male werewolves, to heroes of truly mythic proportions, she believes that everyone should have their happily-ever-after—in fiction and real life.

Sasha lives in the suburbs of the Texas Hill Country with her amazing family. She looks forward to hearing from fans and hopes you'll visit her online: on Facebook at sashasummersauthor, on Twitter, @sashawrites, or email her at sashasummersauthor@gmail.com.

Books by Sasha Summers

Harlequin Heartwarming

The Cowboys of Garrison, Texas

The Rebel Cowboy's Baby

Harlequin Special Edition

Texas Cowboys & K-9s

The Rancher's Forever Family
Their Rancher Protector

Visit the Author Profile page
at Harlequin.com for more titles.

Dedicated to Dr. Bonnie Beaver at Texas A&M University. You've inspired many of my animal-loving heroines—as you've inspired countless veterinary students along their educational journeys. Thank you!

CHAPTER ONE

"HAVE YOU SIGNED the petition yet?" Mabel Briscoe stood outside the Garrison Family Grocery Store with a clipboard in one hand, fanning herself with the straw cowboy hat she held in the other.

"Why, Mabel Briscoe! Is that you?" Barbara Eldridge paused and came around her full grocery cart to hug her. "Look at you. Like a ray of sunshine."

"I am wearing yellow." She smiled, pointing down at her attire. She wore a bright yellow sundress, cowboy boots and one of the large green buttons the Garrison Ladies Guild had made for fundraising. It read, "Save erste Baum. Say No to Quik Stop and Shop."

"Well, you look lovely," Barbara said, nodding with approval. "And, yes, I signed the petition—proudly. But I appreciate you standing out here, getting more signatures."

"I should have known, you being on the

Ladies Guild and all." Mabel tucked a strand of hair behind her ear. "That's why I came home. I want to help." And the only reason she was standing directly beneath the midday sun, melting.

Garrison was home to what was purported to be the oldest tree in Texas. Named erste Baum or First Tree, the tree and the large tract of land around it had always been for public use—a part of the town heritage and a place where the community often gathered. Now, the new city manager was talking to a big-box chain store about selling the prime real estate—erste Baum and all.

"You've always had such a big and giving heart, Mabel. I know having you on our side will give us an extra advantage." Barbara Eldridge winked. "The more signatures we get on this cease and desist petition, the better."

"Yes, ma'am." So far, she'd collected three pages of names—and been hugged and welcomed home more times than she could count. It did make standing in the sun more bearable, but Mabel would have stood out in the rain if it helped. She couldn't think of a better place to stand to catch all the Garrison citizens as they went in and out of the town's only grocery store—even if the temperature was rising. "You should probably get your groceries out of the sun." She nodded at the container of ice cream sticking out of one shopping bag.

"Oh, goodness, yes." Mrs. Eldridge patted her cheek. "I look forward to catching up with you and hearing all about your... What was it again? Donkeys?"

"Mustangs." Mabel smiled. "Wild mustangs."

"Yes, that's right." She nodded. "You take care now. I'll see you at Miss Martha's birthday next weekend?"

Martha Zeigler was the galvanizing force behind the Save the First Tree movement. As the richest person in Garrison, the older, highly opinionated, prickly woman was someone folks tended to accommodate. Miss Martha never celebrated her birthday, as a result no one knew exactly how old she was, but she was doing everything she could to bring attention to the plight of the beloved tree. That was the only reason for her last-minute idea to throw herself a massive birthday party beneath the branches of the First Tree this upcoming weekend—on the heels of last weekend's well-publicized and awareness-boosting community picnic.

Miss Martha was hoping for an even bigger
turnout for her birthday. Mabel suspected it
would be a bigger crowd, too, out of sheer
curiosity. "I wouldn't miss it."

"It's sure to be quite the production. Martha wouldn't have it any other way." Mrs.
Eldridge chuckled. "And good luck getting
those signatures."

Once Mrs. Eldridge was heading across
the parking lot, Mabel went back to fanning herself with her cowboy hat. Harvey,
her brother's massive part Great Dane, part
Great Pyrenees, eyed her from his spot in the
shade against the side of the building.

"You're no help." She shielded her eyes,
smiling at the dog's massive yawn—not in
the least offended by her rebuke.

The doors slid open, and a cool gust of
air rolled over her, giving her a moment's
reprieve from the stifling heat.

"And she said…she said… Daddy, are ya
listenin'?" A little girl with a head full of
black curls came skipping out, pausing to
stare back over her shoulder. "Daddy?"

"Right here, Samantha." The deep voice
was all warmth and amusement.

For Mabel, the sound of that voice had
her heart hammering and her whole body

tightening—torn between running and hiding. But her legs and feet wouldn't cooperate. She was frozen in place. Wide-eyed. Staring. A ball of anticipation and distress formed in her stomach and worked its way up to lodge in her throat. Every bit of her seemed to coil up, waiting for…

Jensen Crawley stepped outside and Mabel had to bite into her lower lip to stop from sighing aloud. Jensen was, to Mabel, the most beautiful man she'd ever laid eyes on.

He'd always been…*different*. Since she lived with four brothers and an uncle who were constantly teasing and arguing and making too much noise, she'd found Jensen's careful use of words and more serious nature highly appealing. He was kind; his smile was shy and warm. And his hair… The girls at school had all been so jealous of his hair. Dirty blond with streaks of gold running through his silky curls. Most of the time, he'd kept his hair short but Mabel had always liked his hair longer— usually right before he'd go for a trim. And, since he was a head taller than everyone and he had that hair, she'd always been able to find him in a crowd.

Because I was always looking for him.

Even though Jensen was the one boy in all of Garrison she shouldn't have been looking for. He was a Crawley. She was a Briscoe. That simple fact was enough for them both to keep their distance. And since that hadn't changed... *I shouldn't be looking now, either.*

From her quick assessment now, it appeared he was, for the most part, unchanged. Older, of course. Taller, too. And thicker. He wasn't the string bean he'd been in high school. Now—she swallowed—his muscles were obvious.

While Mabel was having thoughts about things she shouldn't care one whit about, the little girl with the curls stopped right in front of her. "Hey. I'm Samantha, what's your name?" The little girl stared up at her with dark blue eyes—almost black.

You have your father's eyes. "I'm Mabel." The little girl smiled. "It's nice to meet you, Samantha." She held out her hand to shake.

Harvey, who loved kids, hopped up to trot across the concrete sidewalk.

Samantha backed up, her bright smile fading as she ran around her father and hid behind his legs. "Daddy, is that a bear?"

"No, little miss, that's a dog. One big dog." Jensen Crawley reached around to pat her on the head. "No worries. Miss Mabel's always been able to talk to animals. I'm sure she'd say something if the dog meant us any harm." Jensen's deep blue eyes scanned her face quickly, his smile hesitant. "Probably."

Mabel put her hat on, smoothing her hair from her shoulders. "Probably?" Her laugh was nervous. *Why?* Why was she nervous? It had been years since she'd last seen him— let alone talked to him. He was practically a stranger. *Heat exhaustion.* That was what it was. *I need water.*

He touched the rim of his hat. "It's been a while."

Mabel nodded, her gaze falling to Samantha. "I'd say at least…five years?"

"Hey, I'm five." Samantha held up five fingers. "Almost six."

"Almost. Only ten more months to go." Jensen's gaze fell to the button pinned to the wide strap of her sundress. "Taking up the cause?"

"Of course." Mabel hugged the clipboard. "When Uncle Felix told me, I thought he was joking. I'm still…in shock."

"It won't happen." He shook his head.

"I hope you're right." Which reminded her of why she was standing there, in the sun, hugging a clipboard. *Way to be on the ball, Mabel.* "I know a way you can make sure it doesn't happen." She smiled sweetly and held out the clipboard.

"What's that?" Samantha wasn't budging from behind Jensen—even though Harvey was sitting, patiently, tongue lolling out of his mouth and his thick plume of a tail wagging in greeting.

"It's a petition," Mabel explained. "We are trying to save erste Baum."

"The tree?" Samantha asked, her gaze bouncing from Harvey to Mabel's clipboard. "Is it sick? Does it need medicine?"

"No. Not exactly." Mabel crouched, holding out the clipboard. "This paper says whoever signs it doesn't want anything to happen to the First Tree. I'm trying to get a whole bunch of people to put their names here so we can take it to the city council—the people that make decisions."

"Oh." Samantha nodded, running her fingers over the paper. "Daddy needs to sign it?"

"Only if he wants to." Mabel was aware that Harvey was now belly-crawling, inch by inch, toward her side—closer to Samantha. "What is it, Harvey?" She paused, watching as Harvey turned to look at her, cocking his head to one side. His whimper was soft. "You want me to introduce you to Samantha?"

Harvey's tail wagged.

"He said that?" Samantha asked, moving back behind Jensen, but peering around his legs with eyes round as saucers.

"More or less." Mabel gave Harvey a good scratch behind the ear. "I promise you, Samantha, he's not a bear. But if he was one, he'd be a big ole teddy bear. I know he's on the big side, but he'd never hurt you."

Jensen's hand dropped to rest on Samantha's shoulder. "Mabel knows."

Samantha was studying Harvey now, not convinced. "But he looks like…like a *polar* bear."

Mabel turned, studying the dog. "You know, you're right. He does." She faced Samantha. "But did you know polar bears only live in the Arctic? That's very far away. And much colder than Garrison. So, even though he might look like one, I can assure you Harvey is not a polar bear."

"And zoos," Samantha said. "Daddy took me to the zoo and there was a polar bear there."

Mabel glanced at Harvey again. "Zoos,

too. They do all sorts of work to keep animals safe and healthy."

Samantha nodded. "And they have yummy popcorn, too."

Mabel laughed. "Do they? It's been a long time since I've been."

"You should go." Samantha watched as Harvey continued his snail-paced belly-crawl, scooching closer to her. "So, you're sure he's not a polar bear?"

"One hundred percent. Cross my heart." She drew a cross over her heart with her fingers.

"Okay, then, I guess I can meet him." Samantha shrugged.

"Harvey," Mabel called, patting him when he sat up straight and tall at her side, "Harvey, this is Samantha. You use your best manners and say hello." She held his broad head in her hands and stared into his eyes. "Nice and gentle, okay?"

Harvey blinked.

"Samantha, this is Harvey—the not polar bear." Mabel watched as Samantha leaned forward, hand outstretched, to touch Harvey on the nose. "It's wet." She smiled, stepping around from behind Jensen so her hand could slide up and over his head. "Ooh, he has soft fur."

"Doesn't he?" Mabel nodded, staying close. Samantha was doing well, but it was clear the little girl was uncertain.

Harvey must have sensed it, too, because he flopped onto his back and offered up his tummy.

"He's says he trusts you." Mabel pointed. "A dog does that to tell you that you're in charge and he just wants to be friends." She glanced up to find Jensen Crawley watching her closely, his expression blank.

What did that mean? Had she overstepped? Just because she didn't buy into the whole generations-old Briscoe-Crawley feud didn't mean he didn't. It wasn't like the two of them had ever talked about it. *Not that we've had all that many conversations, period.* For all she knew, he could think like his father did now: the Briscoes were the enemy. "Is this okay?" She nodded at Samantha and Harvey, for clarification.

"It's more than okay." He shook his head, a crease forming between his brows as he turned his attention to his daughter and Harvey.

Harvey, good boy that he was, was perfectly still while Samantha carefully inspected his paws. When she seemed satisfied, she reached out a tentative hand to stroke the thick fur on Harvey's tummy. "Nice, Harvey," she said softly, making Harvey's tail wag.

"Samantha's usually very wary around animals. This is...nice." He shook his head, that slow smile returning to his face.

"Are you friends with Daddy?" Samantha asked.

Mabel tore her gaze from Jensen. "Um..." *I used to be madly in love with your father but, as a mature grown woman, I am totally over him now.* No. That wouldn't work. "We went to school together."

"You did?" Samantha asked.

"Sort of. Miss Mabel's younger," Jensen said, his smile growing as he watched his daughter with Harvey.

Oh, that smile. Mabel swallowed, hard. That hadn't changed. Not one bit.

A sharp whistle reached them, announcing the arrival of her brothers, Webb and Forrest. The sudden tension in the air told Mabel all she needed to know. People might grow and change, but the grudge between their two families wouldn't. *Not that I was expecting anything different.* She stood, smoothing the skirt of her sundress and waving at her brothers. "Is it time already?" she asked.

"Yep," Webb said, giving Jensen a narrow-eyed look.

"Okay." Her gaze shifted to Jensen.

Jensen and Forrest exchanged a stiff nod, before Jensen said, "Come on, Samantha, we need to get home."

"Oh." Samantha stood, taking Jensen's hand. "Did you sign Miss Mabel's papers?" She tugged on her father's hand. "Save the tree, Daddy."

Poor Jensen. Mabel felt certain all Samantha would ever have to do was use that look right there to get whatever she wanted. The big blue eyes. The tiny crease of concern between her brows. The twist to her lips. Samantha Crawley was too adorable for words.

It was no surprise that Jensen took the pen Mabel offered, signed her petition and handed the pen back without saying a word.

"Okay." Samantha went back to wide-eyed, bouncy enthusiasm. "Bye, Harvey. Bye, Miss Mabel."

"Bye, Samantha. It was nice to meet you." She waved at the little girl, her gaze darting to Jensen. "Nice seeing you, Jensen."

Jensen looked genuinely surprised, but he managed a small smile and said, "You, too, Mabel. Thanks for…that." Without another word, he and Samantha walked into the sea of cars in the parking lot.

"What was *that* about?" Webb's tone was sharp as he scowled down at her.

"That was me, being neighborly." Mabel sighed. "Harvey wanted to meet Samantha. Samantha wanted to meet Harvey. And Jensen—"

"Jensen is a Crawley," Webb interrupted.

"Jensen's not so bad." Forrest glanced after Jensen and Samantha. "I can't say I'm a fan of Crawley senior, but Jensen… Well, Mabel did right by being neighborly. He and his little girl have had a hard time the last few years." Forrest placed a hand on his little brother's shoulder. "Besides, go easy on Mabel. You know how she is with kids and animals. We want her to stick around now, you hear?"

Webb frowned, but didn't argue.

"Kids and animals always turn me to goo." Once upon a time, Jensen Crawley did the same. Maybe not goo—but definitely weak-kneed and flustered. Nothing at all like the way she'd reacted today. *Right. Sure. Whatever.* It was fine. It'd been a while, that was all. She'd be better next time she saw him and, since Garrison wasn't exactly a big town, she'd likely be seeing him again. *There's not a thing to worry about.* "Thanks for coming to get me." Mabel hooked arms with her brothers, eager to change the subject to something non-Crawley related. "I could use an ice cream. My treat."

"DOES MABEL REALLY talk to animals?" Samantha asked, bouncing her feet as Jensen buckled her into her booster seat. "Is she magic?"

Jensen chuckled. "I don't think so."

"I dunno anyone who talks to animals, Daddy." Samantha put her hand on his arm. "'Cept the princesses in my movies. They talk and dance and sing with them."

"I don't think Mabel's a princess, either."

"Then how did she talk to Harvey?" Her brows rose. "How?"

He shrugged. "Well, now…" He didn't have an answer for that.

"She's pretty, too," Samantha added. "Princesses are pretty and nice—she was nice, too. I think she was prettier than anyone. Ever. She has long, long, long black hair." She clapped her hands. "And she was wearing a dress, too, and princesses always wear dresses, Daddy."

All true. His daughter was so serious and her arguments made perfect five-year-old sense, so Jensen said, "Maybe."

Samantha's feet stopped bouncing. "Maybe? Maybe Mabel is a...a princess?" She stared up at him with wide eyes. "Really, Daddy? Really?"

"Well... Probably not. I don't think there are any princesses in Texas, little miss." He shrugged, wishing he'd thought before he spoke. Samantha took every single word to heart—remembered every word, too.

"There are. There are. On the floats, Daddy. 'Member?" Samantha waited for his answer.

"Ah, well... Those are for pageants—"

"Queens and princesses and duck-chesses." Samantha counted off on her fingers.

"Duchesses," he corrected.

"Yep." Samantha nodded, crossing her arms over her chest. "See. They are here. In Teshes. And they all wear crowns and stuff."

She looked so proud of herself that he didn't have the heart to argue with her. "Well, little miss, I guess you'll have to ask her next time you see her."

Samantha nodded, a little shell-shocked and a whole lot excited over the possibility that Mabel Briscoe was a princess.

"You all buckled in and ready to go?" he asked.

"Yessir." She reached into the basket beside her and pulled out one of her books. "Princess," she whispered, staring at her well-read fairy-tale book. "A real princess."

Jensen closed the back door, knowing he was going to regret this entire conversation. How was he going to keep her from mentioning this to his father? His father, Paw-Paw to Samantha, was gruff and harsh—with one exception: Samantha. When it came to his granddaughter, his father would do anything to make her happy. But he didn't think that would extend to something that included a Briscoe, even if the Briscoe was Mabel. The origin of the Briscoe-Crawley grudge went back three generations, but over the years, each generation seemed to add their own offense to it.

As he headed around the hood of his truck, he glanced back at the front doors of Garrison Family Grocery. Mabel, arm in arm with her brothers and Harvey the non-polar bear at her side, laughing and talking as they made their way to the crew cab truck with the Briscoe Ranch brand stenciled on the doors. He'd grown up hating that brand and that name.

To his father, *Briscoe* was a dirty word. If his father did utter the name in their home, he spat it out with outright disgust.

When Jensen had walked into his classroom on the first day of kindergarten, he and Forrest had been on the way to being friends—right up until their teacher had called the roll. Then Forrest wasn't just Forrest, he was Forrest Briscoe. *Briscoe.* The bad name. The bad family. That boy was a Briscoe. The ones that had done the Crawleys wrong at every turn—his father had said so, over and over again, and back then, Jensen believed his father's every word. Like Samantha believed him.

Was it any wonder that he and Forrest had wound up in the principal's office with bloody noses and an assortment of bruises? Forrest had called him Creepy Crawley, Jensen had dubbed him Bratty Baby Briscoe— he'd been especially proud he'd gotten in *two* insults—and the floodgates had opened and the fists had started flying. He didn't know half of what he'd said, only that he'd repeated things his father had. That had been his and Forrest's *first* fight. The next ten years were chock-full of playground bullying, athletic rivalry, romantic sabotage, competing over class-rank placement and pretty much anything to get under each other's skin.

After Forrest's parents died, Jensen didn't have it in him to be as brutal as he'd been before. It felt…wrong. Not too long after that, Forrest's older brother, Gene, was killed overseas while on active duty. That had been when Forrest changed. The two of them might not see eye to eye, but Jensen wasn't heartless. Losing so many loved ones? It had been beyond imagining. But when Jensen had tried to tell Forrest how sorry he was, Forrest had…snapped. Later, Jensen understood. Forrest had been grieving and angry and he'd taken it out on Jensen. But even then, as Forrest was beating him senseless, he hadn't fought back. That had been their last fight.

He absently rubbed his nose. The break had long since healed, but he'd never forget that day or the pain that haunted Forrest Briscoe's eyes.

As the Briscoe Ranch truck cut across the lot and onto Main Street, Jensen climbed into his truck, turned on the ignition and peered into the rearview mirror at his daughter. He was thankful none of the Briscoes had a child the same age as Samantha. His little miss wouldn't grow up knowing someone hated them purely because their name was Crawley.

Samantha looked up from her book, her big eyes meeting his. "We going now, Daddy?"

"Yes, ma'am." He winked at her. "First, we gotta go pick up the new microwave from Old Towne Hardware and Appliances—"

"'Cuz Auntie Twyla blew up the old one."

"Because Aunt Twyla blew up the old one." He hadn't laughed that hard in a long time. His little sister had put her brand-new coffee mug into the microwave, not thinking about the gold rim and lettering. Seconds later, a series of sparks and pops began, followed by a deep humming. The microwave started vibrating, the front glass broke, and black smoke started billowing out and into the kitchen. Jensen couldn't remember the last time he'd seen his father move that fast. "After we get the new microwave, we'll go visit with Aunt Kitty and Aunt Twyla for a bit. Then we'll head out for Mr. Earl's place and, finally, the dance shop."

"Okay, Daddy. Lots to do today." She went back to looking at her book.

"Yes, ma'am, lot of errands." During the week, it was his job to oversee Crawley Cat-

tle Ranch operations. If he wasn't out working the land or tending the herds, he was
ordering feed and equipment and balancing
the books. Most days he was up and gone
with the sun and back around suppertime,
so he didn't get as much time with his little
girl as he'd like. On the weekends, he did his
best to spend every minute with her. Lucky
for him, she liked running errands and visiting folk. Just like her mother, Samantha
never met a stranger.

"I like Mabel, Daddy," Samantha said,
turning the page on her book.

"She's nice." He backed up and headed out
onto the main road. Mabel had always been
nice. There'd been times he'd almost forgotten she was a Briscoe. *And now, apparently,
she's a princess.*

"And pretty, too." Samantha turned the
page. "Like a princess," Samantha added,
whispering. "But her hair isn't long enough
to climb…" It sounded like this might be a
strike against Mabel.

Jensen had to chuckle.

Weekends in Garrison meant out-of-
towners shopping up and down Main Street,
sidewalk sales and the occasional church,
school or club fundraiser. This month, things

were a little different. Last weekend, the big community picnic had brought in more tourist and media than ever. This weekend, Miss Martha was throwing a huge birthday party—with a Save the First Tree theme, of course. She'd invited everyone who was anyone from all over Texas. Meaning, Garrison would be bursting at the seams this weekend. On just about every corner and in every shop window were large green banners and posters with "Save the First Tree" printed in large white letters.

The whole town was in an uproar over the city manager, some wannabe big shot from the city, talking to the retail giant Quik Stop and Shop about buying a large parcel of land in town. There were two concerns. First, no one in Garrison wanted Quik Stop and Shop moving in and running the mom-and-pop stores out of business. Second, the parcel of land being considered had the First Tree right smack-dab in the middle of it. That was like taking the Statue of Liberty out of New York City or the Eiffel Tower out of Paris—it was unthinkable.

Maybe that was why Jensen wasn't too worried about it *actually* happening. Between the tricounty-area media blitz, the

Garrison Ladies Guild's activism and the fact that the city council would never approve such a thing, the First Tree was in no real danger. Still, he respected the effort being made by all age levels. From Samantha's kindergarten class making a "Why Trees Are Important" video, the petition going around, the community picnic, Miss Martha's Save the Tree birthday party and the rumored drive-by protest parade and mass attendance at the next city council meeting, it seemed like the whole town had rallied around the iconic landmark that put Garrison on the map.

They headed down Main Street and turned right on the corner of the courthouse square, before doing a U-turn and parking alongside Old Towne Hardware and Appliances.

"Is Mr. Nolan here?" Samantha asked, holding up her hands so he could unbuckle her booster seat.

"I'm thinking so." Jensen lifted her from the truck cab and set her on the sidewalk. Samantha loved visiting Mr. Nolan because Mr. Nolan always seemed to have a lollipop set aside just for her. "But if he's not here, I bet Mr. Rusty is."

"He's okay." Samantha took his hand, shrugging.

Jensen chuckled. Rusty was Nolan's son, good-natured and helpful, but he wasn't always as lollipop-prepared as Mr. Nolan was. Jensen held the door open and followed her in, letting her lead the way—skipping—to the main counter.

"Well, lookee-here, it's Miss Samantha Curly-Locks." Nolan Woodard came around the counter to meet her. "I thought you might be coming in with your daddy."

"Yes, sir." Samantha nodded. "We have to pick up the new microwave since Auntie Twyla blew up the old one."

Mr. Nolan nodded, looking very serious. "Well, now, that happens from time to time."

"Daddy said that's the second time Auntie Twyla blew one up." Samantha nodded.

"I do seem to recall ordering this model at least once before." Mr. Nolan shook hands with Jensen. "Let's get you set up now, shall we?"

After ten minutes of talking about Mr. Nolan's pet bearded dragon, Bongo, Jensen carried the microwave to the truck with Samantha following, sucking on a bright red lollipop. The drive to his sister's shop was the other direction—just long enough for Samantha to get good and sticky.

"Look, Daddy, balloons." Samantha's voice carried from the back seat. "Auntie Twyla and Auntie Kitty have balloons."

He pulled into one of the angled parking spaces in front of The Calico Pig, his sisters' Main Street shop, and peered out the front windshield. "I'd say that's a few balloons." Not only was there an arch of green balloons over the shop door, there was also a large swath of green-and-white-plaid fabric with large calico letters that had "Save the First Tree" sewn on.

"Here ya go." He offered Samantha a wipe. "You got...all over." He waved his pointed finger in a circle over her face, making her giggle.

"Are they having a party?" Samantha asked, less sticky, as he unbuckled her from her seat once more.

"Sort of. Looks like they're helping out, like Mabel." He helped her from the truck.

"To save the tree? Trees are important, Daddy. The give us ox-y-gen to breathe." She took a deep breath. "We need the trees." She took his hand and skipped along at his side.

"Yes, ma'am." He stepped inside to find

his sisters in deep conversation with Hattie Carmichael, the county game warden. "You three look like you're planning something." He tipped his hat. "Hattie."

"Jensen." Hattie waved her fingers, grinning.

"Hi, Samantha. Hey, big brother. We're not up to a thing." His sister Kitty waved aside his question and turned, sliding a stack of folded aprons—newly embroidered with Ellis Family Feed and Ranch Supplies on the bib—into a brown paper sack. "Thanks for taking these to Earl."

"Headed that way, anyway," Jensen said.

"How do, Samantha." Hattie was all smiles. "You keeping your daddy out of trouble?"

Samantha glanced up at him. "I think so?"

Hattie and his sisters laughed.

"Jensen is *never* in trouble," Twyla said, rolling her eyes. "He's as good as gold."

Jensen shot his sister a look. "You're right, I haven't blown up any microwaves recently."

"Who would do that?" Hattie, ever practical, asked.

"Auntie Twyla," Samantha said. "Makin' coffee. Paw-Paw jumped up and sprayed that white stuff *all* over the kitchen."

"White stuff?" Hattie looked among the adults for clarification.

"Fire extinguisher," Jensen murmured, managing to swallow his laugh.

Twyla sighed, covering her face with her hands.

"I see…" Hattie said, then burst out laughing. "That sounds downright exciting, Samantha."

"It was. Oh, and Mr. Nolan just now gave me a red lollipop. It was yum-*my*." Samantha licked her lips. "Mr. Nolan is so nice."

"He did? Well, he *never* gives me a red lollipop." Kitty sighed. "Sounds like he treats you special." She winked at her niece.

"Of course she is." Hattie shrugged, as if it was the most obvious thing in the world. "Anything else exciting happen recently?"

"Oh…" Samantha bounced up and down on her toes, her eyes going round. "Yes. Yes. Something happened." She clapped her hands together and her whole face lit up.

It wasn't just the way her voice wavered or how her whole body seemed to vibrate that drew all eyes her way. It was the pure, unfiltered excitement that rolled off his little girl in waves. He had a pretty good idea what had her all worked up and suspected his sisters wouldn't be as excited as Samantha was. But he waited, along with Hattie and his sisters, to see if he was right.

"Well, don't keep us waiting." Kitty crouched in front of Samantha. "What is it?"

"I met a real live princess this morning." Samantha's announcement was more a giggle and squeak than anything else. But it was just intelligible enough to be understood.

"Here?" Hattie frowned. "In Garrison?"

"Why do you say that, Samantha?" Twyla asked, peering up at him for clarification.

Jensen sighed, ran a hand over his face and offered up the only explanation that wouldn't immediately break his daughter's heart. "Samantha's a lot like Nancy Drew. You give her the pieces and she puts together the puzzle. The way she sees it." Not necessarily the right way... Like this time.

Samantha nodded. "I can't read those books, though."

Kitty lifted Samantha up so she could sit on the wide wooden counter with the large glass front. "I'll read them to you, if you like?"

"Okay." Samantha nodded. "But some of the covers are scary."

"Hold on, I'm still waiting to hear about this princess." Twyla smoothed Samantha's red-and-white gingham skirt.

"Oh, that. She has to be. She is pretty and has long hair and she can talk to aminals, too." Samantha was ticking off the princess list she'd developed on her fingers. "And she was nice, very nice, *and* she wore a pretty dress." She took a deep breath. "She was standing outside the food store holding papers and getting names to save the tree. A princess would save a tree. For her aminal friends."

Jensen smiled. Try as she might, Samantha always said *animal* as *aminal*.

"A princess?" Kitty shot another questioning gaze Jensen's way.

"Your auntie Kitty and I are helping save the tree," Twyla pointed out. "Are we princesses, too?"

"No, Auntie Twyla. Course not." Samantha giggled, her ringlets shaking as she shook her head. "You're funny."

"Nice. Pretty. Long hair. *Talks* to *animals*. That describes the only princess I know." Hattie nodded. "I heard Mabel is back in town. Can't wait to catch up with her."

"That's it, Miss Hattie." Samantha nodded. "You guessed it. Princess Mabel."

But Jensen saw the way his sisters' excitement faded. It wasn't the origination of the Crawley-Briscoe feud or the years of skirmishes since that got his sisters really worked up and feisty, though. It was about protecting their family *now*. They'd watched him come home with cuts and scrapes and a bruised ego since he was Samantha's age. That, coupled with their father's long-standing bitterness, had laid the groundwork for them to have their own feelings about the Briscoe family. And none of it was good.

"She had a dog, too," Samantha said, spreading her arms out wide. "A *big* one. Like this." She stretched out even farther. "Bigger."

"Did it hurt you?" Twyla asked, her hand resting on Samantha's knee.

"Oh, honey, are you okay?" Kitty shot him a look full of reproach.

His sisters knew how fearful Samantha was of dogs…and most animals, come to think of it.

"Uh-uh. Mabel told me he's no polar bear an' he won't ever hurt me an' he didn't. He was so soft on his tummy." She tucked her hands between her knees and grinned. "He was… What was he, Daddy?"

"Like a big old teddy bear?" Jensen offered up.

"Yep." Samantha nodded.

"You didn't have to pet the dog if you

didn't want to." Twyla was giving Samantha a thorough once-over.

Samantha nodded, her little gaze bouncing
between her aunts. "But I wanted to. Mabel
said he was nice. And he was. An' she said
he was soft. And he was soft." She blinked.
"And she was nice and Daddy said she could
talk to aminals an' if she said the doggy was
nice, the doggy would be. Daddy was right,
too."

His sisters both turned to stare at him now.

But Hattie was smiling. "I don't know
about the princess part, Samantha, but I do
know Mabel Briscoe *can* talk to animals."

"Really, truly?" Samantha asked. "For
sure?"

Jensen started to nod, but his sisters'
glares stopped him. Mabel had never done
or said a thing to any of them. He'd always
thought she was *different*. Not just from the
rest of her family, but from…well, *everyone*.
She just had this thing about her—something
empathetic and honest and intense. Like she
could stare into a person's eyes, read their
troubles and offer them help. He'd never forget her kindness after his mother died. Never.
He shook his head, giving his still-glaring
sisters his best disapproving dad face. It

wasn't Mabel's fault that her last name was Briscoe and, when they were alone, he'd remind his sisters of that.

"She can't, honey," Kitty assured her, almost apologetic.

"No," Twyla interrupted, shaking her head. "No one can."

"Maybe not with words, I'll give you that," Hattie agreed, undeterred by his sisters. "But she seems to, I don't know, have a...a connection with them. An understanding, I guess you'd say. I've called her a time or two, before she went off to protect the wild horses, to see if she could help me out when an animal was acting different or worrisome."

"She's protectin' horses?" Samantha's eyes were round once more, absorbing this new piece of information.

"Yes, ma'am." Hattie nodded.

"Did she help you, Miss Hattie? When those aminals acted funny?" Samantha was leaning forward, waiting eagerly for the answer.

Hattie nodded. "She did."

"See?" Samantha nodded. "Mabel *is* a princess. I *know* she is. She's gotta be."

"She did get Samantha to pet a dog. Not just a quick pat, but a full belly rub." Jensen shot his sisters a meaningful look. "A dog that was bigger than she was, I might add."

"He was, he was." Samantha nodded, spreading out her arms again. "Bigger than this."

From the lock of Twyla's jaw, to the deep crease between Kitty's brows, he could tell his sisters weren't going to give an inch on this. When they were in a stubborn sort of mood, like now, the best thing was to wait until the mood had passed. He shrugged, grabbing the paper bag. "We should get going, Samantha. We still have to go see Mr. Earl before we can head to the dance shop for your sparkle tights." When his little girl was clogging, she had to sparkle—from head to toe.

"Okay, Daddy." Samantha let him lift her off the counter. "Bye, Auntie Twyla, Auntie Kitty and Miss Hattie."

"Bye, Sugar," Hattie said, smiling. "You have fun with your daddy."

"I will." Samantha smiled up at him. "We always have fun together, don't we, Daddy?"

That smile, right there, was the thing that got him out of bed every morning. And when the ache in his chest just about brought him to his knees, it was hearing her humming along to one of her sing-along princess tapes that eased the pressure until he could breathe. "We do indeed, little miss." He squeezed her hand and gave her a wink, chuckling as she skipped—still holding his hand—all the way back to his truck.

CHAPTER TWO

"I don't know how Miss Martha arranged it, but you couldn't ask for a more perfect day." Mabel tilted her face up, soaking up the warm Texas sun with a sigh. She was only partly teasing about Martha Zeigler. If there was a person alive who could force the weather to change, it had to be Martha Zeigler. Still, it was Miss Martha's force of will that had brought the last two weekends to life—and the Save the First Tree petitions, too. "She is a force of nature."

Her younger brother, Webb, grunted in response. "Uncle Felix said she's an old battle-ax."

Which sounded exactly like something Uncle Felix would say. "Battle-ax or not, she's doing a lot for Garrison." Mabel had nothing but respect for the older woman. "You know something, Webb? I know it's the same sun in Wyoming, but it feels different here." She tipped her hat forward to shade her now-heated face.

"'Cuz you're home," Webb said. "Everything is better at home."

Mabel nudged him with her elbow. "Says my world-traveling little brother."

"One day, maybe." Webb shrugged. "Still haven't given up on the idea of following in Gene's footsteps." He glanced at her from the corner of his eyes. "Not dying...just serving, is what I mean."

Mabel managed a smile. "I knew what you meant." And she hoped Webb would change his mind. The mention of their eldest brother caused the hole in her heart, the one that would never quite heal, to throb anew. "But I'm not sure our brothers or Uncle Felix could do without you."

Webb rolled his eyes. "We got any soda in there?" He leaned forward, stretching across the quilt they were using for today's festivities.

"Should be." She glanced around her, astounded by the sea of blankets and gathered people. "I think the whole town is here. Maybe even the whole county." She shaded her eyes.

"Well, you're here, aren't you?" Webb

grinned. "Knowing erste Baum was on the chopping block has got *everyone* riled up."

Mabel glanced at the tree in question. Beneath the thick branches, a white tent had been erected for the birthday girl. Streamers and lights hung from the tent and the branches—along with Happy Birthday and Save the First Tree banners. So many celebrations had happened here. Erste Baum, the First Tree, was part of Garrison's soul. The massive tree was a gathering place and landmark. Webb was right, when she'd heard what was going on, Mabel hadn't hesitated. She'd taken the full month of time off she'd accrued at work and hurried home. "It's nice, isn't it? Seeing everyone come together like this?"

"Mostly." Webb chuckled. "Not like I'm going to sing 'Kumbaya' with those Crawleys, though."

Of course not. It was noon and this was the first mention of the Crawleys, so that was something. Mabel swallowed back her sigh. "We wouldn't want to get carried away." Mabel's sarcasm was lost on Webb.

"Exactly." Webb nodded. "You gotta draw a line somewhere."

Did they? Really? While there'd been

bloodshed between the Briscoes and the Crawleys years ago, Mabel had never been able to hold on to the anger and resentment that both families clung to. Then again, she'd had her own personal reason for that. *Nope, not going there.* She took a deep breath. The past was just that, the past. She'd rather focus on all the good, right here and now.

A quick scan of the meadow revealed plenty of good. Her older brother Audy, a self-proclaimed bachelor, appeared every bit the family man. He lay on a quilt, baby Joy held over him, while his sweetie, Brooke, looked on. There was so much love there. So much happiness. Mabel couldn't be happier for them both.

On a blanket nearby was Brooke's sister, Tess, and Mabel's youngest brother, Beau. Webb and Forrest were giving poor Beau all sorts of grief about him being sweet on Tess, but Mabel thought it was sweet. Sure, they were young, but Mabel got the sense that it was more than a teenage crush.

"What are you looking at?" Webb turned, snorting.

"Audy *and* Beau. Look at 'em. It's enough to turn a man's stomach."

Mabel had to laugh then. "Webb, you don't believe that."

"I don't? Audy's old enough to make up his own mind. But Beau? Isn't he a little young to be in *love*?" Webb didn't bother hiding his displeasure as he popped open his soda.

"I don't think there's an age limit." She shrugged, glancing at Beau again.

Webb followed her gaze. "Plus, he is sorta making a fool of himself." He nodded toward the blanket. "Not even trying to act, I don't know, a little *less*…interested."

Why should he? There'd been times Mabel wished she'd been a little less reserved when she'd been younger and more naive. What would have happened if she'd acted on her feelings for… *No*. Even then, she'd known, as she knew now, that having any romantic attachment with a Crawley was impossible.

"What's that face for?" Uncle Felix joined them, setting up his camping chair. Her brother Forrest followed, a large soft-sided cooler under his arm.

Forrest glanced her way. "What's wrong?" He set down the ice chest and dug out cold bottles of water for each of them.

"Nothing." Mabel took a water bottle.

"Thank you." She shrugged. "Why does something have to be wrong?"

"You're making *that* face." Uncle Felix pointed.

"You *are* making *that* face." Forrest dusted off his jeans, then sat on the quilt.

Webb turned, his eyes narrowing as he studied her. "I don't see it." He shrugged.

"That's because there's nothing to see." She rolled her eyes. *Was I making a face? While thinking of Jensen Crawley? That couldn't be right.* She was over him. Jensen was 100 percent out of her system. It was being back home, that was all. Stirring up old things… Memories. *Enough of this.* "But I *do* see an ice cream truck over there so I think I'm going to head that way and take that face with me. Anyone want to come along?"

The three of them grunted.

"Okay, then. I'll take that as a no." She stood, smoothed her pink sundress covered in bright white and yellow daisies, and adjusted her straw cowboy hat. "I'll be back." With a quick wave, she headed across the large meadow, weaving around picnic blankets and folding chairs as she went.

"Mabel." Kelly Schneider, a childhood

friend, sprinted up to her. "Where are you headed?"

"Ice cream." She hugged Kelly. "Keep me company?"

"I'm never saying no to ice cream. Besides, we didn't really get a chance to talk when you were getting signatures at the store." Kelly and her husband, Dickie, owned the grocery store. "Tell me everything. How is it being home? How was Wyoming?"

Heartbreaking. She'd spent the last year as the horse behaviorist for the Wild Mustang Heritage Foundation. The work, protecting the last free mustang herds on public lands, had been rewarding and devastating all at the same time. Mabel had helped out with medical care, relocating herds and, when necessary, helping sell and find homes for mustangs that might otherwise be euthanized. "It was a lot." She sighed. "Lots of good and lots of bad." She forced a laugh, thankful for the month she had here. Hopefully, she'd get the recharge she needed before heading back.

Kelly's gaze sharpened. "It looked hard. I've kept up with your vlog."

Mabel blinked. "Really?" It was part of her tracking process—something the foundation could use as a measuring stick for their successes, weaknesses and any troubleshooting that might crop up.

"You're kind of a celebrity at the high school. Mr. Koch—do you remember Fritz Koch?" Kelly paused for her nod. "He's in charge of the agriculture club and animal husbandry and biology classes and he's been having them watch your vlogs on Fridays, get the kids talking and thinking."

Mabel didn't know what to say to that. But it was reassuring to hear that Mr. Koch was sharing her work with students. If the next generation didn't take on a vested interest in saving the mustangs, the animals' future was all too bleak.

As the two of them queued up in the growing ice cream line, Kelly caught her up on anything and everything she'd missed while she'd been gone. Mabel was so focused on what Kelly was saying that hearing Samantha Crawley's voice, excited and urgent, caught her by surprise.

"Daddy, *it* is her." The little girl was adamant. "See? It is, it is!"

"I see, Samantha." The deep rumble of Jensen Crawley's voice set the hair on the back of her neck straight up. Rumbles aside, he sounded even less thrilled than she was about this surprise meet-up. He continued, "Looks like she's getting ice cream—"

"I want ice cream, Daddy!" Samantha was closer, now. "Hurry up, come on. Miss Kelly, Miss Mabel? Hi."

"Hello." Kelly turned. "Don't you look smart in that dress, Samantha."

Mabel glanced back over the sea of picnickers, but there was no sign of her brothers charging this way. *Stop being silly.* She ran her hands over the bodice of her sundress, took a deep breath and turned to smile in greeting—focusing solely on Samantha. "Oh, that *is* a pretty dress."

Samantha looked as proud as a peacock. "Auntie Kitty made it for me. Auntie Twyla did the stitches, though." Her little fingers ran over the detailed smocking on the front of her pale pink swiss dot dress. "We're both in pink, Miss Mabel."

"We are," Mabel agreed, the little girl's excitement obvious. "Getting ice cream, too?" she asked, taking pains to avoid making eye contact with Jensen. Not that she could ignore him. He was right there, totally visible from the corner of her eye. "It is the perfect sort of day for it, which is good because I love ice cream."

"Me, too." Samantha seemed to find their mutual affection for frozen dairy awe-inspiring. She stared up at Mabel with the biggest, bluest eyes ever. "We don't have any at home 'cuz Auntie Twyla says it makes her hips big. But Daddy gets me some when we are running errands, right, Daddy?"

"Right." Jensen chuckled.

Inside her hand-tooled leather cowboy boots, Mabel's toes curled tight. *Just because his laugh is like velvet? Or warm chocolate? Or... Or... Oh, stop.* Unfortunately, she'd always reacted to him this way. But now, after so long, she'd hoped she'd have…outgrown it? Outgrown him? Or, at least, stopped reacting to him this way. But since she was still suffering from this whole flutter-nervous-awareness thing? *Ha. Guess not.*

"I see you've met Mabel, eh, Samantha?" Kelly's smile was short-lived as she glanced between the three of them. It was the typical response to a Crawley-Briscoe run-in. Bracing for what was to come—but definitely expecting unpleasantness.

Because we should hate each other. "Yes." Mabel nodded, winking at the little girl. "I

met Samantha outside your store yesterday."
As if I could ever hate Samantha.

"We did. With Harvey." Samantha nodded. "And Daddy." She reached back, took Jensen's hand and tugged him forward.

No ignoring him now. Mabel took a deep breath and met Jensen's gaze. "Afternoon, Jensen."

"Mabel," he murmured, touching the brim of his hat.

Maybe the reason she was still suffering from the whole flutter-nervous-awareness thing was because he was still…*Jensen.* No matter how hard she'd tried, and she had, not to compare every man she met with him, it didn't work. Maybe it was because they had a connection—a heightened awareness or a…a subconscious understanding. *Oh, for goodness' sake, enough, Mabel.* It was time, past time, to stop all of this.

"Where is Harvey?" Samantha peered around.

"Oh, he's at home. He's so big that not everyone is brave enough to make friends with him." She winked and added, "Brave, like you."

Samantha beamed up at her. "Harvey is nice an' soft."

"He is. I will tell him you said hello, if you'd like? He'll be sad he missed getting a tummy rub from you." After all, Samantha was just about the most adorable little girl in existence and there was no convincing Mabel otherwise.

"Because you *can* talk to him." Samantha glanced at Jensen, then back at her. "Tell him hello an' I'll rub his tummy again, please."

Mabel wasn't sure what to make of the look, but it meant something. "I will."

"You two want to jump in line here with us?" Kelly stepped aside, ignoring the sighs from the group in line behind them.

Jensen shook his head. "No, we—"

"Daddy, please please please?" Samantha grabbed his hand and turned the full force of her blue eyes on him.

Mabel watched, anticipating Jensen's response. *How could anyone refuse that look?*

"Okay, little miss." Jensen shook his head and stepped in line next to them. "Sorry," he murmured to the man behind them.

"I'd have given in, too," the man said, chuckling.

"What is your favorite flavor?" Samantha asked her, completely delighted.

Mabel pretended to think about it, then said, "Vanilla."

"Vanilla?" Samantha looked confused.

"Oh, yes. You can eat it plain or add all sorts of yummy stuff to it—chocolate sauce or marshmallows or gummy bears or strawberries. You name it." Mabel watched Samantha's confusion clear, turning into a broad smile.

Samantha nodded. "Vanilla."

Mabel laughed.

"I'm guessing we're getting vanilla now?" Jensen asked, also laughing.

Mabel glanced between the two of them, puzzled.

Kelly pulled her ringing phone from her pocket. "Oh no." She sighed. "Alice said she can't get the back of the Suburban open. I'm going to have to go help her so Miss Martha doesn't get upset." She glanced at her watch. "We have her giant, I mean *giant*, custom-ordered birthday cake and she wanted to serve it—" she paused to check her watch "—pretty quick."

"I can come with you? Or hold your spot?" Mabel offered. Kelly leaving meant she'd be alone with Samantha…and Jensen.

"No, no, that's okay. She'll need help setting up, too, at this rate." Kelly typed a quick text, then slipped her phone into her pocket.

"I'll stop by later," Mabel offered, dread swirling in her stomach. *This is bad.* No, it's fine. *It's ice cream.* She just happened to be in line next to them, that was all. *That* was *all*... But if that was the case, she wouldn't be feeling so apprehensive.

"Enjoy your ice cream, Samantha. Have a good day." Kelly waved, distracted, and hurried toward the parking lot.

A stilted silence fell. She risked a quick glance at Jensen, but he didn't seem particularly perturbed by Kelly's departure. Why would he be? It wasn't a big deal, really. *Just me, in line, with Jensen Crawley and his daughter.* She didn't dare look anywhere in the general vicinity of her brothers and uncle now. If they saw her without Kelly as intermediary, they would not be happy. But even if they didn't see it for themselves, word about the three of them in line together would get around fast enough. Just about every member of the Garrison Ladies Guild was close by—if anything unusual or noteworthy happened, they'd find out and share accordingly. *Likely with their own spin on it, too.*

Samantha rocked back and forth on her feet. "I like your boots and your hat, Miss Mabel."

"Thank you. This ole hat fits *just* right." Mabel plucked off her hat and set it on Samantha's head. "It helps keep the sun out of your eyes." She smoothed her hair from her shoulders.

Samantha held the hat on and peered up at her. "A tiara or crown wouldn't do that."

"No, they don't." Mabel had no idea where that came from, but it was true. "I suppose you could wear a tiara or a crown outside when it's not so sunny? And you can wear them all the time indoors—since you don't need to worry about shade."

"Indoors." Samantha seemed to absorb this. "Like indoors in a castle? Or a shallot? Or someplace where a princess would live?" She was watching Mabel closely.

"Princesses do live in castles." Mabel nodded. "Shallot?" It had been a while since she'd read a fairy tale, but she didn't remember one that had a princess living in an onion. But by some miracle, she got it. "Oh, chalet? Yes, I bet they can live in those, too." She'd loved fairy tales when she was little. She'd had her uncle scratching his head when she started singing to the chickens or cows. And her brothers weren't happy when she'd steal one of their dress shirts for a cape. Back then, Briscoe ranch had been her own little kingdom. She smiled. "I guess around here, a princess or a queen would have to live on a ranch since that's sort of like a castle in Texas."

"They *would*, wouldn't they." There was that awe-filled voice again. Samantha seemed so excited, Mabel didn't know what to make of it.

Jensen groaned. He shook his head and ran a hand over his face. Was he upset? Irritated?

"I feel like I'm missing something." Mabel tucked her hair behind her ear.

Jensen's deep blue eyes swiveled and locked onto her face.

She'd been determined to keep it light and upbeat and not get remotely rubber-kneed over anything about Jensen. So far, so good. Aside from the whole toes-curling-in-her-boots thing. But that was *before* he was looking at her. And now that he was looking at her, it was almost like he hadn't truly seen her until now. Now that he had, he almost seemed confused. Like he couldn't quite figure her out.

She swallowed. *No. That's ridiculous.* She might still hold a pathetic fondness for him but Jensen had likely *never* thought of her. And if he did, it was because she was the weird girl who talked to animals and the only Briscoe who hadn't called him a name or punched him in the face. Either way, she knew she didn't inspire even the tiniest rubber-kneed reaction in the tall, handsome, cowboy-hat-wearing, blue-eyed man before her.

JENSEN HAD KNOWN Mabel Briscoe since she was about Samantha's age. Not known her— she was a Briscoe, after all. But known *of* her. Growing up, she'd been an odd duck. At least, that was what grown-ups said about her. His father included. There'd been all sorts of talk among kids, too, and kids could be so mean. Her shyness, big glasses, crooked ponytails and mostly boy hand-me-downs made her an easy target. Then there was the whole talking-to-animals thing, too. Back then, no one would believe her. *Because it's sort of hard to believe.*

Jensen, a good five years older than her, had never thought her odd. Unique? Definitely. He had two sisters and, as much as he loved them, they'd been loud and laughed at silly things and generally acted *girlie*. Even as a little girl, Mabel had been watchful and quiet and not in the least bit girlie.

At the moment, with her long black hair blowing in the breeze and her sundress as bright as the wildflowers growing nearby, she was all spring, sunshine and light. And she was, very definitely, a girl.

A woman.

Her pale blue gaze, no longer hidden by oversize glasses, matched the Texas sky, crystal blue and endless. He remembered those eyes, how steady her gaze had been. And still was.

Little flashes of forgotten memory flitted across his mind—surprisingly vivid.

Little Mabel stopping traffic to move a turtle off the road.

Years later, finding her off trail in First Tree Park with a fox caught in a snare trap. He'd helped free it, but it'd been Mabel, murmuring soft reassurances, that had kept the fox calm enough that it didn't injure itself.

After that, his senior year, when he'd found the barn cat's runt of the litter—sad, scraggly and one-eyed—he'd known the only person who could nurse the kitten to health was Mabel. He'd never questioned why he'd risked life and limb to trespass onto the Briscoe property, after dark, just to leave the kitten in a box at Mabel's front door. To Jensen, it had been the right thing to do.

That cat had followed Mabel everywhere—like a dog—for years. And every time he'd seen them together, it had made him smile.

"Daddy?" Samantha's voice snapped him out of his memories. "Daddy, it's our turn." She tugged on his hand.

Jensen tore his gaze from Mabel and walked up to the ice cream truck's window. Until now, he hadn't noticed the Garrison Ladies Guild sign in the ice cream truck window. Not only was the sign there, but two wide-eyed and interested Guild members were all but falling out the window to watch what was happening. Dorris Kaye, one of The Calico Pig's biggest customers, and Barbara Eldridge waited. Both ladies were absolutely riveted.

Great.

By evening, everyone in Garrison would know he'd been staring at Mabel Briscoe like a…a what? He didn't want to think about it.

"Afternoon, Jensen." Dorris smiled. "And to you, too, Miss Samantha. Look at that pretty dress. Did Kitty make that for you?" Being a seamstress herself, the older woman was always admiring others' handiwork.

"Uh-huh." Samantha nodded. "Auntie Twyla did this." She pointed at her dress front.

"Neat and tidy smocking, if I've ever seen it." Dorris nodded. "What can I get you and your daddy?"

"A vanilla cone, please." Samantha was all smiles. "We both want vanilla. Me and Miss Mabel."

Jensen almost groaned. Almost. But he caught himself.

"You and Miss Mabel?" Barbara Eldridge didn't miss a beat. "Two vanilla cones, coming up." She turned and spoke to Dickie Schneider, who was scooping up ice cream.

"Daddy?" Samantha asked, pulling his hand again. "What do you want?"

"I guess I'll have the same." At the moment, ice cream was the last thing he was thinking about.

Miss Martha's birthday had taken over his weekend plans. Instead of spending time with Samantha, he'd been roped into helping his sisters man the bouncy house Miss Martha had put them in charge of for the afternoon. Then, because no one said no to Miss Martha, Samantha's dance school was putting on a special clogging performance for the woman's birthday. Samantha's excitement had been so contagious even her grandfather was coming into town to watch. But all that was before...*this*.

He went out of his way to avoid having gossip and drama tied to him—being a Crawley already came with enough of that. And yet, here he was, buying ice cream for a Briscoe from Barbara Eldridge and Dorris Kaye. Barbara Eldridge wasn't one to gossip, but Dorris Kaye more than made up for it. *These three vanilla ice cream cones are gonna cost me.* Not money so much as peace.

"That is a mighty fine cowboy hat you've got on, Samantha." Dorris nodded at his daughter.

"It's Miss Mabel's." Samantha adjusted the hat on her head, looking so proud.

"Isn't that nice," Barbara said. "It suits you."

"Miss Mabel is always nice to me. And she's pretty, too," Samantha announced, a little too loudly. "And she talks to animals."

"Don't I know it." Barbara Eldridge handed down an ice cream cone. "My little goat,

Nana, was acting all out of sorts. I'd heard Mabel had a way with animals so, you know what I did?"

Samantha shook her head, captivated. "What?"

Barbara Eldridge grew animated as she spoke. "I'll tell you. I called up Miss Mabel and told her how my Nana was acting, and guess what she did." She paused but Samantha shrugged, licking her ice cream cone. "Why, she came right over that instant to help."

Jensen glanced at Mabel, who was all red-cheeked as she smiled and thanked Dorris for her ice cream cone.

Samantha stopped licking her ice cream long enough to ask, "What happened?"

"Nana had gotten out and taken a nice long stroll around the back pasture. When she'd come home, she'd had burrs and stickers in her hair that I had to comb out. But I didn't know she'd gotten a nasty mesquite thorn lodged way up and under her breast plate." Barbara pressed her fingers against her own chest to demonstrate.

"Ow." Samantha frowned, her little nose wrinkling, and she forgot all about her ice cream.

"I'd say so," Jensen agreed. He'd had a mesquite thorn go through his foot once and it'd hurt something fierce.

"Mabel showed up and sat in the grass in my front garden and the two of them just sort of looked at each other," Barbara said. "Now, if you know my Nana, she is a little bit…"

"Crotchety?" Dorris offered.

"I suppose." Barbara chuckled. "Before I knew it, Nana trotted right over to Mabel and stood still until Mabel had the thorn out. Mabel, here, had found what was bothering my old girl within ten minutes of setting eyes on Nana."

Samantha's eyes were as round as saucers. "You did that, Miss Mabel?"

Mabel nodded, but her gaze stayed focused on her ice cream. As nice as the story was, Jensen got the feeling Mabel was uncomfortable getting such attention. If getting praise over curing Barbara's goat was hard for her, she'd be downright miserable when this whole ice cream fiasco started getting passed around. And that was what was going to happen. He could see it on Dorris's face. As soon as the two of them walked away, she'd be all over this.

"She did." Barbara Eldridge nodded, giving Samantha a wink. "Next time I see you, I'll tell you about the cardinal she found." She handed Jensen his cone. "I have to say, it's nice to see a Crawley and a Briscoe being neighborly. Who knows, maybe you three will inspire your families to do the same. Wouldn't that be something?"

That would be something all right. Something that would never happen, that is. Personally, yes, he'd love for the Briscoe-Crawley feud to end. More than just about anything, he'd love for Samantha to grow up and not have this sort of rancor be a part of her daily life. But there was no way he would say so out loud in front of Dorris Kaye. He knew better. He also knew good and well that what *he* thought wouldn't change the minds of the rest of his family or the other Briscoes, either. He didn't even know if Mabel felt as he did. Out of all the Briscoes, she was the most levelheaded. If she was dedicated to keeping the feud alive, there was no hope of there ever being a reconciliation. Who was he kidding? Even if Mabel did feel as he did, there was little to no chance of reconciliation. Still, he was curious.

Behind her ice cream, Mabel was smiling, her eyebrows arched high and her sky blue eyes fixed on him. He might not be able to glean her opinion on the feud, but he was pretty sure he knew what the look meant. Barbara Eldridge had just asked the sort of question that could lead to all sorts of fodder for someone gossip-prone like Dorris Kaye. Course it helped that Dorris Kaye was practically climbing out the window to see and hear everything.

He chuckled. "Thank you for the ice cream," Jensen said, paying for the cones.

"You don't need to do that." Mabel rummaged through her pocket, pulled out a bill and put it on the service window. "I'll pay for my own." She smiled at him, handing him back one of the bills. "It was nice to see you…all."

Jensen tucked the money back into his wallet, tipped his hat at the three of them and led Samantha away from the ice cream truck and Mabel Briscoe.

"Oh, wait, Daddy. Miss Mabel?" Samantha tugged free and hurried to Mabel's side, her scoop of ice cream listing to one side of the cone. "Your hat." She took off her hat and handed it up to Mabel.

Jensen stayed where he was, eating his ice cream while pretending he didn't have a care in the world.

"I almost forgot. It looked so good on you."

Mabel crouched next to Samantha, took the hat and put it on. "Thank you."

"For your shade. Until you get inside." Samantha smiled broadly.

"Hmm." Mabel cocked her head to one side. "You need to protect your skin when you're out in the sun, too. Sunburns are bad for you. You'll have to get your own hat."

His little girl was staring up at Mabel like she was…as exciting as Santa Claus. *Or a real, live princess.* When Samantha asked, "Can you come watch me dance later?" it was harder for Jensen to hold back his groan.

No. She'd say no. She was just as uncomfortable with all this as he was.

Mabel paused, chewing on her lower lip, her gaze focusing on her melting ice cream. "You're dancing today?"

And it's okay to say no. He held his breath. It'd be for the best. *Say no.*

"Yep. Clogging." Samantha stomped on the ground and spun around. "In a princess dress. And I get to make lots of noise. Oh, an' I have sparkly tights to wear, too." She bent and pointed at her bare legs.

"A princess dress *and* making noise?" Mabel laughed. "That does sound like fun." Her gaze wandered, peering far across the meadow toward erste Baum, before she said, "I wouldn't miss it."

Jensen hung his head. She was going to get just as much grief for their little ice cream expedition as he would from his sisters and father. Agreeing to come to Samantha's performance didn't make sense. It would only add to the chatter that was likely already rolling across the field. While he truly appreciated Mabel's kindness, enough was enough.

He took a deep breath and crossed to where they were still huddled. "Samantha, today might not be the best day for Miss Mabel. She's…" He scrambled for any excuse. "…helping Miss Kelly and Alice. Doing her part for the tree." Surely Mabel heard the desperation in his voice. "You don't have to, Mabel. I'm sure you've got things to do."

But Samantha and Mabel stared up at him wearing identical expressions of disappointment and his heart did an odd flip before lodging itself in his throat.

"Oh…okay…" Samantha blinked, then turned back to Mabel. "You don't have to." Her voice wavered, all forlorn heartbreak.

Mabel stared at his little girl for a solid minute, debating. "I want to." She took Samantha's hand in hers. "I can't wait to see your princess dress *and* listen to you make all sorts of noise and your sparkly tights, too."

Samantha dropped her ice cream and threw her arms around Mabel's neck.

Jensen didn't hear what his little girl whispered to Mabel, but it must have been something because Mabel hugged her tight—her ice cream scoop sliding off her cone and onto the grass. With all the hugging and ice cream casualties, he was pretty sure things couldn't get much worse. It was quite a scene. Still, there was nothing he could do about it. He ran a hand over his face and went back to eating his ice cream.

Mabel let go of Samantha, stood and plopped her hat back on top of Samantha's head. "I'll get it later. Have fun." Her gaze shifted to him, giving him the slightest nod, tossing her empty cone into the trash receptacle and heading back across the meadow—her long black hair blowing in the breeze.

"Daddy." Samantha took his hand. "This is the best day ever." She skipped, swinging their joined arms. "Miss Mabel is coming to watch me dance and there's a bouncy castle later and ice cream…" She stared at her now-empty hand.

"You dropped it." He nodded at the puddle in the grass.

Samantha shrugged, not in the least upset by this development. "Oh, well." She adjusted Mabel's hat.

"Here." He handed her his ice cream.

"Thanks, Daddy." She took it. "Miss Mabel is right. Vanilla is the best."

He grinned down at her. "Is it?"

She nodded, skipping all the way to the massive castle being inflated. His sisters waved in greeting.

"Auntie Twyla." Samantha's words came out in a rush. "Hi. Look, I got ice cream, but I dropped it—this is Daddy's. And look." She pointed at her head. "Miss Mabel's hat. She let me borrow it *and* she's coming to my dance."

While Jensen was normally a plainspoken man, he'd hoped he'd have time to figure out how to present this whole Samantha-Mabel thing to his sisters. They were reasonable women. With any luck, they'd laugh—not shoot daggers at him with their eyes.

"I saw that." Twyla nodded.

Nope, too late. *Daggers incoming.* From both of them.

"An' she wants to see my sparkly tights,

too," Samantha added, unaware of the looks his sisters were giving him.

"Does she?" Kitty's smile was brittle. "How did this all come about?"

"I asked her," Samantha said, enjoying the ice cream. "She said yes. Daddy said she didn't have to, 'cuz we are all real busy. But she is coming." She eyed the thick plastic square Kitty and Twyla had been spreading out. "Is that the bouncy castle? Are we setting it up now?"

Jensen did his best to avoid looking at his sisters. Now was not the time or place for them to launch into some anti-Briscoe rant. Mabel's kindness to his little girl was sincere. Come to think of it, he couldn't remember Mabel ever being unkind to anyone—Crawley or not. Considering the strong opinions her brothers and uncle held, it couldn't be easy. But she did it anyway. *Because it was the right thing to do.* He'd likely get grief for it but… Maybe it was time for him to do the same. Be kind—even to a Briscoe, in full view of most of Garrison, with one of the town's biggest gossips looking on. Just thinking about it made his stomach knot. Until that moment, he hadn't realized how brave Mabel Briscoe was.

CHAPTER THREE

"WHAT TOOK YOU so long?" Uncle Felix was all smiles when Mabel wandered back to the rest of her family.

Better to just come clean and put it out there so they learned from her. "I was—"

"What happened to ice cream?" Forrest asked. "They sell out before you got one?"

She shook her head. "I dropped it." *When Samantha Crawley hugged me and told me she knew my secret.* If only she knew what this "secret" was.

"Sounds like something I would do." Webb started laughing.

Mabel couldn't argue with that. If there was an accident on the ranch, it was safe to assume Webb was involved in one way or another. Growing up, Webb was always the one getting stitches or breaking an arm or a leg or driving the tractor into the side of the barn or a ravine. Uncle Felix had called him What now, Webb? for years.

"You see Beau while you were out walking?" Forrest pulled an apple from the picnic basket. "I blame Audy for that. Throwing those two kids together and all."

Mabel almost laughed. But Forrest's expression was openly disapproving. "You're serious? About Audy?"

"Dead serious. Beau was levelheaded and focused before... Our little brother's still young. Impressionable. They don't know what they're doing." Forrest plucked at the blades of grass lining the edge of the blanket. "I don't want his plans getting derailed over this...this feelings *mess*."

Mabel tilted her head, studying his face. *Feelings mess* could have described any one of her brothers. They didn't do *feelings*. Feelings made them uncomfortable. Like now. Forrest had always been the protective one so it made sense he was worrying about Beau... To a point. "Has Beau changed his mind about college? Said something to worry you?" It was hard to imagine. Since his first day in kindergarten, Beau had known what he wanted: college and rodeo—preferably both. His rodeo scholarship gave him exactly what he wanted. Mabel couldn't have been happier or prouder of her youngest brother.

Forrest seemed to consider this at length before answering, "No." He shrugged. "But it still doesn't sit right, is all I'm sayin'. Beau and Tess are kids."

"It's just a little crush." Webb set his cowboy hat on the blanket beside him and ran a hand over his head. "No harm in it. Over and done with, next week."

"Talk to me this time next week and we'll see." Forrest cocked an eyebrow, not budging.

Mabel couldn't understand her brothers. When had they gotten so jaded? She'd been young when their parents died, but she still remembered how devoted they'd been to one another. It was what Mabel was holding out for—the love that lasts, unwavering and true. Forrest and Audy had more time with their parents, they'd seen it. So how had Forrest gotten so hard-hearted? Webb was just taking his cues from Forrest—like he did on most everything. Did Forrest have a personal reason for being such an anti-romantic stick-in-the-mud? Or was her big brother just an all-around stick-in-the-mud? Audy said it was the latter. More specifically he'd said Forrest was "a boring, uptight, stick-in-the-mud that didn't know how to have fun."

"Where's your hat?" Uncle Felix asked. "Weren't you wearing a hat?"

Here we go. She took a deep breath. "Yes, I—"

"Oh," Forrest held up his hand. "Before I forget, are you free this week? There's a horse auction over in Holsom. Tuesday." He took a bite of his apple. "I'd rather not waste any money."

She nodded. "Of course." Stick-in-the-mud or not, Forrest's faith in her ability to pick the right animals always had her standing tall. Plus, there was something rewarding about finding animals that were meant to come home with them. Cattle. Horses. Even goats—though she had to work on Forrest to get him to come around to her way of thinking on that one.

"Horses. That's *all.*" Forrest used his apple to emphasize his point.

She shrugged. "I'll try but—"

"But she can't turn off her animal whisperer thing," Webb cut in, winking at her.

That was what her brothers called it, her animal whisperer thing. She couldn't remember which of them came up with the term or how long ago it'd been, but it'd stuck. There was no explaining it. Some people called her an animal whisperer, others an animal behaviorist. To Mabel, it was a *connection*. She couldn't remember a time when she'd looked at an animal and hadn't gathered a sense of their thoughts. Not like real words, or words people used anyway, just a…an understanding. And since her uncle and brothers had all seen her having "conversations" with animals, none of them had ever acted like it was out of the ordinary. Most times, it wasn't.

But the people outside her family weren't as quick to accept it. To hear stories, like the one Barbara Eldridge had told today, she had an unusual ability that caused gasps and skepticism and lots of curious looks and disbelief. That was when her connection went from being a part of who she was to an out-and-out oddity. Those were the times she felt like she was back on the school playground, surrounded by kids chanting, "Goggle girl" for her too-big glasses and saying her stories were all "made up" or she was "lying for attention." It had been easier to stop talking about it and pretend, at least outside her family, it wasn't real. Now, she no longer denied it, but she didn't go out of her way to bring it up, either.

"Now, back to *my* question—no more interrupting, Forrest—about you losing your hat. Or is my mind playin' tricks on me and you didn't have one on your pretty little head when we set up this here picnic blanket?" Uncle Felix sat forward, resting his elbows on his knees to give her a narrow-eyed look.

"Your mind isn't playing tricks, Uncle Felix." She swallowed, already dreading the conversation to come. "I had one on when we got here."

Forrest, Webb and Uncle Felix all looked at her. A well-worn hat, one that perfectly fit the head, was a prize to any cowboy. Losing said hat? That was no small thing, it was an outright tragedy—something that required a worthy explanation.

Third time's a charm. She took another deep breath and began, "Kelly and I were headed over to get ice cream—"

"Which you dropped," Webb interrupted, grinning.

"Yes." She cleared her throat, pleating the hem of her sundress with her fingers. "We were walking across the meadow and Samantha—I met her yesterday when I was collecting signatures at the grocery store—came running up to say hi. We were talking and she admired my hat so I let her borrow it and said I'd get it back after she does her dance routine. She's clogging later—and I imagine she will be adorable—so she won't need my hat then."

Uncle Felix's eyebrows had risen higher and higher while she rambled on. Webb looked confused. But Forrest...

"I only know of one Samantha." Forrest's tone was flat. "And that's Samantha Crawley. Is that the Samantha you're talking about?"

"Yes." Mabel nodded.

"Jensen Crawley's daughter?" Forrest's tone didn't change.

"Yes. I'll get it later, after her dance." She could either let them stare her down until she somehow felt like she'd done something wrong—which she hadn't—or she could leave them to stew on their own. "Right now, though, I promised Kelly I'd check in and see if she needed an extra hand with Miss Martha's giant birthday cake so I'd best get going." She stood, smoothing out her skirt.

"Mabel." Uncle Felix's tone was gruff. "I know you have a giving heart and I get that you might feel some sort of...sympathy for the little Crawley girl because she's lost her mother and you...well, you lost your mother but—"

"She's a Crawley." Webb sat up, outright scowling. "And she has her father, grandfather and aunts to look after her."

She's more than a Crawley—more than a name. Mabel swallowed. Samantha was an adorable, wide-eyed little girl who'd decided Mabel was her friend.

"There's too much bad blood there—you know that. After all this time, it can't be fixed. Best leave well enough alone." Forrest's sigh was all impatience. "You... You can't go making friends with his daughter..."

It felt wrong to distance herself from a sweet little girl who sought her out. *What if I want to be friends with Samantha?* Not Jensen, of course. *That would never happen.* There was a horrible finality to that thought, one she couldn't shake. The tightening in her gut was sudden and sharp, but she managed to say, "I just lent her a hat." Her laugh was 100 percent fake and they all knew it. "That's all."

Forrest stared at her, his jaw tight and his lips pressed flat.

"I'll see you later. With my hat. You should come get cake..." She waved and headed toward the birthday girl's tent, her mind spinning. Like it or not, Forrest might have a point. It's not like she could waltz up to Samantha and Jensen, shake their hand and generations of rivalry and grudges would magically disappear.

I wish it would.

Considering how dismissive the menfolk in her family were about love, knowing their great-great-grandfather's love triangle was the cause of the old feud was highly ironic. A Crawley and a Briscoe, courting the same woman, and taking drastic steps to try to win her. Even after she'd married one of them, the other held on to the hope she'd change her mind. *Like some old-timey Western paperback novel.* Too bad for Mabel it wasn't fiction. At times, the lingering anger and resentment was downright suffocating.

Her time in Wyoming had been a challenge in many ways, but it had also been freeing. Out there, she was Mabel Briscoe, horse behaviorist. And while that was just a fancy name the Mustang Heritage Foundation had come up with to validate her animal whisperer thing or connection, *that's* who she'd been. Mabel Briscoe, horse behaviorist. Not the only daughter of Albert and Cecilia Briscoe, not the younger sister of Gene or Forrest or Audy, not the older sister of Webb or Beau, not the poor little Briscoe girl brought up by her uncle wearing her brother's hand-me-downs and making up stories... It had been nice.

Too bad Jensen and Samantha didn't live in Wyoming.

Maybe that was where she belonged? Maybe being there with the horses was truly her home? She still had two whole weeks before she needed to go back, but she could go back sooner—if she wanted.

As soon as the whole First Tree thing is over and done with.

Inside the large white tent, there was a long line of banquet tables set up. The white linen tablecloths with green bunting swagged across the front, and Save the First Tree buttons holding the bunting in place were festive while still supporting the cause. Down the middle of the tables was the biggest cake Mabel had ever seen. At the far end, a table was set up with cupcakes, decorated with little fondant toppers that matched the Save the First Tree buttons.

"Hey, Mabel." Judy Eldridge, Barbara's daughter, waved from behind the table. "It's so good to see you."

"Hi, Judy." Mabel couldn't help but wonder if Barbara had already relayed the painfully awkward ice cream situation. Awkward because of the whole ice cream dropping, hugging and staring thing. Weirdly enough, it hadn't been her staring—it had been Jensen. "They got you selling cupcakes?"

"Oh, so many cupcakes." Judy waved her hand across the table in a dramatic sweeping gesture. "Anything that helps raise money for erste Baum, though, am I right?"

"You came." Kelly peered around the folding screen at the back of the booth—covered in pictures of the First Tree, and the people of Garrison gathered beneath its branches through the years. "How was the ice cream?"

For some reason, Mabel's cheeks felt warm. No, more than warm. Hot. *Am I blushing?* Considering the way Judy and Kelly were looking at her, there was no doubt she was blushing. "After all that waiting, I dropped it." It was an unlikely reason for her to blush, but it was all she could come up with.

"I didn't mean to leave you in a lurch like that… I should have thought." Kelly grimaced, casting a quick glance Judy's way.

Of course Barbara's already told Judy. Barbara and Judy weren't just mother and daughter, they were best friends. Which meant Kelly probably knew. "It's fine." Mabel waved aside her apology.

Kelly and Judy exchanged a long look, the sort of look that gave her pain in her stomach.

"What's wrong?" Mabel asked.

"Nothing is *wrong*." Judy smiled. "It's just… My mother did try to deflate the talk, Mabel, I promise. But people saw you and Jensen *together*. And Dorris… You know Dorris."

Mabel held her breath, waiting. She didn't really know the woman, but she did know that Dorris Kaye was an unabashed gossip.

"Don't freak out," Kelly said, pushing a plate of cupcakes her way. "Eat those. Free."

She'd barely said a thing to Jensen. Really, she'd interacted with Samantha. Pretty much *only* Samantha. *As if that mattered.* Mabel eyed the cupcakes. "What, exactly, is being said?"

"That Jensen Briscoe seemed interested— very interested—in you and that you couldn't wait to get away from him. And, when you did walk away, he sent Samantha after you to stop you and invite you to her recital." Judy frowned. "It's not true, of course. My mother said you two behaved like civil adults and nothing more. Well, she may have mentioned he *was* staring at you… But she also swears the real connection seemed to be between you and Samantha and that nothing untoward took place between you and Jensen."

Untoward? Mabel swallowed. It was worse than she'd thought. If her brothers thought Jensen was pursuing her, against her wishes, and using Samantha to do it, they'd be livid. "Of course that's not true." She picked up the plate of cupcakes. "He didn't do any of those things." *Except the staring.* Her knees had definitely suffered a bout of rubberyness from the staring. "And he certainly didn't use Samantha. She dragged him along, poor man. He was…he was just…being a good father. Tolerating me, really. Well, you know, Kelly. He didn't even want to be in line with us—*you* made him. And Samantha… She's just so precious and irresistible." Being wrapped up in Samantha Briscoe's fierce hug had flooded Mabel's heart with pure sweetness. "It's clear he'd do anything to please his daughter, as he should. And that includes putting up with me. He tried to get me not to go to the concert." She realized that now. Which is what she should have done.

Poor Jensen. "Jensen Crawley was not—is not interested in me. Definitely not *very* interested…" She made a garbled, dismissive snort. "No. Not in the least."

"Then, if one of your brothers catches wind of this nonsense, that's just what you'll have to say to them," Kelly said, nodding.

Considering how they'd reacted to her sharing her cowboy hat with Samantha, she doubted it'd be as easy as Kelly made it sound. *Like they'd listen.* She frowned, hugging herself. If this took off across Garrison, her brothers would feel obligated to do something. *Do what?* Her stomach was officially in knots now and her chest full of lead. *It's not fair.* Jensen had been through enough and now because she hadn't left the ice cream line with Kelly and she'd made the colossal mistake of putting her hat on Samantha's head and had not once glared at Jensen with open hostility, *he'd* have to deal with her brothers. *No. I'll make them listen.* This was all nonsense. All of it.

"Er, Mabel? Careful." Kelly pointed at the cupcakes Mabel was currently cradling against her chest. Thankfully, the layer of plastic wrap covering the baked goods had protected her dress from the sticky green icing, white fondant and sugar sprinkles.

"Oh." Mabel set the plate of slightly mashed cupcakes on the table. "Right. Let me pay for those." Now was not the time to panic. Her brothers were hotheads, but they weren't stupid. No one—*no one*—would believe Dorris Kaye's take on this. She was looking for the next scandal, was all, and she and Jensen had made it all too easy for her. That was all this was. *Gossip, plain and simple.* Somehow, she'd get her family to see that.

Mabel was too busy worrying about how she'd manage to convince her hot-tempered kin and counting out change to pay for the cupcakes to notice the look of true excitement Judy and Kelly exchanged. If she had, Mabel probably would have packed her bags and run back to Wyoming that very second.

"You look like a princess." Jensen adjusted the bow in Samantha's hair.

"I do?" She spun, her sparkly dark blue tulle tutu a glittering cloud around her tiny waist. "Do you think Miss Mabel will like it?"

Jensen nodded.

He didn't want to dim his little girl's excitement, but truth be told, he'd be fine never hearing the name *Mabel* again. Ever. He'd scarcely thought of the woman the last few years and yet, today, she seemed to pop up everywhere he went—in conversation or in person. How could he have known that a simple ice cream cone purchase would knock down the first domino in a long and winding chain of zigzagging dominoes? What else had he expected? He knew Garrison loved its talk.

The entire time he'd been standing guard outside the rented bouncy castle, one or the other of his sisters had kept up an ongoing lecture about his public *fraternization* with Mabel.

"You're the one that said you didn't want Samantha knowing about the feud," Twyla had said. "You think that sort of…spectacle won't cause talk? Talk Samantha might hear?"

Spectacle? He'd bought an ice cream. Since when had partaking in a dairy treat become a spectacle?

"What happened to your 'Keeping her away from the Briscoes' policy?" Twyla had continued. "You get all bent out of joint when people talk about the family. What do you think that little stunt will cause?" Twyla had whispered, all the while smiling at a family whose little one was jumping inside the castle.

He did his best not to respond. Initially, he'd taken it as a sign of concern for Samantha. But they didn't stop. And with each passing reprimand or disappointed headshake, his patience slipped—more and more—until he'd had enough. He wouldn't deny there might be a sliver of truth to everything they'd said. There was. What he objected to was adding any more fodder to the fire. And seeing the three Crawley siblings in heated conversation following his and Mabel's ice cream spectacle… Well, that was more fodder, all right. He'd finally managed to get both of his sisters together long enough to say, "We will talk about this at home. For now, drop it." And they had.

He might have come across a little short, but that couldn't be helped. He'd apologize—later.

Right now, Samantha was all that mattered. He stood behind the curtains of the makeshift stage waiting for Samantha's big dance—and her solo. Her dance teacher,

Gretta Williams, looked as calm as ever among a dozen or more four- and five-year-olds swarming around her. He, on the other hand, was ready for this performance to be over.

"You ready?" he asked his little girl. It was her first solo. Even though he knew she'd practiced and practiced and practiced some more, he was nervous.

Samantha, on the other hand, didn't seem the least bit nervous. "Don't forget her hat, Daddy."

Jensen eyed Mabel Briscoe's cowboy hat. "How could I forget the hat?" He might have sounded gruff, so he offered Samantha a wink. "I'll be right up front."

"Okay." Samantha clapped, jumping up and down so her clogs thumped, too.

"All right." He pressed a kiss to her forehead, grabbed Mabel's hat and walked out from behind the curtains. His sisters were holding his seat in the front row with his father.

His father sat, arms crossed over his chest. He wore his usual scowl, making no pretense that he was happy to be there. Dwight Crawley didn't mind people talking about how crotchety and gruff he was, he preferred it that way. If he was a bear, people kept their distance—something else he preferred. The only exception was *his* Samantha. Sweet Pea. Cookie. Butter Bean… His father's nicknames for Samantha were endless—and mostly food related. As far as his father was concerned, Samantha was just about the only thing worth leaving the comfort of the ranch for. His father wasn't much for dancing or the fuss of the costumes or the loud music, either, but he never missed one of Samantha's recitals. Not ever. Even now, when it meant leaving the ranch *and* engaging, minimally, with the rest of Garrison.

"Dad." Jensen nodded in greeting, sat in his seat and slid Mabel's hat beneath his folding chair. "You good?"

His father gave him a side-eyed grunt.

"Samantha is so excited," Kitty gushed. She was the one who had brought Samantha's costume idea to life. Ideally, Samantha's costume would lead to Kitty getting other commissions and she'd be sewing fancy costumes for most of the dancers in Garrison. And since dance or karate was the only thing available to Garrison's youngsters, there'd be plenty for Kitty to sew for. "I love how dedicated Samantha is. She's worked so hard."

"She really doesn't need to." Twyla leaned forward, whispering to the three of them, "She is the only one who has any talent."

Twyla's comment had their father laughing.

"Twyla." Kitty's tone was mildly scolding. "They're all precious." She didn't like to speak ill of anyone. Even when the Briscoes came up, Kitty more or less nodded instead of hurling insults and calling names.

"Humph" was their father's only response. He took a long look down both sides of the row they were sitting on, his scowl back in place.

Jensen had a hard time not chuckling. He'd heard his father compared to Mr. Potter from *It's a Wonderful Life* more times than he could count and, at times, Jensen was hard-pressed not to agree. From his squinty-eyed glare to the twist of his mouth, there were times his father's determined glower was almost comical.

"Well, as I live and breathe. I never thought *you'd* come to *my* birthday party." The flinty voice of Martha Zeigler had his father wincing. "You *are* still alive, you old dog."

"Martha." Dwight nodded, barely sparing her a look.

"Glad to see you coming out, supporting your community." Miss Martha sniffed. "Those of us able to put a stop to this ought to put our money where our mouth is."

"I should have known you weren't stopping by to exchange pleasantries, Mrs. Zeigler." He peered up at her now, his hands folded on top of his walking cane. "If you think I'm going to write a check to save some…some tree, you've got another think coming."

And then something happened that Jensen had never seen before. Barbara Eldridge walked up, standing beside Miss Martha, and his father smiled. Not a forced smile or one strained with civility. No. A real smile. If his sisters hadn't gasped in shock, he'd have thought he'd imagined the whole thing. But no, he hadn't.

Because his father was still smiling. At Barbara Eldridge.

"Barbara." His father's voice was soft. Almost warm.

What is happening?

"Dwight." Barbara's slight head tilt and pink cheeks only added to the bizarreness of the whole exchange. "It's lovely to see you out on such a fine day."

If they weren't sitting outside, Jensen would have suspected a gas leak—causing him to see things. But since they were outside, he was forced to consider the possibility that his father didn't hate *everyone* after all.

"It is. It is, indeed," his father agreed, his tone warmer.

"For Martha's birthday *and* for such a good cause, too." Barbara nodded. "I saw your little Samantha earlier, getting ice cream." She paused, and for a second, Jensen held his breath. "Her smile is just about the sweetest thing I've ever seen. And her manners—that little one puts half of the adults in Garrison to shame. Is she dancing here today?"

"That's why I'm here." Dwight Crawley nodded, puffed up like a proud peacock.

For being such a private man, his father's outspoken and public devotion to Samantha never failed to surprise Jensen—or make him happy.

Barbara dared to take the empty seat beside his father. "I suspected as much. And I don't blame you one bit. I keep hoping my Judy will find a man with a whole passel of little ones so I can spoil them all rotten."

His father chuckled. *His* father. Dwight Crawley.

Chuckling? Jensen knew he *had* to be seeing *and* hearing things. Maybe he'd hit his head? Eaten something bad? He turned to his sisters. But they were staring, open-mouthed, at their father, too. So, this was real. *Not imagining this.*

Even Martha Zeigler looked downright confused.

"Well, now, don't you worry on that front. Judy is a smart woman, Barbara. Sharp as a tack. She's not going to settle for just any ole fool." His father's declaration was oddly comforting.

"I'll hold you to that, Dwight." Barbara patted his father's hands. "Am I taking up a seat?"

"No, no." His father cleared his throat. "I'd be pleased for you to join us."

"Why, thank you, Dwight." Barbara smiled. "I think I will."

"While you're sitting there, Barbara, see if you can talk the miserly, hardheaded old coot into parting with some of his money to help save the First Tree. I swear, Dwight Crawley, you hold on to your quarters so tight, you make the eagles scream." Martha crossed her arms over her chest. "If you want erste Baum to still be standing for your granddaughter,

you need to do your part. We all do." With
that parting shot, she stalked off.

"Excuse me for saying so, but that woman
could make a preacher cuss." His father
shook his head.

Now my father is making jokes? And Barbara Eldridge was laughing as if it was the
most hysterical thing she'd ever heard. If Jensen didn't know better, he'd think... *No.* It
wasn't possible. *It couldn't be.* They weren't
flirting with each other. *Or were they?*

"She's not short on opinions, that's true."
Barbara chuckled. "I think she feels partly
responsible for this whole mess."

"Because her nephew's the one that's been
talking to those good-for-nothing Quik Stop
and Shop people?" his sister Twyla asked.

Barbara nodded.

"It's not her fault that boy's porch light
is on, but there's nobody home." His father
shook his head. "There's one in every family, after all."

"Daddy." Kitty sounded horrified.

But Barbara Eldridge was laughing all
over again. She had a pleasant laugh. All in
all, she was pleasant woman. It would seem
his father shared that sentiment. But Jensen wasn't sure what to make of this. He'd

never seen his father like this. Not since his mother's passing, anyway, when Kitty was still in elementary school.

He remembered how kind the Garrison Ladies Guild had been to his family when his mother had passed away. Especially, come to think of it, Barbara Eldridge. She hadn't just dropped off casseroles and collected the mail. No, she'd come to lend a hand and—even when his father tried to chase her off—had taken hold of running the house and keeping he and his sisters fed and cared for until his father had regained his faculties.

He'd never considered Barbara Eldridge had done all those things out of fondness for their father. Now, however...

"Now, Kitty, come on, now. You know I'm right." Their father waited. "Your cousin Matthew?"

Jensen couldn't help it, he chuckled. Poor Matthew. He was a good man, book smart and successful. But he lacked the things his father prided most—common sense and ingenuity. According to Dwight Crawley, a man was a real man only if he had both.

Miss Gretta's appearance on the stage brought the murmur of the audience to a stop.

It was right about then that, from the corner of his eye, Jensen saw Kelly Schneider and Mabel Briscoe wander up. They stood at the end of the row—not blocking anyone's view, but close enough that his sisters saw them. Worse, his sisters were now whispering. And once again, they were shooting daggers his way. His sigh was bone-deep. He didn't want to think about Mabel. Or her hat. Or how he was going to have to return her hat—likely drawing attention to the two of them all over again.

A ripple of applause drew his focus back to the stage. Samantha was up first, with her solo, and even from his seat he could tell she was tickled pink. Seeing his little miss walk onto the stage alone, smiling, all tulle and sparkles and excitement, made him set everything else aside. She deserved his full attention and that's just what he was going to give her.

Miss Gretta was murmuring with the high school theater tech student who was in charge of sound for the production. From their frowns, it looked like something wasn't working. Not that Samantha seemed the least bit worried.

"Hi, Daddy," Samantha whispered so

abel. *Everyone* knew it. She'd been happy
nd bouncy and excited before, but now his
ttle girl looked ready to pop.

"Miss Mabel!" Samantha cried out, spinning. "Look, look. My princess dress."

He braced himself for Mabel's reaction.
This wasn't the three of them, amid a crowd,
standing in line for ice cream. This was in
front of a packed audience, his family and
the entire Garrison Ladies Guild, and, for
all he knew, the Briscoes were here somewhere, too. He ran his fingers along the scar
on his nose.

Silence descended. Absolute silence. Even
Miss Gretta turned and glanced into the audience.

Mabel had been put on the spot and now
the whole town was waiting to see what she'd
do. He'd understand if she didn't respond, but
he knew his little girl would be devastated.

"You look beautiful, Samantha." Mabel's
voice was strong and sure. "Just like a princess."

He shouldn't look at Mabel Briscoe. People were watching. His family was watching. But he looked anyway. How could he
not? Most folks would have caved under such
pressure. But there was Mabel, smiling at his

loudly everyone in the first few ̶ ̶ ̶ M
hear her.

He blew her a kiss.

"Hi, Paw-Paw." His little girl wave
excited then. "I see you."

"I see you, too." His father, also kn̶
Paw-Paw, tipped his hat. "And don't yo̶
pretty, sugar plum."

"Hi, Auntie Kitty and Auntie Twyla.'
mantha waved, tapping one foot.

Jensen chuckled. Knowing Samanth
she'd hold things up saying hello to ever
one she recognized... And that's when hi
heart stopped and his throat dried out. *No*
But he knew... He knew there was nothin̶
he could say or do to stop what was coming

As far as his little miss was concerned
Mabel Briscoe was a princess straight ou̶
of one of Samantha's favorite fairy-tale stories. His little girl had no idea that, if this
was a fairy tale, Mabel would be cast as the
wicked witch or the evil stepmother or queen
or... *She'd be the villain.* At least according
to his family. Not because she'd done anything warranting that title other than having
the last name *Briscoe*.

I need to get her interested in dinosaurs.
He knew it the moment Samantha found

little girl with the same happy excitement his Samantha was gushing. He wasn't prepared for the sudden thump in his chest—or the flood of warmth that washed over him.

The sudden burst of music erupted from the speakers. All at once, the entire audience jumped, the creak and squeak of their folding metal chairs surprisingly loud.

"Are we ready now?" Miss Gretta asked, laughing.

There was laughter from the audience.

At Samantha's nod, the music started and she began to dance with such glee that Jensen set his worries aside. This was about his Samantha. At the moment, he didn't care if Mabel was a Briscoe or a real-life princess, all he cared about was his daughter feeling loved and special. Mabel had made his little girl feel both.

Whatever happened when the music stopped, Jensen would deal with it.

CHAPTER FOUR

UP UNTIL NOW, Mabel had considered herself an animal person. As in, she gravitated more to animals than to people. Animals weren't complicated and they didn't ask for much and Mabel appreciated that. People… They tended to make things as complicated as possible for no apparent reason. But children weren't like that. Samantha Crawley wasn't like that.

With her bouncing black curls and a smile that put the Texas sun to shame, Samantha was the most precious thing Mabel had ever seen. She danced without a care in the world. Spinning and clogging and enjoying every second of it. Her glee was infectious.

And for the moment, watching Samantha allowed Mabel not to worry about what happened once the music stopped. While Samantha's sparkly tulle tutu and her bejeweled clogs kept moving, all was right with the world. But once the music ended and bows and curtsies were given, Samantha and the other students in her class left the stage and there was nothing left to delay the inevitable.

From the moment she had answered Samantha, she'd known there would be consequences. But how could she not respond? Samantha had been so proud and excited that it didn't matter she was a Crawley. What she was, *was* a child. A child Mabel had become surprisingly attached to in their two short meetings. She took a deep breath and braced herself.

A glance at Kelly was hardly comforting. She was chewing on the inside of her lip, a deep V between her brows. As her friend's gaze flitted around the audience, her agitation increased. But when Kelly caught Mabel looking at her, she did her best to smile. Mabel didn't buy it.

She sighed. It would probably be easier to let Samantha have her hat and leave. The last thing she wanted to do was taint this little girl's day with something that had nothing to do with her. She'd grown up knowing the animosity between their families had nothing to do with the here and now, it was the way things were. And there was no changing it. Watching Samantha, Mabel got the impression the little girl was unaware of their families' history or offenses. Why would she? She *was* a little girl. And unlike Mabel and her brothers, Samantha had no Briscoe rival in her classroom or picking fights on the playground. Still, she wasn't under any illusion that *the Briscoes* didn't come up in conversation in the Crawley household from time to time. And if it was anything like the conversations her family had about the Crawleys, the talk wasn't flattering.

"Are you ready to go yet?" It was Forrest. When he had arrived, she didn't know. It was possible he'd witnessed the whole thing. If he hadn't, he'd likely hear all about it later.

She turned...and realized everyone in the front row was staring at her.

Twyla and Kitty Crawley.

Barbara Eldridge.

Mr. Crawley.

The only person not staring at her in the front row was Jensen. He was too busy reaching under his chair for what looked like her hat. But once he had it, he became fully aware of the mounting tension surrounding them all.

"I can get it," Kelly offered.

Was she really going to have her friend get her hat? It seemed cowardly. This whole thing was ridiculous.

"I think that would be a great idea," Forrest answered for her.

But then Barbara Eldridge stood, a smile on her face as she walked toward them. "Felix? Land sakes, it's been a while since I've seen your face."

"Well now, Barbara, a ranch the size of mine doesn't run itself." His tone was brusque, but uncle Felix took his hat off, ever the gentleman. "You know you're always welcome."

"Call me old-fashioned, but it doesn't feel right to show up without a proper invitation." But if the woman was chiding her uncle, there was nothing but warmth in her tone.

"I guess I'll have to ask proper like." Uncle Felix held his hat in both hands against his chest.

Mabel couldn't help but notice the red hue staining her uncle's cheeks. Or the fact that he seemed more than a little *flustered* by Barbara Eldridge. Not in a *bad* way. Just in a way Mabel had never seen before.

"Good. I look forward to that." Barbara's gaze swept over Felix's face. She blinked several times, as if she was waking from a dream, and stepped back. "Goodness, I should go find Judy. It's getting late." And she hurried off, looking almost as flustered as uncle Felix.

"What was that about?" Forrest grumbled.

"Nothing," Felix answered, his tone extra gruff.

But that was when things went from bad to full-on terrible. Mabel watched as her uncle and Mr. Crawley made eye contact. If it had been an old Clint Eastwood movie, this was where they'd line up for the duel. Narrow-eyed glaring and clenched jaws, all that was missing was ominous music. Nothing like seeing two seventysomething-year-old men sizing one another up. It was almost comical, really—almost—if the tidal wave of hostility hadn't slammed into everyone in their path. As it was, she, her brother Forrest, Kelly, the Crawley sisters and Jensen seemed equally rattled by the older men's open aggression.

The air was so taut, Mabel could scarcely breathe—her nerves stretched to their limit.

"I'm getting that hat now," Kelly whispered.

Mabel turned away, hooking her arms with her brother and uncle. "Let's head this way." This way, as in away from the Crawley family and any potential incident.

"Why?" Uncle Felix practically growled. "I have every right to stand here if I want to."

"And you want to?" Mabel waited, tugging on his arm in a silent plea.

His gaze swept over her face before he sighed, impatient and irritated, and grumbled something that sounded a lot like, "I didn't want to be here in the first place," before letting her turn them.

In a few minutes, they'd be back at their picnic blanket, Kelly would have her hat and the whole thing would be over and done with. Easy-peasy.

Or not.

"Miss Mabel, Miss Mabel." Samantha's voice rang out like a bell, light and full of motion.

Mabel stopped, her heart in her throat.

"Did you see me?" the little girl asked, the thump of rapid footfalls coming to a stop right behind them.

Mabel disengaged herself from her brother and uncle and turned. "I did, Samantha." She knelt, unable to resist the little girl's eager smile. "You sparkled brightest of all."

"Thanks to Auntie Kitty." Samantha spun. "She added all the sparkles and made my skirt nice and poofy." She fluffed the tulle fabric, her deep blue eyes gazing up.

"Your aunt Kitty did a perfect job." Mabel

ran her finger over the delicate needlework. "They almost look like snowflakes."

"I wanted to be a snow princess." Samantha laughed. "'Cuz I'll never see real snow."

Mabel had to laugh then. "No. It doesn't snow in Garrison very often." And when it did, it brought the sleepy little town to a standstill. "Texas isn't built for snow and ice."

Samantha nodded, her gaze wandering higher. "Hello."

Once again, Mabel's heart got lodged in her throat, but she cleared her throat and stood. "Samantha, this is my uncle Felix and my brother Forrest."

"Forrest?" Samantha smiled up at Forrest. "Like being outdoors? In a forest? Where you go camping and ride in canoes and roast marshmallows and sing songs." She nodded, her curls bouncing as she turned toward Felix. "And Uncle Felix." Her grin grew. "I like the name Felix. That's fun to say. Fe-Lix."

Mabel turned, hands on her hips, to see their reaction.

Forrest shook his head, but gave up. Really, what choice did he have? "Nice to meet you, Samantha." He held out his hand.

"You, too, Mr. Forrest, sir." She shook his

hand, then her eyes went round. "You're Mabel's brother?"

"I am." Forrest glanced at Mabel.

"So, you...you are a..." Samantha covered her mouth with both her hands, then stared—more wide-eyed than ever—up at Felix. "And you are a... Oh my." She curtsied. "It's very nice to meet you, sir, Uncle Felix, sir."

Felix chuckled, a deep resonant, honest-to-goodness chuckle. "You *are* something, aren't you?"

"I'm a dancer." Samantha answered. "And a little girl, too." She leaned forward to whisper. "But I'd rather be a princess. Oh, or a fairy."

Too adorable. "I think you're perfect, just the way you are," Mabel assured her.

"Got it." Kelly arrived, holding Mabel's hat. "Why, Samantha, you did such a good job."

"Thank you, Miss Kelly." But Samantha was watching Mabel put on her cowboy hat. "For shade." She tried to wink—but it was more like an overexaggerated blink.

"We should be going." Mabel tucked her hair behind her ears and adjusted her hat. "I'm so glad I got to see you dance, Samantha."

Samantha launched herself at Mabel's knees. "Thank you so much for coming, Miss Mabel. You made me happiest of all."

Mabel knelt again, welcoming the hug Samantha gave her. "Well, now you've gone and made my day the happiest of all, too."

Samantha stepped back. "Really? Truly?"

Mabel had never seen a more expressive face. It left nothing to the imagination. "Really."

Samantha sighed. "Good." She waved up at Forrest and Uncle Felix. "Oh…" She paused, then curtsied. "G'bye." And she ran off, all glitters and sparkles and bouncy curls.

"And that is why she had my hat," Mabel said, knowing her uncle, brother and Kelly would hear her. "Because of that smile and that sweetness… I don't care what her name is."

"Funny little thing," Uncle Felix said, running his hand along his chin. "Curtsying like that."

Forrest chuckled. "She did like your name."

"I'm going back to get some cotton candy," Uncle Felix said, heading away from the stage and the Crawleys, with Forrest at his side.

Mabel risked a glance in the direction Samantha had gone. Luckily, the Crawleys all seemed to be entranced by whatever Samantha was telling them. Samantha's curls were bouncing as she spoke, going up on her tip-toes and hopping a little, too. *A ball of energy.* Mabel smiled—her gaze colliding with the deep blue eyes of the very person she should *not* be making eye contact with.

Jensen gave her a slow smile, touching the brim of his hat, and the slightest nod of his head.

Every time she'd almost convinced herself that he wasn't the most handsome man in the world he went and... Well, what was the point? He was the most handsome man in the world. She could try to convince herself otherwise, but it wouldn't change the truth. And, if she needed any more evidence of that fact, her knees went into full rubber mode.

"You good?" Kelly whispered.

"Yep." She was fine. If she took a step, she might fall over, but she was fine. "I'm great."

"Uh-huh." Kelly nodded. "Well... Good?" Her brow rose and she leaned in to whisper, "Maybe stop staring?"

Mabel almost pointed out that she wasn't the only one who was staring. Jensen was, too. That was why her knees were still rubber... And her lungs were just about out of air because she seemed to be having difficulty breathing.

Kelly nudged her, hard, in the ribs with her elbow.

"Ow." Mabel winced, rubbing her side and shooting a glare at Kelly. "Your elbows are sharp."

"Desperate times..." Kelly shrugged.

"Right." What was she thinking? Staring. At Jensen. After the wild tale Dorris Kaye was spreading. The last thing she needed to do was...well, anything else. "Thank you." She gave Kelly an apologetic smile.

"Sure." Kelly nodded.

"For the hat," Mabel clarified. "And the elbow."

Kelly laughed. "I figured you needed them both."

With a sigh, Mabel spun on her booted heel, determined to glue herself to their picnic blanket until it was time to pack up and head home.

"Who'd have thought today would be so interesting?" Kelly asked, walking at her side. "Tyson Ellis and RJ Malloy exchanging words over a trailer missing from the fairgrounds—"

"Oh no." Mabel hadn't heard about that.

"Well, you know RJ. What was it Miss Patsy said? 'If something smells rotten, RJ's likely somewhere nearby.'" Kelly used her best Miss Patsy voice. Miss Patsy was one of the members of the Ladies Guild. Yes, she was a gossip, but she managed to sprinkle sage life-advice into her stories. "How do you accidentally steal a stock trailer?"

Mabel had to laugh. "Poor RJ."

"I used to feel the same, but that boy—man—is just a trouble magnet. Trouble *he* causes."

Considering her brother Webb often found himself in trouble, Mabel couldn't help but feel a little bit of sympathy for RJ. Then again, Webb had never stolen a stock trailer... Even *accidentally*.

"So, we can hope that the whole you-and-Jensen-and-Samantha thing isn't the most-talked-about thing from today." Kelly gave her an almost hopeful look.

"And Miss Martha's birthday?" Mabel offered. After all, that was why they were all here.

"Oh, right. Good news. Miss Martha said almost the whole town signed the petition." Kelly smiled. "If that's true, there won't be a bit of resistance voting down further talks with that Quik Stop and Shop person."

"That's amazing news." Mabel's heart felt lighter.

"I knew you'd think so." Kelly nodded. "So, maybe, don't worry so much over...today?"

There's not a thing I can do about it. It was done and over. And besides, Samantha's dance had been worth it. "I have to admit, it was kind of gratifying to see Forrest and Uncle Felix with Samantha. No matter how crusty Uncle Felix likes to pretend he is, he was no match for her. Her smile and those little curls had him melting."

"Samantha Crawley is an angel. On the inside *and* the outside." Kelly nodded. "She's a lot like her mother was. She had Samantha's smile and spirit."

"Meaning she was impossible to resist?" Mabel smiled. She'd never officially met Casey Crawley. Sure, she'd seen the woman from time to time, but she was a Briscoe and Casey was a Crawley so...

"She was. And too young to die from a heart attack. After that, I walked straight into Doc Johnston's and told him to make sure I didn't have a heart arrhythmia. Poor Casey." Kelly sighed.

Poor Samantha and Jensen. After today, she needed to face facts and put a stop to this silly infatuation she had for Jensen Crawley. He didn't need this sort of drama. He'd dealt with more than enough. If she didn't put a stop to this, she was going to wind up making a fool out of herself, and she'd continue to give folks something to talk about. Namely, her, making a fool out of herself. And even if it was something more than infatuation, nothing could come of it. *How could it be something more than infatuation?* It couldn't possibly be. He wasn't an animal—the idea that she had that sort of connection with him and only him was ridiculous. *I'm being ridiculous.*

Sometimes her brothers liked to tease her about her need to find the good in any situation. But she couldn't find a single good thing about staying stuck on Jensen Crawley. It was long past time for her to find someone else to turn her knees to rubber… Someone whose last name wasn't Crawley.

JENSEN LEANED AGAINST the door frame of Samantha's room. No matter how hard his day had been, this made it better. His little girl, sound asleep, surrounded by the detailed murals Casey had painted for their daughter. Casey, like Samantha, had an abundance of imagination. She was the one who had read Samantha fairy tales each night before bed. She was the one who clapped her hands and oohed and aahed over the princess dresses Kitty and Twyla would create for Samantha. *She was the one who should be here now, looking in on our little girl.* But Casey was gone and it was left to him to make sure Samantha knew her mother. That was why he continued to read the fairy tales each night— even if he couldn't do all the voices right.

He ran a hand over his face, sighed and gently closed Samantha's door before heading down the hall and into the great room. He'd lived his whole life under this roof, save his college years. It was a big, sprawling home—big enough for him and Samantha to inhabit one wing and have room to spare. He and Casey had talked about building their own place but… He was glad that hadn't happened. Here, Samantha was surrounded by people who loved her. That was what Jensen reminded himself of when his father succumbed to one of his foul moods.

Like now.

Ever since Felix Briscoe had shown up at the dance recital, his father had been madder than a wet hen. Jensen wasn't sure if it was simply because Felix was there or if it was because Barbara Eldridge had seemed so happy to see the elder Briscoe. What he *was* certain of, once he'd recovered from shock, was that his father was carrying a torch for the woman. And that his father wasn't the only one smitten with Mrs. Eldridge. It appeared Felix Briscoe was, too.

Jensen had barely stepped foot inside the great room before his father started in on him. "Samantha in bed?" his father asked, waiting for Jensen's nod before he carried on. "Good. Now, you can clear a few things up for me." His father crossed his arms over his chest. "Was I seeing things?" His scowl grew. "Or was my granddaughter hugging that...that Briscoe woman." He huffed.

"You weren't seeing things." Any hope Jensen had had of having a levelheaded conversation went right out the window. When his father got worked up like this, there was no talking him down.

Kitty stopped stitching beads onto the front of the dance costume she'd been working on all evening. "Daddy, remember your blood pressure." She shot a look Jensen's way.

Jensen shot a look back. His father was the

one making a mountain out of a molehill—
not him.

"*Why* was *my* granddaughter hugging that
Briscoe woman? Come to think of it, *why* did
my granddaughter know who *that* woman
is?" Whatever his father said then was a garbled angry mess. But he paused long enough
to gather himself and add, "It's because of
that woman that my granddaughter came
into contact with that no-good, thieving,
lying Felix Briscoe."

Twyla peered over the edge of the book
she was reading.

"I won't have it, Jensen," his father blustered, thumping his fist against the table. "I
won't."

"Daddy," Kitty soothed.

"You know Samantha." Jensen spoke carefully. There was no winning here. No matter
what he said, his father wouldn't be satisfied.
Jensen filled a mug with coffee and sat in the
chair opposite his father, cradling the mug in
his hands. "She makes friends wherever she
goes." His father wouldn't want to hear that
Mabel and Samantha had that in common—
even if it was true. "Today it happened to be
with—"

"If Mabel Briscoe is being sweet to my

granddaughter, there's a reason. Likely one I'm not going to like." His father shook his finger at him. "You mark me, son. Nothing good ever comes from a Briscoe."

Jensen knew his father's hatred for all things Briscoe ran deep, but he'd hoped, somehow, Samantha's show of affection for Mabel would give the woman a pass. What had he been thinking? *That we're all adults and we can act like adults?* Obviously, that was asking too much.

"I think there's just been…a sort of mis-understanding, Daddy." Kitty went back to stitching, but half-heartedly. "Samantha's excited because she thinks Mabel is a prin-cess."

His father made an unintelligible sound— something between a snort and a laugh. "Where in the Sam Hill would she get *that* idea?"

Jensen was torn between explaining his daughter's deductive reasoning and finding a way to end this whole conversation.

"Samantha came into the shop today talk-ing about how Mabel was a real-life prin-cess. How Mabel was pretty, nice and that she could talk to animals just like her fairy-tale princesses could." Twyla placed a bookmark between the pages, closed her book and set it in her lap.

"And you set her straight, didn't you?" His father's narrow-eyed gaze locked with his. "You explained that Mabel Briscoe was nothing but a…a…"

"What is she, Dad?" Jensen set his coffee cup on the table and stood, regretting the edge to his voice. If there was ever a surefire way to get his father to dig in his heels, it was using a less-than-respectful tone of voice. He took a deep breath and tried again, suspecting the words were wasted as soon as they were out. "As far as I know, Mabel Briscoe has never done anything to anyone. Except, maybe, help when an animal needed helping."

His father was staring at him like he'd grown a second head. *Yep. Pointless.*

"People were talking," Twyla announced, not in the least bit happy. "About you. And Mabel."

His father was slowly turning a deep shade of red.

"About how you might be interested in Mabel?" Kitty almost looked apologetic.

Twyla cut in. "And how *you* were *pursuing* her."

Really? Jensen shook his head. The only

person Mabel was interested in was Samantha and making her happy. That was it. Nothing to talk about. "People are always talking. Most of the time you all laugh it off right along with me. Why is this any different?"

"Because they are talking about *you* and a *Briscoe*. They're saying you made unwanted advances and used Samantha to do it." Twyla crossed her arms over her chest.

Which brought him up short. "Why would anyone say such a thing?"

"Jensen." Twyla barely kept her patience in check. "Guess who's saying this. One guess."

He knew exactly who'd be spreading rumors. He'd seen the gleam in the woman's eyes as she handed out ice cream. "Dorris Kaye."

"No, not Mrs. Kaye." Twyla shook her head. "Mabel."

Kitty nodded, definitely apologetic then. "That's who was supposed to have said it."

"That makes no sense." He ran a hand along the stubble lining his jaw. Why would Mabel say something like that? She'd barely said a word to him, to anyone, besides Samantha. He couldn't imagine her saying such a thing—to anyone. It didn't fit.

"It doesn't have to." Twyla rolled her eyes. "She is a Briscoe. You know, the same family that sent you home bruised and bloodied more times than I care to remember."

The Briscoes didn't do that. Forrest did. "Mabel didn't do that." Jensen instantly regretted saying a word.

"Is there some truth to this?" his father blustered. "About you and Mabel? Are you interested in the woman?" His father was so red, Jensen grew concerned.

Not only had their father's doctor warned him of his high blood pressure, the doctor had also reminded him to avoid stress and eat better—neither of which his father had bothered paying any attention to.

"No." Jensen made a point of looking each of them in the eye. "No, I am not." He drew in a deep breath. "However, I have a hard time being rude to anyone who shows my daughter kindness."

"Kindness?" his father sputtered. "Filling my granddaughter's head with nonsense is hardly kindness. Telling her things about talking to animals? Horse-pucky, that's what that is. And when Samantha goes around talking to people about all that, you think she won't get picked on?"

Jensen didn't answer right away. Mabel's abilities were a little out of the ordinary, but that didn't make them any less real. As far as he knew, no one in Garrison seemed to question it. *Other than my family.* There was no point mentioning that Mabel wasn't the one to bring up the whole talking-to-animals thing. *He'd* started it outside the grocery store and then Barbara Eldridge had offered up her story about Nana the goat at the picnic today. If he thought pointing that out would change things, he would. But now that he'd heard what people were saying about him and Mabel, trying to convince his family Mabel wasn't the bad guy was pointless. "Fine." He held his hands up in defeat. "If I see Mabel Briscoe, I'll turn around and head the other way." That didn't mean Samantha was going to cooperate. His little girl saw Mabel, and she made a beeline straight for the woman.

"See that you do." His father nodded his head. "I just don't know what's gotten into you, boy." But his father paused, his color returning to normal as he gave Jensen a long look. When he did speak, the edge was gone. "It's normal for you to be lonely. There are times I miss your mother so bad I can't stand it. I know you feel the same. About Casey. It's been a while since Casey passed—"

"We are not talking about Casey, Dad."

Jensen sounded harsher than he had intended.

"All I was going to say," his father muttered, "was that there are plenty of fine-looking, goodhearted women that would be a *good* fit for you and Samantha—"

"I said we're not talking about that." Jensen ran a hand along the back of his neck, barely managing to keep his temper in check. He was out of patience and this wouldn't help. The only surefire way he could change the subject was by turning the tables on his father. "You seem more worked up than usual tonight, Dad. I think it might have something to do with Barbara Eldridge. If Dorris Kaye had seen the way you and Barbara were acting tonight, I have a feeling people would have been talking about the two of you."

Jensen didn't miss Kitty's smile or the way Twyla suddenly seemed absorbed in brushing lint from her jeans. Yes, it was a shameful attempt at changing the topic of conversation, but he was okay with that. His grief over losing his wife wasn't something he felt comfortable sharing with anyone. There were some things too personal and raw to put into words.

His father made another garbled sound of irritation. "You're seeing things."

"Then I'm seeing them, too." Kitty set her sewing in her lap. "Why don't you give her a call? Or even take her to dinner, Daddy?"

"She'd say yes," Twyla added.

"I don't know where the three of you are coming up with this cockamamie notion, but there is no way I'm calling Barbara Eldridge." He'd gone back to scowling, his color darkening.

"Why, Daddy?" Kitty, ever the empathetic one, studied their father's face.

"You're not afraid of a little competition, are you?" Jensen knew he was walking a fine line, but he did it anyway.

Both of his sisters went wide-eyed, staring back and forth between him and his father.

"What?" Kitty frowned.

"You mean Felix Briscoe?" Twyla leaned forward in the recliner. "There is no competition there."

"Daddy, if you're interested in Mrs. Eldridge, then you should let her know it," Kitty said with a gentle smile.

"The sooner, the better. You don't want Felix beating you to it." Jensen crossed his arms over his chest, doing his best not to laugh.

His father glared at him. "I'd like to see Felix Briscoe try it." But his father's sigh sounded defeated. "I had my day. I'm not saying Barbara Eldridge isn't a good woman, she is, but... Well... It may be that I'm content with the way things are, ever think of that?"

But Jensen saw the hesitation on his father's face. Was his father serious? He was content? Or had Jensen struck a nerve? Surely Felix Briscoe wasn't the reason his father was going to give up on Barbara Eldridge? Growing up, Jensen had learned many things from his father. One was, if you wanted something bad enough, you focused and worked single-mindedly toward that purpose. His father lived by those words, too. Jensen couldn't remember a single time that his father let anything or anybody get in his way. *Until now.*

"And before the three of you stick your nose even further into my business, I'll say good night." He pushed himself up from the kitchen table. "Remember, Jensen, I need you to go to that horse auction on Tuesday.

I've heard tell there will be some mighty impressive stock."

Jensen nodded. "I'll be there."

With a final nod, their father left the room. The three of them stayed silent long enough to hear the click of the latch on their father's bedroom door. After that, the three of them started talking at once.

"What was that?" Twyla looked downright confused.

"He looked sad." Kitty glanced back and forth between the two of them. "Didn't he?"

"Maybe." Jensen stared down the hall after his father. "Or maybe he was telling the truth."

"You know that's not true. You saw the way he looked at Barbara." Twyla stood, clutching her book to her chest. "I haven't seen him smile that way in years."

"What are we going to do?" Kitty went back to chewing on the inside of her lip.

Jensen held up both of his hands. "*We* aren't doing a thing. This is one time I'm going to agree with Daddy. This is his business, not ours. If he doesn't want to pursue Barbara Eldridge, that's his choice." But Jensen knew, deep in his bones, that it wasn't that his father didn't want to pursue Barbara.

No, it was because—maybe for the first time ever—his father was scared. Not just over having his heart broken, but of losing the girl to a Briscoe. *History repeating itself.* In a way, Jensen understood why his father would choose not to put himself in that situation. But for a man who taught the three of them not to live their lives in fear, it was a shame to see him give up on something that could bring him such happiness.

Happiness might not always be easy to get, but it *was* always worth trying for. Jensen missed that most of all. He missed the bond he had with Casey. That unspoken communication. The sense of comfort and shelter. The knowledge that, no matter what, the love he felt for her was unconditional and fundamental to who he was. Better yet, knowing she'd felt the same about him. He didn't hold out much hope that he'd ever find something like that again. But if there was the slightest chance he could, he'd like to think he'd try.

CHAPTER FIVE

MABEL WALKED SLOWLY, stopping now and then to give a horse a longer look. She'd picked out three horses so far. Since Forrest was hoping to leave with five, she was taking her time, going from pen to pen, lingering long enough to get a feel, and seek out their best options.

"Pretty crowded." Forrest trailed after her, a hint of impatience to his words.

"Uh-huh." She kept walking, pausing by the next pen. A large buckskin gelding stood in the middle of the pen, eyes and ears alert. She walked closer, draping her arms over the top bar of the metal pipe fencing and letting her hands dangle. "Who are you?" she whispered, smiling when he lifted his head and looked her way.

The horse flicked his ears and nickered, then trotted to her. She rested her chin, watching the way he moved. He was cautious but hopeful. Alert but not wary. He had a strength about him—but he wasn't stubborn. He'd be a good horse. A solid horse. She nodded, smiling when the horse was near nose-to-nose with her.

"So...this one?" Forrest asked, chuckling.

"Yes." Mabel rubbed a hand along the horse's neck. "I think you're pretty perfect for Webb. You'd keep him out of trouble."

The horse turned into her hand, his big brown eyes looking her over.

"You'll like it on the ranch. We'll make sure you get home, where you belong." She patted his neck again. "I'll see you later."

The horse nickered again, watching as she and Forrest moved on.

"One more," Forrest said, circling the tag number on the buckskin.

There were plenty of animals and Mabel did her best to sort through them. It wasn't that an animal was bad; she'd *never* met a bad animal. But when she met an animal that seemed to recognize her, she knew that animal was hers. Or, rather, part of her family.

She wandered the length of two aisles of pens, but none caught her eye.

"Mabel." Forrest made a big production out of checking his watch. "We're going to need to find seats pretty quick."

"Only if you find horses you want to bid on." She waved him away. "You can go on. I'm not done."

Forrest chuckled. "I'll save you a seat. Hurry... If you can."

"Uh-huh," she murmured, walking on.

At the end of the row, a paint horse stood—pressed tight against the wall. It wasn't just its blue-gray coloring that caught her eye, or the large scar that ran along the horse's left flank. It was the wariness in its stance. Mabel stopped, studying the animal for some time. It shied away from all eye contact, seeming to press itself against the wall. *Like you're trying to make yourself invisible?*

She approached the fence, folding her arms on the top pipe and resting her chin. She tried to quiet her mind, to focus only on the animal, but the horse wasn't cooperating. It wasn't angry. Or hostile. It was...sad. So sad, Mabel wasn't sure what to do—only that she had to do something.

"You can come home with me, if you like?" She spoke softly, hoping to draw the horse out. "You'll be okay."

But there was no ear flick or tail swish, no acknowledgment of her presence. And yet, Mabel knew the horse was aware of her. She could feel it—inside. She shook her head, her arms slipping from the bar. *This is a first.* She'd never been ignored by an animal before. In her experience, when an animal recognized her as a kindred spirit, they were just as curious about her as she was about them.

She's not interested. And yet, Mabel lingered. The scar. Mabel couldn't shake an unease tied to the scar. It was long healed… *On the outside maybe.* Something had happened to the mare. Something that still troubled the animal. Mabel took a deep breath, trying to separate her feelings from what was right for the ranch. After all, she wasn't staying. She couldn't bring the horse back and expect her brothers or uncle to give the paint the time, attention and patience she'd likely need.

But *if* Mabel walked on and let the mare go home with someone else, she might find the perfect owner… Or? *You might never heal.* A vise tightened around her heart.

The mare shifted her weight and dropped her head forward. For no more than a second, the paint mare's eyes looked Mabel's way.

"You're not going to make this easy on me, are you?" she asked.

The mare swished her tail and went back to ignoring her, turning her back on Mabel.

Mabel sighed, glanced down the remaining row of pens. *Pens full of perfectly good, low-maintenance, hardworking horses that won't need attention—or need me to stay in Garrison longer.*

The static from the speakers was faint, but enough to tip Mabel off that the auction was starting. If she was hoping to get a seat beside Forrest, she needed to hightail it toward the main arena—two stock barns away. With a parting glance in the mare's direction, Mabel headed toward the large expo hall where the sale was taking place.

"Mabel?" a voice stopped her. "Hey."

Mabel spun to find Hattie Carmichael, in full game warden getup, standing next to a table covered in informational brochures, maps of Texas parks, bird-watching and generally everything Texas had to offer for nature lovers. "Hattie! Oh, Hattie." Mabel ran to the other woman, giving her a big hug. "It's so good to see you."

"You, too." Hattie straightened her hat. "I kept hoping we'd catch up—"

"I know. Me, too." Mabel took her hand and squeezed. "I'm so sorry. I've been going nonstop since I got home. After this, I was going to call you and beg you to go have a burger and shake for dinner tonight. After the city council meeting? The Buttermilk Café—our usual booth?" It was their staple hangout place—since high school. They'd order a plate of fries, kid-sized burgers and large milkshakes and settle in for hours of talk and laughter. *Exactly what I need right now.*

"You're going to the meeting, too? I'm so ready for this mess to be over and done with."

"Hopefully the vote tonight will do just that." Mabel nodded. She couldn't imagine the city council not voting down any sale of land to Quik Stop and Shop. But Mabel had never imagined this situation in the first place.

"I'm thinking extralarge shakes might be in order tonight." Hattie sighed, closing her eyes. "That sounds perfect. Seriously. You have no idea."

"Yay." Mabel hugged her again. "Oh, I guess I should stop hugging you? Are you here on duty?"

"Yes." She grinned, hands on hips—going into full presenter mode. "Officially, I'm here as Warden Carmichael and I'm going to present outdoor safety tips to a couple of local scout troops and an outdoor adventure club." Hattie shrugged. "The big Texas state parks Camp-Out Weekend is coming up so all the troop leaders are trying to get the kids as prepared as possible."

Mabel's phone was vibrating so she pulled it from her pocket. "Forrest." She sighed, reading the text. "The auction is starting." She slid her phone back into her pocket. "I should go. But I'll see you tonight?"

"I wouldn't miss it." Hattie nodded, pointing in the direction of the main arena. "But you better get a move on or he'll give *me* a talking-to for holding you up. That man's about as pigheaded as they come. Seems to be getting more so every year."

"I'm glad you see it, too." Mabel waved and set off. A night with Hattie would help her clear her mind. They had one of those relationships where, no matter how much time had passed or how long it'd been since they last talked, they could pick right up where they left off.

She left the cattle barn, hurried through the goats and pig barn, and landed at the back of a packed auction. She murmured, "Excuse me," at least a dozen times, smiling apologies at the impatient or irritated faces she had to squeeze past to get to the chair Forrest had doggedly held on to for her. "Sorry," she whispered, sliding into the metal chair. "Hattie."

"I figured." He nodded.

"We're going to have a girl's night out tonight," she said, glancing over the list.

"Sounds nice." He shrugged. "You haven't missed much."

She nodded, her thoughts returning to the paint horse again and again. There was no point fighting it. If she didn't try to help the animal, she'd never forgive herself. And she'd be too distracted and worried to be any use elsewhere. "Found the fifth," she murmured, handing the list back to Forrest— with the paint horse's number circled—and sat back in her chair.

The barn was surprisingly full. But according to Forrest, it'd been a while since they'd had this large a sale. Her gaze swept the crowd—some faces familiar, others not. But one face in particular caught her full attention.

Jensen.

He was staring down at the auction list in

his hands, his tan cowboy hat shielding the top part of his face… But it was him. She knew it was him. She *always* knew… *Stop staring.* She forced her gaze onward—and locked eyes with Dwight Crawley. If looks could kill, Mabel would be in serious trouble.

I get it. Mabel drew in an unsteady breath. *You don't like me. Like* might not be a strong enough word. Still, she managed a smile and nod in greeting. He might send her a shrivel-up-and-die glare, but how she responded was up to her. And since she'd never mastered the art of scowling or glaring or giving anyone the stink eye, a smile and nod would have to do.

Mr. Crawley must have made some sort of noise, because Jensen shot his father a peculiar look—before searching out the cause of his father's irritation. When those deep blue eyes met hers, a flush of warmth crept up her neck to settle into her cheeks.

"Mabel?" Forrest asked, nudging her gently and leaning closer. "This one, right?"

Mabel was glad for the nudge and the need for focus. She blinked, staring at the page until she was calm enough to say, "Yes. Go for it."

Auctions were terribly exciting events.

While Mabel found the idea of bidding anxiety-inducing, she did love watching her brother in action. He was fast, his hand popping up with a calm that belied the energy rolling over the crowd. For a split second, Mabel thought they'd lost the red quarter horse with the white blaze on his face, but Forrest managed to place a final bid.

But as the auction carried on, Mabel began to think her anxiety might have more to do with Mr. Crawley's continued narrow-eyed stare over the furor of the auction itself. It wasn't like she was trying to look in their direction—she wasn't. Forrest was seated beside her. When she looked his way, the Crawleys were two rows behind his shoulder. It got so uncomfortable that she stopped looking at Forrest to avoid any accidental eye contact with Mr. Crawley. Things were going well; they'd secured the horses she'd picked out. All that was left was the paint. And when she leaned over to tell her brother that, she did her best to ignore Mr. Crawley, openly scowling her way.

"We're down to the final horse today. This lovely little blue roan paint has an impressive lineage and a mild disposition," the auctioneer read, flipping the index card over.

Mild disposition? Mabel wasn't so sure about that. *Timid* was more like it. Maybe even *frightened*.

"You're sure?" Forrest asked, zeroing in on the scar marring the horse's flank.

Am I? She sucked in a deep breath. "I'm sure."

But something in her voice must have tipped Forrest off because he turned to look at her. "Mabel." Forrest sighed, shaking his head. "I know that look." Another sigh. "I can't spend money on a pet project—something you feel the need to fix. Especially if that horse will wind up costing me more money in the long run. It's not like you've said you're staying, either." He paused. "This is business."

Valid points, all of them. But... "I'll buy her." Mabel knew, in her heart, this horse needed help.

"That's fine. You buy her... But where are you going to keep her?" Forrest was sounding far too logical for Mabel's liking. "Because I can tell you right now, it won't matter who pays for her if you leave her at the ranch and you go back to Wyoming."

Mabel refused to look at her brother. He was right. If she looked at him, he'd see her uncertainty and put his foot down. He always said the worst time to make a decision was when emotions were high. And now that she could see the paint's withdrawn reaction to the crowd of people and the constant murmur of conversation, Mabel was feeling all kinds of emotions. "I'll buy her." It was what needed to be done. "I'll stay and take care of her." She'd figure it out. Work. All of it. She would. All she could do was *hope* it sounded like that had been her plan all along. "But you have to bid for me."

"If she's living on the ranch, the ranch will buy her," Forrest grumbled. "But I'm holding you to the rest—staying and all." He gave her a quick nod and jumped into the bidding.

But the dollar figure kept climbing and, one by one, the other bidders dropped out. The only two left were Forrest and… Dwight Crawley. Which meant Forrest would keep right on bidding, no matter what. As the bid started edging its way up to a ridiculous amount, Mabel's heart sank. Her uncle and brother kept a fixed cost on livestock purchases—with *very* few exceptions. She knew how hard they worked for every dollar they made and how fickle ranching could be. Asking Forrest to spend this much money, on a horse who might never be a working animal put a knot in her stomach.

"It's okay," she whispered, her hands fisting in her lap. "Don't break the bank, Forrest." She might not be fond of Dwight Crawley, but he and Crawley Cattle Ranch had a reputation for treating their animals well. There was some comfort in that. "You hear me?"

The muscle in Forrest's jaw was so rigid, Mabel worried he'd chip a tooth.

"I don't want Uncle Felix having a heart attack over this." She placed a hand on his arm. "You neither, Forrest."

Forrest glanced her way, disappointment and frustration bracketing his eyes and mouth.

"You know I'm right." She couldn't look at the horse. She'd lost out on animals before—auctions weren't always fair—but she couldn't deny this was hard. There was something in that mare that tugged at Mabel's heart. *She'll be fine. I'll be fine.* And now she wasn't forced into staying put in Garrison. *That's something.*

It wasn't easy for Forrest to cross his arms over his chest, Mabel could tell, and she loved him all the more for it. But frowning and rigid, Forrest yielded the bidding to

Dwight Crawley and that was that. When the gavel slammed down for the final time, she winced.

"I don't like losing—especially to *those* people." Forrest stood abruptly, turning his back on the people he was referring to and offering her a hand. "Guess we'll get the paperwork done, load them up and hit the road?"

She nodded, walking with him to the business office.

Sometimes the best course of action is to retreat—with dignity. The words were so clear Mabel could swear she could hear them. She couldn't, of course. She hadn't heard her father's voice in years. But he *had* said that to her once, long ago. It was a treasured memory, warm and comforting. She'd been sitting on the corral fence, watching as one of the ranch hands worked patiently with a horse who'd yet to be broken.

Her father had been talking softly, walking her through what Bossier was doing and why. Mabel had listened, quietly, but her attention kept wandering back to the horse. Over and over… Mabel had been struck by a notion.

"But the horse wants to make friends with Bossier, Daddy," she'd said. "He wants Bossier to talk nice to him and stop waving that rope in his face."

Her father had looked at her for a long time, those sky blue eyes of his searching her face until Mabel worried she'd said something wrong. Finally, he'd called out, "Bossier, put the rope down and talk soft. Talk to the horse like he's Mrs. Bossier." Her father had chuckled then.

Bossier had pushed his hat back on his head, swiped his forehead with the back of his forearm and dropped the rope.

It was the first time Mabel had dared share her *connection* with someone and her daddy believed in her. Thankfully, it had worked and Bossier and the horse got on much easier after that. Since everyone else took their cues from Albert—Albie to his friends—Briscoe, no one on Briscoe Ranch batted an eye over Mabel's *ability*. She could help out now, in her own special way, and it felt good. It had always been a part of her, nothing odd or unusual.

But once she'd started school, she realized the truth. Not only was her connection *highly* unusual—she was odd. A weirdo. Goggle girl. After the single-engine plane crash that took her parents' lives, it got worse. She was old enough to "know better" and her "lying" had to stop. Yes, it was sad she'd lost her parents, but telling stories for attention because she was some "sad little girl wearing her brother's clothes and Coke-bottle glasses" wasn't acceptable behavior. She'd been telling the truth. What they wanted her to do was lie—lie so she'd fit in. But she didn't fit in. Hiding her connection from people helped them accept her, but it didn't change how she felt. Sometimes Mabel wondered if life would be easier if she couldn't communicate with animals. Easier, maybe. But it would also be lonelier. *As if that were possible.*

JENSEN STARED AT his father. There was no way he'd heard that correctly. "For Samantha?"

"She's old enough." His father nodded, leaning against the horse trailer. "You'd been in the saddle since you were out of diapers—"

"She's not ready for a horse," Jensen cut him off. Maybe his father was telling him the truth and he'd been planning to buy Samantha a horse all along. Maybe. But would his father have been as insistent on buying *that* horse if he hadn't been bidding against Forrest Briscoe?

"She's not ready because *you're* not pushing her. It's what parents are supposed to do, Jensen." He sighed, frowning at Jensen. "You want her running and hiding from every thing on four legs for the rest of her life? Of course you don't. This is a good thing, you'll see. A little push now and then won't hurt."

"A little push?" Jensen shot his father a look. "Buying her a horse is your idea of a *little* push?" He opened the back doors of the trailer and pulled out the ramp as he added, "And what was it, exactly, about *this* horse that made you think of Samantha?"

"Well, now..." His father huffed. "That mare comes from good stock."

"It's not the only one." He stood, tipping his hat back on his head to get a better look at his father.

His father was squirming—looking for just the right thing to say. Finally, he pushed off the trailer, red-faced and scowling, to snap, "I didn't want... It felt like... Well, that animal deserves someplace better..."

"Than Briscoe Ranch?" Jensen finished, waiting. "And you didn't want Forrest Briscoe to have it."

"I didn't say that." His father crossed his arms over his barrel of a chest. "But it's good to know you're thinking like a Crawley again."

Only his father would twist his words to suit his purposes. He'd been scolding his father—his tone should have said as much. But nope, his father had perfected the science of hearing only what he wanted to hear or what suited him best. Like now. Jensen walked into the trailer, making sure everything was stowed away before the horses arrived. His father was too proud of publicly thwarting the Briscoes to consider the spectacle their little bidding war had caused. Mabel just happened to reel in Forrest before Jensen attempted to do the same with his father. Though, he likely wouldn't have had much luck. *When has my father ever listened to me?*

"You need to be careful, son." His father cleared his throat, giving Jensen an assessing look before he continued. "I get that she's... sort of attractive. I suppose. A fact she's likely well aware of."

Jensen stopped what he was doing and looked at his father.

"The way she seemed to be sizing you up, today... She's up to something, I know it. A woman like that will play dirty, too. Best remember where she comes from and who she is. A Briscoe."

Jensen rolled his neck, stretching out the knots that'd set in once his father and Forrest were going toe-to-toe over the pretty little paint mare and still showed no sign of easing. He turned his back on his father, heading into the interior of the trailer to check the medical kit—or at least that was what he was pretending to do. He'd done this before they hit the road this morning. What he needed was a few minutes to clear his head, away from his father.

Sort of attractive? Jensen swallowed. From where he'd been sitting, he'd had an unobstructed view of Mabel. Oddly enough, Jensen had a hard time seeing anything *but* Mabel. Every smile, every twitch or eyebrow raise, and every time she brushed one long strand of that midnight-black hair from her shoulder, Jensen knew. Instinctive. Reflexive. She had a dimple in her left cheek. He hadn't known that before today.

Mabel wasn't sort of attractive. She was mesmerizing. Anyone with eyes could see there was an honest-to-goodness genuine sweetness to her. Anyone, that is, except his father. The very notion of Mabel using her looks for some dastardly purpose was downright laughable. For that matter, Mabel being involved in *anything* dastardly was absurd. He took a deep breath and headed down the loading ramp and out of the horse trailer.

"What now?" his father asked, scowling once more. "You look like you swallowed a bee."

The day was only half done. Jensen still had to load the newly purchased horses, drive them—and his father—home, unload them all, get them sorted and settled. Then, it was Samantha time. Homework, playtime and bedtime. If he voiced even the slightest difference of opinion on Mabel, his father would load every second of every minute of the rest of the day with hostility and snide comments.

"Nothing." Jensen shrugged. "Just thinking logistics. You know I like to load by personality. I don't know much about these horses."

"You worry too much." His father shook his head. "I saw Tom Parker over in the swine barn. I figure I'll head that way while you wait on the horses."

"Sounds good." As far as Jensen was concerned, his father spent too much time on the ranch and removed from people. Then again, his father wasn't overly fond of most people. Tom Parker was an exception. Tom had worked on the Crawley place for years. Upon the death of his sister, he'd inherited her small farm and quit the ranch, but they'd stayed friendly. "Give him my best."

"That I will." His father set off, his stride slow but confident.

Jensen watched his father until he'd disappeared in the sea of livestock, people and what looked like the arrival of a school group or two. The kids were lined up in twos, wearing name badges, school T-shirts and grinning from ear to ear. He smiled, thinking about Samantha... But his smile faded.

Would she enjoy being here? The only time she ever ventured into the barn, it was to see a new baby animal, rabbits or chicks. The small ones were fine, most of the time. Grown animals—like the horse his father had bought today—plain terrified his little girl. No one thing had caused it, Samantha just panicked over something bigger than her being on all fours. His father might be going about it the wrong way, but he was trying to help. Jensen was pretty sure buying Samantha a horse wasn't going to cure her fear, but what did he know? Maybe his little girl would take one look at the pretty paint and fall in love.

Wouldn't that be nice.

He'd planned to leave with two horses, horses that knew how to work cattle and were easygoing. And he was. But the little paint? She was pretty to look at, but did her temperament match? There was only one way to know. He walked down the aisles, heading straight for the mare's pen.

The last person he'd expected to find there was Mabel. But there she was, her arms draped over the top rung of the fence and one booted foot resting on the lowest rung. Today, she wasn't wearing a dress. He wondered if her boot-cut jeans and red-and-white shirt with the frilly neck would make Samantha rethink the whole princess thing. *I doubt it.* As Samantha had pointed out, some Texas royalty wore boots and jeans "'Cuz we live in Texas, Daddy," she'd said. There was no arguing with that.

As he drew closer, he realized Mabel was studying the mare.

The mare seemed to be studying Mabel right back.

He slowed, torn. The last thing he needed

was to get caught out in the open talking to Mabel Briscoe again. There was still all sorts of chatter about the two of them at the picnic, or so his sisters said. Twyla had gone on to say, "It didn't help that Mabel had spoken out at the recital, making sure there wasn't a single solitary person that didn't know what was happening." She'd said a whole lot more, too. So, *this* probably wouldn't help.

But the paint was now his horse; he had every right to be there. And it wasn't like he could just turn and head the other direction. People had noticed them and they were watching. *There's no turning back now.*

"Mabel." His voice was low, but it still startled her. "Sorry."

She stared up at him, eyes wide. "No," she murmured. "No, not at all."

A lump hung in his throat the moment he caught sight of her face. *Is she crying?* Her eyes were red-rimmed. And her nose was red, too.

"I shouldn't be here." But other than blinking rapidly, she didn't move. "I just… She…"

That was when it clicked. "*You* wanted the horse?" He hung his head, his hands on his hips—silently cursing his father's pigheadedness. The lump in his throat doubled in size and felt jagged when he swallowed. He looked up to find her staring at him.

"I... Yes." She was staring hard. Looking for something. "What do you plan to do with her? The mare?"

It took a minute to draw air into his lungs. The uncomfortably sharp lump in his throat didn't help. "Samantha." He ran a hand over his face, breaking the hold she had on him. The less time he spent getting caught up in those blue eyes, the better. But if she'd wanted this horse, there was likely a reason. It gutted him something fierce to know he'd gotten in the way of that.

"Oh." Luckily, Mabel's gaze swiveled back to the horse, but there was no missing the surprise on her face. "I thought... Isn't Samantha afraid of animals?"

"Yes." He hadn't realized how long and dark her eyelashes were. Almost inky black.

"Does she want a horse?"

"No." He watched as she ran her fingers through her hair. Samantha said Miss Mabel had beautiful hair. And...he agreed. It was getting hard to breathe again. The lump wouldn't budge. "I don't know," he admitted.

"Does she know she's getting one?" She looked down at her boot, resting on the bottom rung of the fence, and her long hair fell forward to hide her face.

"No." His fingers itched to tuck her hair behind her ear. *What is wrong with me?*

"Did *you* know?" She turned to face him them, openly concerned.

At the moment, Jensen was pretty concerned, too. It'd been a long time since he'd noticed a woman, let alone little details… like the tiny mole by Mabel's right eyebrow or that one eye seemed just a hair darker blue than the other. But he was noticing all right. How could he not? She was… She was Mabel. *Briscoe.* And wherever this train of thought was headed, he'd best make it stop. *Immediately.* Yes, she was something— staring up at him with worry creasing her brow. And, no matter what his father thought or said, he knew she *was* truly worried and concerned. *About the horse.*

"Jensen?" Mabel raised an eyebrow.

Clearing his throat didn't do a thing to ease his discomfort. "No. No. My father bought her the mare. He was…full of surprises today." *Was it warm in here?* It was warm. Too warm. He tore his gaze away and forced himself to focus on the paint mare in the pen.

"Can I ask a favor?" She paused. "I know it'll sound weird, but can you... Can you be extra patient with her?"

"Samantha? Or the horse?" he asked, knowing the answer, but hoping to ease the tension.

Her laugh was reward enough. "Both, I guess."

"I can do that." He glanced her way and froze. Her eyes were very definitely full of tears now. Tears that looked ready to spill over any second. The lump in his throat was downright painful now. "Mabel—"

"Thank you," she whispered. "Jensen." She swallowed, her gaze searching his. "I know we're supposed to hate each other and all that, but I can't help but feel like you and I—"

"Mabel?" Forrest Briscoe's voice was sharp enough to cut glass. "I've been looking for you all over."

"I told you where I was going." She sighed, quickly swiping at her eyes.

"What's going on?" There was no denying Forrest was worked up. "What's wrong?"

"Nothing." Mabel waved aside her brother's question. "I was just saying goodbye." She nodded at the paint horse, standing on the far side of the pen.

"Goodbye?" Forrest crossed his arms over his chest. "To the horse?"

Now might not be the best time to want to laugh, but Jensen couldn't help it. He was standing right here, clear as day. He and Mabel had been talking, also apparent— they hadn't been trying to hide it. But Forrest showed up and she was supposed to, what? Pretend he *wasn't* here? That they hadn't just been talking five seconds before? That Mabel hadn't been about to say something that Jensen would never get to hear? All because Mabel saying goodbye to him, a Crawley, wasn't acceptable. *But it's fine for her to say goodbye to a horse.* He tried to hold back, he really did, but a soft chuckle slipped out.

Mabel's eyes went round, but she didn't look at him. "Yes. All done, now." She pushed off the pen. "You ready, Forrest?"

"I've been ready," he snapped. "Loaded up and ready to go."

"Good," she said softly.

Jensen heard the slight hitch in her voice and turned to look her way.

Forrest's gaze met his. "You need something?" Each word was edged with hostility.

Jensen didn't flinch. "Just making sure

Mabel's okay." He'd done nothing wrong. Neither had she. But her tears… They got to him.

Mabel's gaze bounced between them. "I'm fine."

"Why wouldn't she be?" Forrest's eyes narrowed.

The last thing he wanted to do was fight Forrest Briscoe—again. But he'd learned a long time ago, when Forrest Briscoe was determined to fight, there was no stopping him. "Because she was meant to have this horse," Jensen explained, nodding at the paint horse. "And she's worried about it. Sad, too, I expect. For my part in that, I'm sorry."

Forrest's brow smoothed, he was so shocked. Jensen felt the odds of being pummeled tipping in his favor.

Mabel, on the other hand, was looking at him with…what? What was that look? What did it mean?

"I am." Jensen spoke directly to her. "I didn't know."

"How could you have known?" Her smile didn't quite reach her eyes and there was only a hint of her dimple. "At least I know you'll take care of her. That helps." She took a deep breath. "Really, Jensen, it does."

Now she was trying to reassure him? Even tear-filled, he found himself getting lost in those blue eyes. A massive weight seemed to drop square in the middle of his chest, knocking the air from his lungs and rattling around everything in his rib cage. She was… something.

She didn't seem bothered by the fact that her brother was standing there, looking at her like she was speaking another language. If she noticed the small crowd of folk gathering close to the pen, hoping to see some Briscoe vs Crawley action up close and personal, she didn't let on. Instead, she smiled. At him. Warm and gentle—pretty much exactly how he'd describe Mabel.

Before he knew it, he was smiling back.

Forrest's sharp indrawn breath was enough to end all the smiling. "Come on, Mabel," he grumbled. "I don't know what's gotten into you."

Mabel blinked, her gaze widening as she took in the cluster of people pretending a sudden fascination in the paint horse. "Oh." Her cheeks turned a deep pink as she hooked arms with Forrest.

She didn't look back as she walked away. He knew, because he watched her go—

hoping her departure would dislodge the lump from his throat or ease the weight off his chest. It didn't. Not one bit.

And while she was walking out of the stock barn, he was left to sort through the jumble of confusion making his head spin. He wasn't sure what was real or inferred or how to tell the difference. He did know he didn't want to be *just* a Crawley to her—although he wasn't focusing on *why* that was the case. Probably because he didn't see her as a Briscoe. To him, she was Mabel.

What he was beginning to realize was, right or wrong, he *liked* Mabel. Why wouldn't he? There was plenty to like. Her kindness toward Samantha. The dedication to causes she valued. Her abiding family loyalty. She had, according to everyone who knew her, a heart of gold. Not to mention her way with animals. *Like the horse I now own.* He looked at the blue-gray paint mare eyeing him from her place across the pen. *Yeah, I know. Mabel has that thing. I don't.* He sighed.

Today he had taken a detour and he'd no idea how to get back to where he was before. *Before* he'd gotten caught up in Mabel, caught up in a way that left him off-balance and flustered. Since he didn't seem able to rein in whatever this was she'd stirred up, the only thing left for him to do was to stay as far away from Mabel Briscoe as possible. How hard could that be?

CHAPTER SIX

MABEL SAT IN the back row of the meeting room, her green Save the First Tree button pinned to the front of her green dress. The room was packed wall to wall for tonight's city council meeting. Some folk were standing along the walls. From her spot, Mabel couldn't tell who was here and who wasn't.

"Is Forrest wearing a bolo tie?" Hattie whispered, covering her mouth with her hand to stifle her snort of laughter.

Mabel had to fight to stop herself from laughing, too. Hattie's giggle-snort thing was impossibly contagious. "I'm afraid so," Mabel whispered back, wrinkling her nose. "He seems to be getting fashion advice from Uncle Felix and Webb. Neither of which should be giving fashion advice—clearly."

Hattie giggle-snorted again, earning them a long-suffering look from an old man, with a squeaky hearing aid, sitting in the row in members and to all of you. I admit, your impassioned pleas and sincere love of the Old Tree…" She paused, glancing at her notes. "The First Tree, excuse me, is lovely."

If she'd been hoping to ingratiate herself with pretty words and flattery, she should have taken the time to get the correct name of the thing her company was planning to bulldoze. Mabel knew this was business—emotions wouldn't affect the bottom line. The bottom line being profit, of course. But this wasn't the first time she'd seen commerce steal from nature.

Her work with the mustangs had been eye-opening on that front. There were so few herds left in the wild and ever fewer places available for them to roam. In Wyoming, when the national parks boundaries were being adjusted, she'd spoken out about the damage that "minor" shift would have on the food and resources for the animals that lived within the parks. When a private sponsor had suggested rounding up the mustangs, selling the land for their upkeep and putting them on a preserve they'd pay for, Mabel had protested. It wasn't just that the area was less than a quarter of the land the herds had been roaming for years—it was

front of them. "Sorry," Hattie murmured, her cheeks red.

Mabel leaned closer to Hattie, barely making a sound. "He's too young to dress like he's seventy. And he's too old to wear painted-on jeans and skin-tight button-ups." Thankfully, he'd decided against the jeans. He was, however, wearing a too-tight shirt and a ghastly turquoise Texas-shaped bolo tie. "I did try to talk him out of it." She'd even tried to hide the bolo. But Harvey had emerged from her room, the bolo tie hanging from his mouth and his tail wagging. "It's like he doesn't know how handsome he is."

Hattie leaned back, crossing her arms over her chest to study Forrest. Tonight, she was just Hattie, not Warden Carmichael, meaning no tan polyester uniform or badge. Instead, she was in faded jeans and a plaid button-down shirt two sizes too big, and her strawberry blond curls had been twisted and clipped at the back of her head. She was nibbling on the inside of her lip, her eyes narrowing, and she cocked her head to one side.

"Don't you think?" Mabel asked, glancing from Hattie to Forrest.

Hattie shrugged. "He's been my friend for too long, I guess. I mean, he's all right. He's not ugly." Which, from Hattie, was sort of a compliment. She didn't put much stock on a person's outsides; it was the words and deeds that influenced Hattie's opinion.

Mabel grinned.

There'd been almost two hours of testimonials. Old Towne Hardware and Appliances owner Nolan Woodard had gone first, followed by his sons. Mikey Woodard was a county EMT and well liked. Rusty Woodard knew everyone from working in the family appliance store. Then just about every shop owner took a turn. Brooke Young stepped up, with baby Joy on her hip, and stressed the importance of the town's heritage and traditions for the generations to come. One by one, the members of the Garrison Ladies Guild took a turn at the podium. From Miss Patsy's fire-engine-red hair and earnest plea to Miss Martha's clipped and rapid-fire promise that each and every council member who voted against saving the "very foundation that Garrison was built upon" would be sorry—all while shaking her finger at each and every one of them. Finally, it looked like everyone had talked themselves out. Which was good considering the noises coming from Hattie's stomach.

One particularly loud gurgle had M red-faced from trying not to laugh.

"Now, we'll hear from Miss Elsa Nas Quik Stop and Shop," Council member pert Langford announced, peering over top of his reading glasses to watch, blar faced, as the woman walked across the ti floor.

"Look at her," Hattie murmured. "How does she walk in those things?" Her brows shot up.

Mabel eyed the ridiculously skinny heels of Miss Nash's red-soled shoes and shrugged. Mabel wore a dress—she loved dresses—but boots were her shoe of choice. She'd owned one pair of heels, something Uncle Felix had bought her for some high school dance. She'd come home from that dance with a twiste ankle and bruises on her hip and thigh a her ego. The heels were put back in t shoebox, buried deep in the recesses o closet, never to be seen again.

The whole room seemed to hold its watching as the woman approac weathered lectern. The tension was Mabel found herself pulling at th neckline of her dress for more a

"Good evening, distinguished

the concerns over what the land would be used for if it was sold off. How could they expect the wild mustangs to thrive in a confined space smack-dab in a commercial- or residential-zoned space?

Money. It was always money. She'd begged, borrowed, written grants and done everything within her power to have the financial backing she needed in order for people to listen to her. It hadn't been enough. The private donor won out and the preserve was created—with a good number of mustangs being relocated.

Hattie elbowed her. "Did you hear that?"

Mabel shook her head.

"She's saying they'll pay local employees above minimum wage and provide health care for all employees working over twenty hours a week." Hattie shook her head. "For how long?" She was referring to the Quik Stop and Shop that had opened in a town about the size of Garrison, two counties over, and the devastation it'd left behind when it closed.

"You should ask, Hattie," Mabel whispered. "That's the sort of thing people need to be reminded of."

Hattie's face went beet red. "I can't. I'm

not in uniform, remember?" Hattie's fear of public speaking had almost stopped her from being accepted into the Game Warden Academy. Mabel and Forrest had helped her think of her warden's uniform like a costume. When she was wearing it, she had no problem standing in front of a packed room—just like this. But without it? Hattie hadn't figured out that, with or without the uniform, she was one and the same person. "No way."

Mabel patted Hattie's leg. "Right. Sorry."

"But you should." Hattie elbowed her. "You look nice and everyone loves you."

Mabel made a noncommittal noise. When she and Hattie had walked into the courthouse, there'd been a low buzz. She'd heard enough, though—her name, *Jensen*, *horse auction*, *picnic* and *Samantha* murmured in various volumes. Did she really want to get up there and draw more attention to herself? First, she'd lost the horse to Jensen. Then they'd had that weird staring-contest thing in the barn after. Followed by all sorts of warm tingles and a full mind-muddle that kept her silent most of the way home. It was like she'd gotten stuck on some sort of Jensen Crawley–themed merry-go-round: exhilarating and unsettling and dizzying and spinning too fast for her to think straight or get off the ride. When he'd said her name in that barn... She shivered. It wasn't fair. It wasn't fair that the one man who was 100 percent off-limits to her could do *that* to her. *By saying my name?* One look, one word and she was a ball of jumbled nerves.

"We will open the floor to questions," one of the council members said, startling her.

Hattie elbowed her again, harder this time, and nodded at the newly vacated podium. "Go on, Mabel."

What am I doing? Hattie was right. This had nothing to do with her. This had everything to do with her home. She took a deep breath and stood, walking down the aisle, past rows packed full of curious faces, to the waiting lectern.

"Good evening." She cleared her throat.

"Good evening, Miss Briscoe," Council member Buck Williams, owner of the only honky-tonk in Garrison, greeted her "You have some questions?"

"I do." She nodded, gripping the lectern to steady herself. "About three years ago, Quik Stop and Shop opened a store in Dripping Springs." She smiled. "They came in, making big pay and benefit promises—similar to what Miss Nash outlined this evening. I remember because Myrna Ingells was working there and excited over the benefits for her children—being the breadwinner of the family and all." She took a deep breath, willing her nerves aside. "Within six months or so of opening, the store went through restructuring. Hours were reduced, benefits cut and employees like Myrna were left working odd shifts without everything they'd been promised. And, with all the mom-and-pop shops run out of business, there weren't a whole lot of places to look for work." There was a murmur of conversation now. "Then Quik Stop and Shop closed, leaving an empty big-box store and the town in all sorts of financial trouble. What sort of binding guarantees could Quik Stop and Shop give us? Not only do we risk losing a part of our heritage, we risk the substantial financial toll their business will take on local shops like Old Towne Hardware and Appliances, Young's Beauty Salon, Old Towne Books and Coffee, Schneider's Family Grocery Store and The Calico Pig. These people are our neighbors. They've invested in our community knowing that we'd invest in them. Allowing Quik Stop and Shop to set up shop here guarantees Garrison is forever changed—with no guarantee those changes would be good for any of us."

Buck Williams had been nodding. Now he stopped. "Was there a question in there, Miss Briscoe?"

Mabel laughed, her cheeks going hot. "I suppose not. Not really. I guess I'm asking you, as the city council, to put your town and your neighbors before the short-term financial gains that might be hard to resist."

There was a brief silence—so silent that the whole room heard Hattie's stomach growling from the back of the room.

Amid the laughter, Hattie mumbled, "Sorry."

"Duly noted." Rupert Langford nodded, his steely gaze fixing on Mabel. "Well said, Miss Briscoe."

"Thank you." She nodded and stepped away from the lectern, refusing to look at the sea of faces or to slow until she plopped down next to Hattie once more.

"You should run for city council," Hattie said, not bothering to whisper.

"I'd vote for ya," the old man sitting in front of them said loudly.

"See." Hattie nodded.

"I'm not sure two votes would do it," Mabel said. "But it's kind of you two to say so."

"Let's get right to the vote, shall we?" Rupert Langford had leaned into his microphone. "I know I'm not the only one anxious to get home to their supper."

A few people chuckled and poor Hattie looked ready to slide onto the floor, but that was forgotten when the seven city council members scribbled their votes onto the cards and passed them in for the clerk, Valeria Hillard, to read aloud. "The vote to cease negotiations with Quik Stop and Shop is unanimous. The vote and results will be recorded and published within this meeting's minutes for record."

Mabel hadn't been this relieved in a long time.

"Your talk made all the difference. I just know it did." Hattie gave her a fierce hug.

"I'm pretty sure they all came in already knowing their mind." Mabel hugged her back. If anything, Jensen had been right. There'd been no need to worry.

"Whatever." Hattie stood and pulled Mabel to her feet. "Now, let's go eat before my stomach makes another horribly embarrassing noise."

"Was that what that was?" the old man sitting in front of them asked, smiling over his shoulder at the two of them.

It took a while for Mabel and Hattie to make their way out of the city council chamber. Folks were clustered together, celebrating and talking, the general sense of relief overwhelming. Mabel understood. Whether or not the First Tree had been in any real danger, there was something about seeing a community come together to fight for a common purpose. Garrison had rallied. And won.

But before the two of them could get outside, Miss Martha had caught up to them. "Hold up, Mabel. You just knocked my socks off, young lady. Not that I'm wearing any socks." She took Mabel by the shoulders, giving her a head-to-toe inspection. "That was quite a pretty speech you made."

"It was Hattie's idea." Mabel didn't like where this was headed. "If Hattie hadn't brought it up, I wouldn't have thought to do it myself."

"Is this true?" Miss Martha's attention zeroed in on Hattie. "Why didn't you speak at the meeting, Officer Carmichael?"

"I'm off duty tonight, Miss Martha. Besides, I'm pretty sure I could never be as elo-

quent as Mabel here." Hattie looked at Mabel
with such pride.

"I have to say, I agree. About the eloquence part. I had no idea you were such a
gifted speaker, Miss Briscoe." Miss Martha
was still looking at her like she was a blue-
ribbon-winning pie. "And I heard your little
comment about running for city council—"

"That was a joke," Mabel hurried to explain. "Hattie's joke. Not mine. I have no intention of running for any office." She wasn't
sure she was staying in Garrison after her
two weeks were up now that her horse belonged to Jensen.

"Well, now, that's where I hope I can
change your mind." Miss Martha's smile was
more than a little intimidating. "But I know
Miss Hattie is starving, we all know it, so
you and I will catch up later, Miss Briscoe.
Just keep an open mind, will you?"

Luckily, Mabel didn't have to answer before Miss Martha was already headed back
toward the Garrison Ladies Guild—all huddled together and smiling.

"What have you gotten me into?" Mabel
hissed at Hattie. "Once that woman gets a
hold of an idea, she's like a dog with a bone."

"Then I guess you better get used to the

idea of running for city council." Hattie was laughing as they made their way outside onto the sidewalk. "What's wrong with that, anyway? I think you'd be a great city council member. Have we ever had a council member under the age of sixty?" Hattie shrugged. "You'd be groundbreaking."

"I have no interest in being groundbreaking. Or serving on city council." She nodded a few "hellos" as they passed others leaving the courthouse. "The only thing I'm interested in right now is an extralarge milkshake. And since you've gotten me into this mess with Miss Martha, you can pick up the tab."

"Fine. But we are not sharing a burger this time. I'm starving."

The two of them took their time strolling along Main Street. It'd been so long since they had just chatted, there was a lot to catch up on. Mabel had always appreciated that Hattie was a straight shooter. When they were together, Mabel knew she could be herself. Hattie never expected anything from her, except good conversation and, of course, a milkshake. And right now, that sounded pretty perfect to her, too.

Mabel opened the front door of the Buttermilk Café and stood aside for Hattie. "After you."

"Why, thank you." Hattie waved at the owner and headed toward their booth.

But Mabel stopped short when she caught sight of Samantha Crawley sitting on one of the high stools at the counter. Alone. "Well, hi there." One look at the little girl's wide, sad eyes had Mabel sitting on the stool next to her. "What's the matter, Samantha?"

"Hi, Miss Mabel." Samantha perked up a bit when she saw Mabel, but not with the same bounce and eager grin Mabel had become accustomed to. "Nothin'." But the quaver in Samantha's voice said the exact opposite.

"Where's your daddy?" Hattie asked, her gaze sweeping the restaurant. "Or your aunties?"

Mabel was wondering the same thing. With any luck, Samantha was here with her aunts. Even Mr. Crawley would be better. She'd rather get scowled at and ignored than face Jensen. Again.

"He's in the restroom. Miss Lucille is keeping an eye on me." Samantha sighed.

Mabel waved at Miss Lucille, ignoring the alarming surge of tingles that tightened her stomach. Really, she had to stop this. Somehow, some way, she had to figure out how to cure her reaction to Jensen Crawley. Right now, the smart thing to do would be to give Samantha a hug, then she and Hattie would head to their booth and enjoy their evening as planned. The more time she spent with Samantha, the harder it would be to get Jensen out of her head. And she desperately needed to get him out of her head. And heart. *Heart? No.* He was not in her heart. The very idea was...was...*true?* The realization was as effective as being doused with ice water. "Well, it was good to see you," she said, her heart hammering in her ears. It was. And as much as she wanted to make Samantha smile that infectious, light-up-the-room smile, getting involved wasn't her place.

But then Samantha leaned forward and threw her arms around her neck with such urgency that Mabel realized something else. Jensen wasn't the only Crawley who had touched her heart. She pulled the little girl into her lap. "Hey, hey, now. I've got you."

JENSEN GLANCED AT his reflection in the Buttermilk Café restroom. He looked stressed out. *I am stressed out.* Thanks to his father. All the way home from the auction, he and his father had discussed the best way to introduce the idea of the horse to Samantha. His father had been surprisingly receptive. Calm and levelheaded, listening as Jensen insisted they take things slow. *That should have tipped me off.* There were times he forgot how his father worked, is all. He should have known better.

Once they were home, his father had made it almost ten minutes before he clapped his hands together and told Samantha he'd brought her a very special present. Jensen had cut him off, hoping the glare and head shake would stop him. "Dad, we agreed."

His father had glared right back. "Who agreed? You were talking—I listened. I never agreed to a thing."

It took a lot to get Jensen angry, but that had done it. "When we discussed Samantha and me living here, you agreed that I would raise my daughter the way I saw fit. If you can't abide by that, then it's time for us to find a place of our own." He'd scooped up Samantha, ignored the shocked looks on his sisters' faces and carried her out to his waiting truck.

Did I take it too far? He sighed, staring at his reflection. *No.* His father had crossed a line today. First, buying the horse without discussing it first. Then, going against everything Jensen had said about introducing the horse to Samantha. His *father* had taken it too far.

The worst part of it was how upset the whole argument had made Samantha. Luckily, Samantha hadn't known what the argument was about—the paint mare waiting in the barn was still a secret. But he'd been so upset on the drive into town, he hadn't done much to soothe her fears. He'd left her alone with Miss Lucille for five minutes—just enough time to calm down. She needed him to be calm. He took a deep breath. *I'm calm.*

Some ice cream, maybe a visit to the playground… Anything to assure Samantha that everything was fine. It was, too. He splashed some cool water on his face, dried his face and hands and headed back out into the Buttermilk Café's dining room. His smile had been in place. Until he found Samantha hugging Mabel Briscoe. Not just hugging, clinging. As if her little heart was breaking and only her favorite real-life princess could fix it.

Hattie's gaze met his, and she shrugged. *Yes, I know.* He didn't know what was happening, either. Whenever Mabel was around, everything seemed to get flipped upside down. *Maybe that only happens to me.*

Samantha got an extra bounce in her step whenever Mabel was around. Even talking about Mabel seemed to perk his little girl right up. Was it any surprise that Samantha was turning to the woman now for comfort? *No. No surprise.* But his daughter's growing affection for Mabel Briscoe was sure to complicate things. *As if they weren't complicated enough.* In that moment, he felt bone-tired. Single fathers didn't get to be tired—not when their little girl needed them. "What's all this?" It took effort to keep his voice upbeat, but he managed. "Are they out of vanilla ice cream?" It was a lame joke, but it was all he could come up with.

Mabel had Samantha cradled in her lap, running a steady hand over Samantha's curls while his little girl buried her face against Mabel's shoulder. The sight of the two of them put an ache in his chest.

"We do have vanilla," Miss Lucille chimed in. "I'll get Samantha here a double scoop. Want some sprinkles, sugar?"

"Do you want sprinkles?" Mabel whispered. "I bet that would be yummy."

Samantha nodded, her voice muffled against Mabel's shoulder. "Yes, please."

"Coming right up." Miss Lucille turned, ice cream scoop in hand, and headed to the ice cream case at the end of the counter.

"Little miss." He rested a hand on Samantha's back. "Let Mabel breathe. You're squeezing her awful hard."

Samantha let go. "I'm sorry—"

"I'm fine." Mabel cupped Samantha's cheek. "I'm not breakable. I like tight hugs. They make me feel extra special." She smoothed a wayward curl from Samantha's forehead. "A good hug can cheer a person up."

"Ice cream can help with that, too." Miss Lucille handed over a waffle cone with vanilla scoops, and extra sprinkles, stacked high.

Samantha's eyes went round when she saw the ice-cream-heavy cone. "This should help lots, then, huh?"

Mabel's eyes were just as round. "A whole lot." Her laugh was free and easy and the only thing that had made Samantha smile since before he and his father's standoff.

It was a whole lot easier for him to breathe all of a sudden. And yet, hearing Mabel's laugh made the ache in his chest bigger—almost hollow. He swallowed against the tightening of his throat.

Samantha held the cone with both hands. She turned her head, inspected the ice cream, leaned in, then turned her head the other way. "It's too big." She giggled then.

"I was going to say that there is the biggest ice cream cone I have ever seen," Hattie said with a laugh.

"Sharing might be in order," he added. Without being asked, Miss Lucille slid three empty cups and spoons across the table—with a wink. "Thank you, Miss Lucille."

"Oh, but..." Mabel's gaze darted from the cups to him to Samantha. "Um... Hattie and I—"

"Are eating some ice cream." Hattie slid onto the stool beside Mabel. "I'm so hungry, I could eat a horse—tail and all."

Samantha carefully handed over her cone to him and shot Hattie a confused look. "You'd eat a horse, Miss Hattie?"

"No, no," Hattie chuckled. "That's a silly expression. I am hungry, though. Mabel and I were over at the courthouse just now and my stomach was grumbling so loud, everyone could hear it. Interrupted Mabel's speech.

But even with my tummy grumbling, Mabel made a big enough impression that Miss Martha came over after, wanting her to run for city council."

Interesting. He risked a glance Mabel's way.

She didn't seem all that excited. She was red-cheeked and shaking her head and clearly uncomfortable. Her eye roll was adorable. He cleared his throat. *Adorable?* Better to focus on divvying up ice cream instead of how lovely Mabel looked. *Really?* He tapped his spoon against the cup with a little more force than necessary, almost tipping the cup over. *First, adorable and now lovely?* He glanced up to find Hattie and Mabel and Miss Lucille watching him.

"What'd you talk 'bout?" Samantha asked, too busy staring at Mabel to notice his overly aggressive ice cream scooping.

"The First Tree." Mabel nodded her thanks as he slid a cup her way.

"And?" Miss Lucille asked. "I heard some hootin' and hollerin' so I'm thinking it's good news?"

Hattie nodded. "Unanimous. Miss Nash and her fancy high heels and Quik Stop and

Shop can make their way out of Garrison city limits."

"I was hoping that was the way it'd shake out." Miss Lucille heaved a sigh of relief. "I can't remember a time when I've been so worried over something. Now, if we can get that yahoo who got this nonsense started on his merry way, I'll be pleased as punch."

The yahoo in question was one Lance Devlin, the city manager. He was some big-city hotshot hoping to make a name for himself by putting his stamp on Garrison. He'd made a name for himself, all right, but Jensen was pretty sure "yahoo" wasn't what Mr. Devlin had in mind. Word on the street was the only reason he'd been hired in the first place was his relation to Martha Zeigler. Being one of the richest people in three counties came with a lot of perks, like nepotism. Not that she was claiming any relation to Lance now. According to Twyla, Miss Martha was this close to disowning Lance from the family— on account of his involvement with this Quik Stop and Shop business.

He had a feeling the city manager position would be open soon enough. "Give it a week." Jensen handed Samantha back her ice cream cone.

"I'm just glad the First Tree is safe." Mabel looked almost wistful as she said, "Growing up, I thought it was a magic tree. I used to pretend elves and fairies lived there—along with the birds and possums and squirrels, too. It was where only good things happened. Birthday celebrations and parties and family reunions and weddings, all happening in the shade of that giant tree." She smiled at Samantha. "I like to think my children and grandchildren will create memories there, too."

Samantha was now enjoying her much more manageable ice cream. "But you have to find a prince, first." She stopped licking, her eyes wide. "I mean a—"

"A prince would be nice." Hattie's spoonful of ice cream paused halfway to her mouth. "To get whisked off our feet and go to balls and all that." She sighed, all dreamy, then giggled.

Samantha grinned broadly.

"I don't need a prince." Mabel wrinkled up her nose, a gesture he'd seen her do before.

He stopped himself before he did something foolish like label the nose-wrinkle thing as adorable or lovely or anything else along those lines. *I'm gonna sit here and eat ice cream.*

"You don't?" Samantha was confused by the announcement. If Mabel was a princess, she'd have to marry a prince. All the fairy tales said so. "You don't want to marry a prince?"

"I think a real prince would be too… stuffy." Mabel leaned forward to whisper, "I'd be happy with a nice man. A nice man with a big heart and a good head on his shoulders."

"Sounds like a prince to me." Hattie rested one elbow on the counter. "Let me know if you find one."

Jensen knew firsthand that the dating pool in Garrison wasn't exactly deep, but there were a few men who fit Mabel's description. "What about Mikey Woodard?" he offered, looking at Hattie. "Or Rusty, for that matter." He paused. "And Tyson Ellis and Fritz Koch. Oh, and don't forget, there's also Lance Devlin."

Hattie rolled her eyes then. "Ha, ha, very funny."

"I was only teasing about the one." He scraped the last ice cream from his cup. "What's wrong with the rest of them?"

"Are you playing matchmaker, Jensen?" Hattie chuckled.

"No." He was the least qualified person to

help with romance. He'd been lucky. Casey had had a great sense of humor and endless patience, and had no problem taking him by the hand and leading him through the courting process. A fact he was forever grateful for. "But if you're looking, there might be a few that match your description."

"Mabel's description," Hattie clarified. "She was the one talking about kids and weddings and grandkids under the tree. I'd settle for the good-man part, to start."

Did that mean Mabel was looking? And if that were the case, why did the idea of her considering any one of the men he'd listed off rub him the wrong way?

"And there's you, Daddy," Samantha piped up. "You could marry Miss Hattie or Miss Mabel. You're a good man. And you love me so you can love them. And you have a head on your shoulders 'cuz I see it and it's good and pretty."

"Thank you, little miss," he murmured, flattered and embarrassed at the same time. He was acutely aware of the fact that Hattie and Miss Lucille were sizing him up. Mabel, however, was staring into her ice cream cup—a deep red flush creeping up her neck and into her cheeks.

"You know what, Samantha?" Miss Lucille rested an elbow on the counter, staring at him intently. "I'd say *pretty* fits."

"Pretty?" Hattie shook her head. "You can't call a man pretty. Good-looking, sure. Handsome, fine. Even smoking hot. But not pretty."

"If they're smoking hot, shouldn't they go to the doctors?" Samantha looked concerned. "That sounds really too hot for a person to be okay."

Mabel let out a little laugh, and he couldn't help smiling.

"It's another expression." Hattie was grinning from ear to ear. "I guess I use a few too many?"

"Well, Daddy is ham-some, I think. Don't you, Miss Mabel?" Samantha turned her wide eyes on the even-redder Mabel.

"I do," Mabel said, not bothering to look at him.

He wasn't sure how to feel about that. Was she just agreeing to make Samantha happy or did she find him attractive? The real question was, shouldn't he be concerned that her answer mattered to him? The answer to that was yes. A big, fat yes.

Jensen's phone rang, dragging him firmly

back to reality. His sister's name popped up on the screen. No doubt she was calling to chide him for upsetting their father. He hit Ignore and set the phone on the counter. Twyla wasn't one to shy away from speaking her mind and she was fiercely protective of their father. While those were two things he normally admired, he wasn't in the right frame of mind to deal with either at the moment.

"Daddy, I'm sticky." Samantha held up her hands.

"Me, too." Hattie slid off the stool. "Let's go wash up."

"Okay." Samantha followed. "Be right back."

And since Miss Lucille was now on the phone taking an order, he and Mabel were left alone in awkward silence.

"Thanks for…this," he murmured, unable to stop himself from looking her way.

"I had to." She stirred the remains of her ice cream. "She was pretty upset." She barely glanced at him. "I hadn't gotten around to asking her why yet."

"I messed up." It was hard to get the words out.

"Jensen…" She took a deep breath, flustered. "I adore Samantha. I know I shouldn't, me being a Briscoe and all, but I do. And if I can ever help or if she needs a hug or, well… I'm here. Samantha is not, she *never* could be my…enemy." She tripped over the last word, wincing as she said it.

Don't. Don't ask. There was no point. It wouldn't change anything. But there was something in her blue eyes that pulled the words out of him. He had to know. "Am I, Mabel?"

CHAPTER SEVEN

MABEL HAD SEEN movies where, for a snippet of time, the whole world would disappear or go into a full slow-motion state because something important was happening. Since it was a movie trick, it had never happened to her. But it was happening—right now. Here she sat, on a stool in the Buttermilk Café, staring at Jensen Crawley over her cup of melted vanilla ice cream and sprinkles and everything and everyone else had faded away. The low murmur of conversation, the ring of the phone—all of it seemed muffled.

It was just her and Jensen. Jensen, who was watching her. His dark blue eyes didn't waver or blink. They were locked with hers. Waiting.

"Am I your enemy, Mabel?" he asked.

No. She swallowed. *Of course not.* But the words wouldn't come.

Her heart was racing along.

Her lungs were drawn and tight.

Her stomach was a jumble of nerves.

Jensen, however, didn't seem especially worked up. He seemed…curious but not particularly upset or troubled. *Or maybe he's better at hiding things.*

She almost laughed then. *What does he have to hide?* He hadn't had some secret crush on her for the last way too many years. He wasn't the one who got all rubbery in the knees because she walked into a room. He wasn't the one who used her as a measuring stick for all other members of the opposite sex. *That's all me.*

Even now, she was too aware of him. Acutely so. The years had changed him— but they had been kind. On the whole, he seemed more defined. More substantial. And at the moment, he was all too real. Probably because those deep blue eyes were unshakable. He seemed so…so…

Enough. She closed her eyes and drew in a deep breath. *Stop it.* There was no place for this man in her life. He didn't fit. He never would. *And the sooner I accept it, the better.*

"I guess that's answer enough." Jensen's voice was hard.

Her eyes popped open in time to see the

muscle in Jensen's jaw clench and his gaze turn away.

She wanted to answer him. The word *No* was struggling to force its way out. But she pressed her lips tightly together and focused on her melted ice cream. And just like that, the world returned to normal. Lights and color and sound and movement all buzzed around them. The café seemed busier. *Great.* From the looks of it, a good portion of the people who had attended the city council meeting were here. Which meant, if she didn't move soon, the two of them sitting together at the counter wouldn't go unnoticed and they'd have a much larger audience than just Miss Lucille. The older woman stood behind the counter, pretending to look at the menu. But she'd been holding it upside down the entire time.

Staying moony-eyed and giving in to the urge to set Jensen straight was not an option so she slid off the stool and carried her cup of melted ice cream to the trash can. Instead of heading back to her stool, she made a bee-line for the bathroom—right when Hattie and Samantha were coming out.

"Go ahead and grab our booth, Hattie," Mabel said. "It looks like half of Garrison has shown up. And I'm still craving a burger."

"Me, too." Hattie pressed a hand to her stomach. "Though that ice cream did quiet things down a bit."

With a grin and a wink for Samantha, Mabel headed into the bathroom. She took her time, washing her hands, fixing her hair and generally doing anything she could to stall. If she went back out before she'd collected herself, she feared she'd march straight up to Jensen and tell him how she felt. Maybe not how she *felt*—only that she did not consider him her enemy.

She frowned at her reflection, washed her hands again and threw the paper towel away on her way out of the bathroom.

Jensen and Samantha were preparing to leave when she came out.

"Daddy is taking me to the playground." She wasn't quite as sad as she had been when Mabel first laid eyes on her, but the little girl's smile had definitely lost its sparkle when she added, "So Paw-Paw can calm down."

Mabel could tell from Jensen's reaction that he wasn't exactly thrilled Samantha had shared with them. However, he didn't reprimand his little girl. In fact, Mabel had only ever seen Jensen treat his daughter with affection and patience. He was a good father. A good father who loved his little girl to the moon and back and would do anything to make her happy.

"Well now, those granddads can be awfully opinionated." Hattie gave Jensen a sympathetic look. "I imagine you and your daddy will have fun at the playground, though."

Jensen was holding Samantha's hand and he gave her arm a playful wiggle. "That's the plan."

"You wanna come?" Samantha looked far too hopeful.

"I was kind of looking forward to having time for just the two of us." Jensen wiggled Samantha's arm again.

"And I've got to feed Miss Hattie. We don't want her stomach making those strange sounds again. Trust me," Mabel teased.

"Now, Samantha, I want you to think long and hard about what we talked about." Hattie had stooped to make eye contact with Samantha.

"Do I want to know?" Jensen cocked an eyebrow. "Is it gonna cost me a lot of money?"

"It shouldn't." Hattie stood and laughed. "Well, not much."

"Miss Hattie asked me to become a Junior Ranger." Samantha didn't look convinced.

"Does it really sound all that bad?" Hattie laughed again. "You don't have to. I won't get my feelings hurt. Some kids enjoy the field trips and hikes, but it's not for everyone."

Mabel thought this was a great idea. She remembered visiting the wildlife rehabilitation center when she was little—and loving all the animals. It might be just what Samantha needed to help her get over her fear of animals. "Hattie and I were Junior Rangers together," Mabel said. "I remember singalongs, campfires, campouts, all sorts of arts and crafts."

"You do, huh? Well, that's good to know. Because I could use a couple of Ranger parents to help out. Obviously, they don't *have* to be parents. Any able-bodied volunteer that can pass a background check will do." Hattie was staring at her now, her hands on her hips, looking every bit Officer Carmichael.

From the corner of her eye, she saw Jensen pretend to wipe his nose—to cover his smile.

It *was* kind of funny. *I did walk right into that.* "Well, I'm not sure—"

"You and Miss Mabel would both be

there?" Samantha asked, her eyes going wide and hopeful.

"Your daddy can be there, too." Hattie smiled sweetly at Jensen. "The more hands the better."

Jensen held up both his hands. "Now, hold on a second. This is the first I'm hearing about any of this." He chuckled. "How about we take some time to think this over, okay?"

Mabel couldn't help but notice that he glanced her way again.

"Okay, Daddy. Let's go swing." Samantha seemed much happier already. "Can you tell Harvey I said hi, Mabel?" She was already leading Jensen across the restaurant.

"I sure will." Mabel nodded, waving.

"Y'all have fun. And think about the Junior Rangers." Hattie waved, too, spinning on her heel to face Mabel the instant Jensen and Samantha were gone. "Well. That was something." She gave Mabel an assessing look.

"How about we get some food and not talk about anything to do with the Crawleys." She followed Hattie to their booth, sat and slid the menu across the table to Hattie.

"I'm on board with the whole food idea." She sat on the red vinyl seat and opened her menu, peering over the top at Mabel. "But I'm not making any promises about the other thing."

Mabel rolled her eyes and pretended to read the menu. She knew what she was getting—she always got the same thing—but the menu prevented Hattie from continuing her inspection. Tonight was supposed to have been about relaxing and having fun. Not worrying over what Jensen thought of her or worrying over Samantha being sad or wondering what Mr. Crawley and Jensen had been fighting over... *It's none of my business*.

"You know people are talking, don't you?" Hattie asked, her voice low. "I've even heard there might be a bet or two—involving you and Jensen."

Mabel set her menu aside. "What?" She shook her head. "I can't believe it. I don't understand. What is there to bet on? And why can't people find more constructive things to do with their lives?"

Hattie's brows rose high. "Did you want me to tell you or you don't want to know? You started asking a lot of questions there at the end."

Mabel propped her elbows on the table and

rested her chin on her hands. "Sure. I guess," she murmured.

"You sure?" Hattie frowned. "You don't seem very—"

"Oh, Hattie, spill the tea, already." Mabel sighed.

"First, there's been a lot of talk about fights."

"Fights?" Mabel sat back. "Like Jensen and I arguing or actually throwing punches?" She was smiling now.

"Ha ha. You're hilarious." But Hattie did laugh. "Not you and Jensen. Forrest and Jensen. Or Webb and Jensen. Or Audy and Jensen." She shrugged. "You've got a lot of brothers."

"Don't I know it." Mabel blew out a long, slow breath. "Why, exactly, would these fights happen?"

"You." Hattie gave her an are-you-serious sort of look. "Duh. Jensen courting you—"

"You were right there. Did you see any courting going on, Hattie?" She paused as Alice Schneider, Kelly's teen daughter, approached the table. She wore an apron, had a pencil tucked behind her ear and carried a small tablet in hand. "Hey, Alice, I didn't know you were working here now."

The girl nodded. "Gotta help pay for my junior class trip."

"Where are y'all going?" Hattie asked. "Someplace exciting, I hope."

"It's either New York or San Francisco." Alice shrugged. "I don't care as long as it's not Garrison. I've never been outside of Texas."

Mabel remembered that feeling. "When Garrison is all you know, it can feel small. But once you've been out and about, you'll find Garrison is the perfect size."

Alice didn't buy it.

"I'm starving." Hattie put the menu back in the holder and rattled off her order.

After Mabel had done the same, Hattie circled back around to their earlier conversation. "Now, you'd asked me if I thought Jensen was courting you."

Mabel slumped. "It was a rhetorical question, Hattie. We know he's not."

Hattie stared at her for a bit, like she was working through what she needed to say. "Maybe… Maybe he's looking for a sign from you." She pointed her straw at Mabel for emphasis.

"Or not." Mabel blinked. "His little girl has taken a shine to me so he can't exactly be rude to me."

Hattie frowned. "That's not nearly exciting enough."

"If you're looking for excitement, you've come to the wrong girl." Mabel dodged the straw wrapper Hattie had balled up and launched her way. "So, basically, you're saying everyone is betting that one of my brothers is going to pick a fight with Jensen over some imaginary *thing* between him and me?"

"That's part of it." Hattie nodded. "The rest is more about you and Jensen. How long before you get together. Whose family will disown who. If it's for real or an act for—"

"Okay, hold on. If it's for real? We know it's not. But let's pretend for a minute that something was going on. Why would either of us fake something?" She couldn't wait to hear this.

"Some people think Jensen's mad because Samantha adores you and he's worried you'll turn her against him. Others say it's all to get even for the original feud. You know, whose grandfather did what to who again?" Hattie broke off. "This is where you remind me how all this started."

For some reason, Hattie loved the story. *Because she's not living it.* "It was started by our great-great-grandfathers." Mabel felt ridiculous telling the story. Again. "My great-great-grandfather Cyrus Briscoe and Jensen's great-great-grandfather James Crawley. They both fell for Hannah Monroe, the daughter of a wealthy East Coast merchant that was some distant relation to Miss Martha's family, I think? Hannah was a horsewoman and quite a beauty—and a handful, apparently. From the sounds of it, she led them both on a merry chase before her father stepped in and told her to pick. She set a challenge."

Hattie leaned forward to prop herself on one elbow. "I love this part."

Mabel shook her head, but she was smiling. "She said they both needed to find her the perfect horse. That the man that truly loved her would know exactly what she wanted. James Crawley about bankrupted the ranch to buy some prize mare with ancient bloodlines while Cyrus Briscoe went out to the Rio Grande, where wild mustangs still roamed free, and lassoed a stallion. The horse fought, of course, but—according to my great-great-grandfather's surprisingly romantic journal—the confidence of his affection for Miss Monroe saw him bring the stallion back to Garrison for her approval."

SASHA SUMMERS

"He literally went out and tamed a wild horse for the woman." Hattie sighed.

After seeing so many wild stallions broken, in spirit and body, Mabel no longer saw it through the rose-colored lenses Hattie did. But the sentiment remained.

"Hannah picked the stallion—and Cyrus—on the condition that it be freed. Cyrus agreed. James did not take losing well. He and Cyrus fought, but Hannah broke them up. James went after the stallion with a shotgun. For years, on and off, James would go after the stallion and Cyrus would ride after him—at Hannah's request. The horse was never hurt, but both the men suffered all sorts of injuries and wounds by the other's hand.

"Meanwhile, Hannah was having a whole passel of Briscoe babies. It was number five—five in five years mind you that was difficult. Cyrus had been out chasing James when it happened—because Hannah had begged him to go. When she passed, James blamed Cyrus for not taking better care of her and Cyrus blamed James for putting Hannah under constant stress and taking her away from him. A huge fight erupted. Cyrus's eldest daughter jumped between the two of them. James saw how much she looked like Hannah and left.

"But every time they saw each other after that, they fought. James managed to round up the stallion—he didn't kill it, though. He wanted to torment Cyrus. The two of them did terrible things to each other, to their ranches, anything to lash out. They were always looking for a fight—and they passed along every petty grievance to their children. Those children developed issues of their own, fueled by the hate at home. On and on and on and here we are." Mabel leaned back, smiling her thanks as Alice placed the food on their table. "Not so romantic now, is it?"

Hattie still looked dreamy-eyed, but that could have been because of the burger Alice placed in front of her. "I don't know, Mabel. How can you not see the romance in all of that?"

"Because every day I live with the hate that was born out of a…a frontier love triangle." Mabel had to laugh then. "I do find it funny that my uncle and brothers, some of the most emotionally constipated humans on the planet, continue to let that *romantic story* dictate their daily life."

Hattie was coughing, hard.

"Hattie?" Mabel jumped up. "Are you okay? Are you choking?"

Hattie waved her away, taking a big sip off the straw tucked into her extralarge milkshake. "Emotionally constipated?" She went back to laughing, until tears were streaming down her face.

"You know my brothers, you know it's true." Mabel ate a fry, pausing. "And to think, people are placing bets thinking that Jensen or I would play each other to get even for…for what? Cyrus or James? Or Hannah?"

"I think it's more the duping the other than the actual vengeance part of it." Hattie shrugged, pouring a large dollop of ketchup onto the side of her plate. "Whatever the reason, people seem to be favoring you on that one."

Mabel frowned. "That's horrible. People think I'm capable of…of faking feelings for sport?"

"Is it just me or are these the best french fries you have ever tasted?" Hattie closed her eyes, moaning, as she devoured a ketchup-coated fry.

"Good thing you have the metabolism of a teen boy." Mabel never got over her friend's ability to eat. Boy, howdy, could Hattie eat.

"I'm lucky. What can I say?" Hattie winked, smiling slowly. "Emotionally constipated." She snorted. "That's a good one."

Mabel was all too glad for them to change the topic of conversation. But hours later, when she was staring up at the thick wooden beams holding up the ceiling, she couldn't help thinking about what Hattie had said. Not about the betting or the gossip or that there was any romance in the origins of the feud. She was thinking about what Hattie had said about Jensen. Was he waiting for a sign from Mabel? *No. Of course not.* That was all Hattie. There was no way Jensen was interested in her. None. But deep down, there was a part of her that hoped Hattie was right. If he was then… *Then what?* That was the question that kept Mabel tossing and turning into the wee hours.

Two weeks had gone by since he'd unloaded the little paint into the barn and Samantha still had no idea she had a horse. He'd tried, time and again, to get her to help him organize the tack room or go for a ride with him on the tractor—but she seemed to sense there was more to it than that and didn't budge.

His father did not approve of Jensen's

tactics, glaring and grumbling soft enough that his words were unintelligible but loud enough for everyone to hear he was unhappy. Other than the grumbling and glaring, his father wasn't talking to him. Not one word. Even at the dinner table, his father would ask Twyla or Kitty to relay things to him. *Like a ten-year-old.*

Samantha didn't know what to make of it. She'd tried to get her Paw-Paw to be nice, but Jensen worried his father was so bent out of shape he might snap at her. That wouldn't do. The idea of Samantha growing up and pulling this sort of thing to get what she wanted also wouldn't do. Like it or not, he was going to have to offer up some sort of explanation for his father's behavior—without being a disrespecting son.

After agonizing over just the right thing to say, he decided short and sweet was the best bet. Samantha had listened as he'd explained that Paw-Paw was out of sorts because he and Jensen hadn't seen eye to eye on something but that, in time, Paw-Paw would get back to normal.

"I hope so, Daddy. Malcolm, in my class, makes faces and grumbles like that and he's always in trouble. He has to sit right by the teacher's desk and never gets special class-room jobs." Samantha sighed. "Mrs. Wilkes says he causes aches in her head with his... attics."

"Antics?" Jensen had to grin at that.

"That." Samantha had nodded gravely. "I don't want Paw-Paw to give people aches."

"Me, neither, little miss. Me, neither." Jensen had given her a quick hug and hoped that would be the end of it.

That had been ten days ago.

"Are you taking her to Junior Rangers tonight?" Kitty asked, rinsing off the night's dinner dishes as Jensen handed them to her.

"Planned on it." He handed her the last plate and carried a rag to the large wooden kitchen table. "I was thinking... I'd be happy to go." Kitty put a dish into the dishwasher and looked his way. "I loved Junior Rangers and I wouldn't mind having some time with Samantha."

"I'm sure she'd like that, too." He started wiping down the table. If he were being honest, the last thing he wanted to do was go spend a couple of hours with a bunch of five- and six-year-olds but... "But getting out of the house might be good, too." He swept the crumbs from Twyla's fresh-baked rolls into his hand.

"Did you know there are other places to go in Garrison, Jensen?" She gave him an innocent grin. "There's a restaurant or two. A coffee shop and book shop. And there's even a place where you can go play pool and watch football and eat wings and drink beer. With friends."

"You don't say?" He dumped the crumbs into the trash and washed his hands, shooting her a narrow-eyed look.

"Come on, Jensen." Kitty stowed the stack of kitchen towels in a cabinet. "You could, I don't know, call up Tyson and go have a beer and play some pool? Or something."

He and Tyson Ellis had spent many a night playing pool at Buck's in their younger days. The two of them were like-minded, avoiding drama and fine with minimal conversation. Considering he couldn't remember the last time he and Tyson Ellis had spoken—let alone had a beer together—his sister might have a good idea.

"Be men," Kitty added, shrugging. "Do whatever it is that men do."

Jensen had to laugh then. "Whatever it is

that men do?" He shook his head. "I'm curious now. What do you think we do?"

"I don't know." Kitty pulled the broom from the pantry. "Why don't you grab that dustpan and lend a hand."

"I've been helping, haven't I?" He collected the dustpan and followed her. "Not going to answer the question?"

"No. I don't think so." She swept up the area under and around the table and swept it all into the dustpan he held before she asked, "Are you going to call Tyson?"

He dumped the pan and returned it, and the broom, to the pantry. "Sure." Why not?

"Really?" Kitty stared up at him.

"You don't have to act so shocked." He chuckled. "It was your idea."

"I know. I'm a genius. Nobody around here seems to notice that, though." Kitty gave a long-suffering sigh. "It's sad to be so underappreciated."

Jensen loved both of his little sisters dearly, but they were as different as night and day. Where Twyla was assertive and independent, Kitty was shy and careful with her words. Kitty was also more empathetic—making her the peacekeeper of the family. He didn't envy her that.

Kitty handed him the phone. "Here you go."

Jensen took the phone. "Thank you?" He glanced at her. "You trying to get rid of me? Is something going on?"

Kitty shrugged, dodging his gaze. "No." She made a dismissive sound. "Don't be silly." But her voice sounded funny.

"Really?"

"Yes, *really*," she sassed—something she rarely did. "I thought you were more likely to call and go out if you had a witness. Not that I'm telling you what you have to do. You are an adult. You're an adult who spends all of his free time with his five-year-old daughter, nosy sisters and curmudgeon of a father." More sass. "Hmm. I can't imagine why I'd encourage you to have a social life. Just because the rest of your family are hermits doesn't mean you have to be." She blinked. "Besides, if you don't call him, you'll find some reason to hang out at the Junior Ranger meeting and we both know it."

"Someone's full of attitude this evening." But she was right. He didn't have a leg to stand on now—she'd called his bluff. Since Casey's death, he hadn't spent a lot of time away from Samantha. It wasn't planned. It was just the way it was. He didn't like to be away from her. He hadn't been there when Casey collapsed…

"You know, it wouldn't hurt her to have some non-Daddy social time, too, Jensen."

"What, are you reading my mind now?" He grumbled and started dialing. Kitty, he noticed, was grinning when he held the phone up to his ear. "Don't gloat," he murmured.

"I'd never do such a thing." Kitty waved. "I'll go get Samantha ready."

"Tyson Ellis here." Tyson was short and clipped, all business.

"Hey, Tyson." He cleared his throat. "Jensen here."

There was a moment's pause. "Jensen. How's it going? Been a while."

"Kitty was just telling me the same thing." He chuckled. "You got plans tonight?"

"Me? Oh, only eight hours of that reality television show following Texas game wardens while they do their job. So… That'd be a no." Tyson sighed. "You up for getting a beer or something?"

"Yeah. If you're okay postponing your television watching." He nodded. "Buck's? Half hour or so?"

"I'll be there. Glad you called." And Tyson hung up.

When Jensen put the old phone back on its charging stand, he was surprisingly excited. It'd been a while. A long while. Before he'd lost Casey. *More than two years ago?* Maybe Kitty was right.

"Kitty said you're going out." He hadn't even noticed Twyla coming into the room, but she was standing behind him, opening the refrigerator door. "Not like that, I hope?" Her brows rose.

He stared down at his jeans and button-up shirt. "I'm going to have a beer, Twyla. I guarantee Tyson doesn't care."

She rolled her eyes. "You never know, Jensen. Someone might walk in, your eyes might meet across a crowded room, and—"

"You've been watching that channel again, haven't you? The one that plays romance movies all day and all night?" He'd watched one or two in his time. Samantha liked them. Especially the ones with the princesses.

"Or I could just be wishing you'd find someone that made you laugh again." She wasn't teasing now. "Besides Samantha, that is. You're a good father, but you don't have to spend every minute you're not working with her, Jensen. It's not good for either one of you."

"Fine, right. I get it. First Kitty. Now you." Then he pointed at her. "Why aren't you and Kitty going out? You two are young and lively and single. You're staying home knitting and watching romance movies and Kitty is reading—"

"Romance novels," Twyla cut in. "And a spy novel or two."

"The point is, this is a double standard." He frowned. "If I'm going out, you two should do the same."

"What's wrong?" Kitty asked, leading Samantha into the great room. "Why are you two scowling at each other?"

"Yeah, Daddy, are you mad at Auntie Twyla?" Samantha looked worried.

"I'm not scowling." He smiled at his daughter. "I'm just getting Auntie Twyla to agree we should always take turns."

"*Ooh*. Takin' turns is polite," Samantha said.

"It is," Kitty added.

"Kitty," Twyla snapped. "You might want to know what we're taking turns *doing*."

"What? Oh." Kitty saw the look on Twyla's face and panicked. "What would that be?"

"Going out." Jensen clapped his hands together, making all three of them jump. He scooped up Samantha and spun until she was giggling. "While you go to your Junior Rangers meeting, I'm going to see Tyson Ellis. And tomorrow, we will do some puzzles here and your aunties will go out—"

"With Tyson from the stock-show-farmyard?" Samantha finished. "He's the ham-some one, right, Auntie Kitty? The one you like?"

Jensen's brows arched high as he cast his little sister a questioning look. "Tyson's ham-some, is he?"

Kitty went beet red.

"Kitty?" Twyla asked, smiling. "Well, I never."

"Why are you so red, Auntie Kitty?" Samantha tugged on her hand. "Are you okay? Do you have a fever?"

"I'm fine." Kitty stared up at the ceiling. "More embarrassed than I've ever been in my whole life, but fine."

Kitty. Tyson. *Huh.* Jensen would *never* have guessed. Then again, his little sister tended to keep this sort of thing to herself. Considering she lived with Twyla and their father—and their very strong opinions on *everything*—it made sense. But even the two of them would be hard-pressed to find something wrong with Tyson Ellis. Hardworking. Respected. Ethical. A man of his word. *Kitty could do a lot worse.* The more he thought about it, the more Jensen liked the idea. He'd always worried his sisters would end up taking care of their father and never find love for themselves.

"He is a hardworking, upstanding sort of man," Twyla agreed.

"I didn't…" Kitty broke off, blinking furiously. "He's…just…" Her hands flailed.

"You said he was ham-some and the best man in town. After Daddy, prob-ly," Samantha announced.

Kitty's head fell forward and she covered her face with her hand, muffling a squeak of mortification.

"*Probably* true." Jensen nodded, having a hard time not laughing at Kitty's reaction. He had never seen her squirm this way.

"It doesn't matter." Kitty looked ready to pop, her words rapid-fire. "He doesn't know I exist. At all." She was redder than ever. "I don't know why we're having this conversation. I did say he is ham-some, handsome, but that's all. He is. You have eyes. You know I'm right." She grabbed her keys. "Samantha and I are off to Junior Rangers so I'd appreciate it if you two would wait to say anything else until we are gone and out the door." As she spoke, she led Samantha across the great room to the front door. "Ready?" she asked Samantha.

"Ready." Samantha nodded. "Bye, Daddy. Have a fun playdate with Mr. Ellis."

Jensen was still laughing when the door closed.

When Twyla had stopped giggling, she said, "I had no idea."

"Me, neither." Kitty tended to look after others instead of bringing attention to herself. He glanced at the now-closed front door. "Or, are we making a mountain out of a molehill?"

"Have you ever seen Kitty that color, Jensen? Ever? She's shy so she's had her fair share of red cheeks, but *that*." She nodded at the front door. "Those weren't your run-of-the-mill red cheeks. Those were a whole caught-with-her-hand-in-the-cookie-jar-and-her-secret-is-out sort of red."

All the evidence did imply his little sister was sweet on Tyson Ellis. And, no matter what she said, Tyson knew she existed. *Everyone* knew Kitty. Everyone *liked* Kitty. She was a likable person.

Twyla turned to face him. "If it happens to

come up in conversation tonight, you *could* find out if he's dating? Just to see. You don't have to bring up Kitty or anything."

"I won't bring up Kitty." He arched a brow. If they thought Kitty had been red now, he couldn't imagine what'd happen if she heard he was asking Tyson about her. Growing up in a town where gossip was traded with recipe cards at Sunday's church potluck or Tuesday night's bingo games, he'd never been one to get involved with someone else's business. If anything, he tended to avoid conversation that strayed into personal matters or potential scandal. Even something innocent. *Like ice cream with Mabel.* He shoved all things Mabel aside—like he'd done every time she'd popped to mind over the last two weeks.

Kitty. He'd been thinking about his sister. And Tyson. *Right.* Kitty was shy. Tyson was aloof. Kitty was on the sensitive side. Tyson was…not. Not openly, anyway. If Kitty didn't give Tyson some sign or hint of interest, it was possible Tyson Ellis would never find out he had an admirer. Now that he knew, Jensen couldn't let that happen— not if there was a chance saying something to Tyson gave the both of them some happiness. "But if it comes up, I'll see what I can find out."

Twyla didn't bother hiding her excitement.

"But no matter what happens tonight, you two are going out tomorrow." He grinned.

"Go on, then." Twyla sighed, but she didn't argue. "Go on in your wrinkled-up shirt and dusty boots."

Jensen didn't let her jabs get to him. He grabbed his wallet and headed out the door. It took a good fifteen minutes to get into town. As he was parking out front of Buck's Honky-Tonk—the one and only honky-tonk in four counties—Tyson was walking up the steps to the front door. Jensen sat there for a second, mulling things over. Somehow, someway, he had to find out if Tyson was seeing someone or not. Not that he had the slightest idea of how to go about it. It'd been years since he'd talked about dating and courting let alone *actually* dating and courting. It'd all been pretty simple. Two people liked each other and they spent time with each other to see how they'd fit. At least, that was the way it should be. Easy.

Then again, he'd had Casey. All he'd had to do was follow her lead. Now… Well, the only woman to spark *his* interest considered him her enemy. He sighed, beyond frustrated. Why did his brain go there? Why did *she* keep popping up uninvited?

Tonight was about getting out of the house, relaxing and, maybe, seeing if Kitty had a chance at something more with Tyson Ellis. With any luck, the Briscoes wouldn't even come up in conversation—especially Mabel…

Mabel Briscoe was off-limits. But it took effort to box up the memory of Mabel's smile and the sway of her hair in the spring breeze or the sound of her laughter… He groaned, shaking his head. *No more.* He wasn't going to waste any more time on Mabel Briscoe. *Starting now.*

CHAPTER EIGHT

"How does it look?" Samantha asked, tilting her rock toward Mabel.

"It's lovely, Samantha." Mabel inspected the painted rock closely. "I especially like the blue."

For the gazillionth time, Mabel was acutely aware of Kitty Crawley looking her way.

"That's Auntie Kitty's favorite part, too." Samantha went back to adding blue to the butterfly's wings. "I like blue, too."

"Just a few more minutes now," Hattie said, walking around the room, leaning forward to offer a word of encouragement or praise to one of the kids gathered. It was a decent turnout. Six kids in all. Four boys and two girls.

When Samantha had arrived, Mabel's relief had been twofold. Mostly, it was because Samantha was here. Not only was she glad the little girl was giving Junior Rangers a chance, but it had also been a whole two weeks since Mabel had last seen her. She welcomed the little girl's exuberant hugs and listened as Samantha chattered away about her new clogging routine, the discovery that strawberry jam was yummy on her peanut butter sandwiches and that she had to write her own story for school and she was going to write a princess story.

The other reason for Mabel's relief? Jensen had not accompanied his daughter. If he'd shown up, tonight would have been all sorts of challenging. But he hadn't.

During the meeting and arts and crafts time, Mabel had done her best to circulate among all the children and offer help when needed. Since Samantha had Kitty to help her out, Mabel didn't hover. But Samantha called her over, again and again—something that set Kitty Crawley's back up.

"Next time, we'll be taking a nature walk through erste Baum park so you'll want to wear good walking shoes and pants. We will take your painted rocks with us and you can find a special place to leave them along the path." Hattie held up a piece of paper. "I've got a letter for your parents, so make sure they get one before you leave."

Mabel sat beside little Levi Williams and

did her best to scrape up the globs of paint he'd managed to cover his work area with.

"Accident." He grinned.

Mabel knew full well it wasn't an accident. She'd watched him dip his brush into the cups of paint and hold the paint-laden brush over the table until paint rolled off the brush and splatted onto the table. "I think there's more paint on the table than your rock."

He shrugged. "So." He'd painted a large red X on his rock and nothing else. "It's a pirate rock."

"Like X marks the spot? For buried treasure?"

He sighed, irritated. "Duh."

It was quickly becoming apparent that— unlike her connection with animals—Mabel didn't have a universal connection with children. Levi Williams was case in point. He seemed too young to be all sarcasm. But he was. At the ripe age of "almost six," he was a handful. Then there were the Travis brothers. Seth was seven, the oldest of the group and not happy about that fact. Pete, his adoring five-year-old brother, was all wide eyes and long-winded stories. Poor little Eddie Hillard was painfully shy. Hattie had put Pete Travis beside Eddie, hoping it would help. Instead,

Pete had carried on a one-sided conversation for most of the meeting. And last, but not least, was little Abigail Koch. She'd started crying the minute her father had dropped her off. She'd calmed down while Hattie told them about the importance of taking care of nature and the rocks they'd be painting that night. But the tears started up again once Abigail decided she didn't like the shape of her rock or that her paintbrush was too big. She'd quieted while she was painting. Once she'd finished, Abigail saw Samantha's butterfly painting and burst into tears over how she wanted to paint a butterfly, too. Mabel did her best to soothe the little girl, but there was only so much she could do. Hattie, distraught over the little girl's sobbing, offered Abigail another rock for a butterfly. So far, Abigail seemed mollified.

When cleanup started and parents started arriving, Mabel almost sighed with relief. She pulled the book she'd brought for Samantha from her bag.

"What's this?" Samantha asked, staring at the cover. "It's so pretty."

"It's one of my favorite stories." Mabel sat beside Samantha, acting like she wasn't aware of Kitty's rigid posture or her heavy sigh. "It's about this horse, see." Mabel pointed at the picture. "And the little princess, right here." She opened the book so Samantha could see the beautifully detailed and whimsical illustrations. "The princess was scared of the horse, because the horse was so big and tall. But the horse wants to be friends so it follows the princess around—like Harvey, remember?"

Samantha nodded, smiling. "I do like Harvey. He's silly."

"He is." Mabel agreed. "The horse and the princess become friends, just like you and Harvey."

Samantha turned the page, taking her time studying each picture. "What happens?"

"You'll have to read the book. But I will tell you that the little princess and her horse go on all sorts of adventures together." Mabel glanced at Samantha then.

"She wasn't scared anymore? Of the horse?" Samantha asked.

Mabel shook her head. "Nope. Don't you think the little princess looks like you? And the horse looks like yours."

Kitty made an odd sound—one that drew Mabel's attention. She was shaking her head, shooting a meaningful look at Samantha.

Mabel frowned. What did that look mean?

"I don't have a horse," Samantha said.

Oh. That's what that look means. What had happened to the paint mare? If Jensen had sold it, surely he'd have given her the chance to buy the horse. *Or would he?*

Samantha continued, "And I don't want one. They *are* too big and if I fell off it would be a long fall." She stretched out the word *long* to make her point. "And if I fell, it could step on me and that would hurt."

"Or bite you," Levi Williams added. "They have sharp teeth."

"Sharp teeth?" Levi's announcement side-tracked Mabel from worrying over the paint mare—for the moment. "I've *never* met a horse with sharp teeth."

"A horse can bite?" This was new, distressing information for Samantha.

"Or stomp on your head." Levi nodded. "And rear back real far right before they do it." He leaned back in his chair, flailing his arms like he was a wild, rearing horse. "Smash!" He slammed his hands against the tabletop—making them all jump.

"They can?" Samantha was truly horrified by the boy's display of horsey ferocity.

Wonderful. Just what Samantha needed.

Mabel eyed the boy, wishing he had an off switch.

"We have all sorts of horses and we have never had one stomp on anyone's head." Kitty Crawley said.

Yes, good. "Not on our ranch, either," Mabel hurried to agree, then added, "No sharp teeth, either. Do any of yours have sharp teeth?" she asked Kitty.

Kitty's gaze met hers and, for a minute, Mabel wasn't sure the woman would answer her. She had breached established Crawley-Briscoe protocol by asking Kitty a direct question. "No." Kitty cleared her throat. "Not a one," she said. For Samantha, they could work together. "Where did you see such a horse, Levi?"

"On the television." Levi shot an irritated look Kitty's way. "The horse is called Killer and he belongs to Krollo the Barbarian Conqueror. He can shoot lasers out of his eyes, too."

Mabel and Kitty exchanged a look.

"Real horses don't do things like that." Mabel sighed. "I'm not saying Killer doesn't sound like he'd help out Krollo do whatever it is that barbarian conquerors do."

"Conquer, I suppose?" Kitty shrugged.

"Exactly the sort of magical pretend horse you'd need for conquering." Mabel tried to give Samantha her most reassuring smile.

"He's cool." Levi puffed out his chest. "Grampa says he's gonna get me a horse just like Killer. You'll see." He stuck his tongue out at Samantha, grabbed the permission slip from Hattie and ran to his waiting grandfather.

"Let's hope your grampa sets the record straight." Kitty sighed, watching the man and boy leave.

"Levi was making that up?" Samantha asked. "There are no horses like Killer?"

"On TV, maybe. But not here or in real life." Mabel had met her fair share of wild horse, but none had sharp teeth or laser eyes and only rarely did they rear back and stomp at anyone. "Not on the Briscoe Ranch. Not on the Crawley Ranch." She patted the storybook. "Just like some of the pretend magical stuff in storybooks."

Hattie took in the paint and mess on the tables used for tonight's class. "That boy is going to make me rethink this whole Junior Ranger program." Hattie pulled out the chair opposite the three of them.

"I think it went well." Mabel's memories

of her Junior Ranger days were all good. Then again, she'd been a kid—not an adult having to wrangle the kids. Kids like Levi. "Levi is…"

"A *handful*." Hattie added extra oomph to *handful*. "Big-time. What's that you've got, Samantha?"

"A book." Samantha cradled it against her chest. "It's about a princess that looks like me and a horse that becomes her friend."

And a horse that looked like Samantha's little paint. *If it's still Samantha's paint?* After Kitty's weird throat-clearing cough thing, she knew asking outright wasn't an option.

"I know that book." Hattie nodded. "It's a good one. All princesses need a good horse, after all." She winked at Samantha.

Samantha glanced up at Mabel then. "Do they, Mabel? Do all princesses need a horse?"

"I would think so." Mabel saw this as an opportunity to try to bolster Samantha's interest in horses. Samantha loved with her whole heart—which is just what the little paint mare needed. Mabel could almost picture them together, the best of friends. *If the paint horse was still on Crawley Ranch?* "To get them around, all over their kingdoms. I'm not sure a car or truck could reach some of the castles. Especially those on the tippy-top of mountains."

"Oh." Samantha nodded. "Do you have a horse?"

"I have two." Mabel smiled. "One is named Tinker Bell. She's a big Clydesdale so it's sort of funny since Tinker Bell is a tiny fairy. She pulls things, heavy things, because she's so strong and sure-footed. She could pull a princess carriage easily—*if* I had one." Mabel laughed. "And then there's Firefly."

"He is a character." Hattie laughed. "Have you ever been hugged by a horse, Samantha?"

"No." Samantha shook her head. "Horses can hug?"

"You better believe it." Hattie nodded. "You'll have to meet Firefly."

If it wasn't for the whole Crawley-Briscoe thing, Mabel would invite Samantha out to meet Firefly tomorrow. But… There was the whole Crawley-Briscoe thing.

"I guess it'd be okay 'cuz you'd be there to tell me if the horse wanted to be friends." Samantha held the book away from her chest to stare at the cover. "Like you did with Harvey."

"You know something, Samantha? I bet

your daddy and aunties and grandpa would only let friendly horses near you." All a person had to do was see the Crawleys together to know Samantha was the apple of all their eyes.

Which brought her back to the paint horse. Mabel had known there was something about the horse. Something sad. Wounded even. Had it behaved in a way that worried one of them? Did they decide it wasn't a good fit for Samantha? If that was the case, surely Jensen would have called so she could buy the horse—

"We should be going, Samantha." Kitty stood, all distant and rigid once more. "I'm sure Hattie and…Mabel have things to do now."

"Daddy might be home from his playdate." Samantha stood.

Playdate? A coldness seeped into Mabel's chest, making her lungs heavy. She swallowed. As in, a date? A real date date? Her throat tightened. *It's none of my business.* Jensen was young and handsome and a good father and kind and…and… She swallowed again, wishing the tightness in her throat would ease. Worse, a sudden hollowness gnawed at the base of her belly. *What is wrong with me?* She stood quickly, knocking the chair behind her over. "Oops," she murmured, her cheeks hot, before righting the chair—and knocking the chair she'd been sitting in into the table.

"Oops, again," Samantha giggled.

Mabel's laugh spilled out on the breathless side. *Pull yourself together, Mabel.* She turned, straightened the second chair and pressed her hands against her hips to stop them from shaking. Not that it worked.

Hattie and Samantha were watching her.

Kitty Crawley was *staring* at her. Those deep blue eyes, so like Jensen's, didn't miss a thing.

But there wasn't a thing Mabel could do about her red cheeks or her sudden clumsiness or the fact that she was…upset. *Am I? Upset?* She swallowed again, flexing her hands at her sides before crossing her arms tightly over her chest. *No. Why would I be?* She had no reason to be upset. Not about the unknown fate of the horse or Jensen dating… or anything.

"You good?" Hattie waited for Mabel to nod before asking, "What sort of playdate did your daddy go on?"

Kitty's eyes remained fixed on Mabel.

"Oh, you know, a night out. He and Tyson went to play pool or something," Kitty said.

Tyson? Not a date. Relief bowled Mabel over. *What is* wrong *with me?*

"We all need a night out now and then." Hattie sat back in her chair. "After tonight, I think I've earned one."

"You going to go play in the pool, too?" Samantha asked.

"In the pool?" Hattie asked. "Do you mean, play pool, sweet thing?"

Samantha frowned. "Is playing pool pretending you're a pool?"

Kitty laughed. "Pool is a game. You have a big table with pockets around the sides and corners and you try to hit balls into them."

"Oh." Samantha's eyes widened. "That sounds like fun."

"It can be." Hattie shrugged. "If I recall correctly, Mabel here was a good pool player. What do you say, Mabel, wanna go crash their guys' night?" Hattie was up to no good. "Something tells me it'd be interesting. Guaranteed to entertain." Her smile was pure glee.

Hattie was Switzerland. Anyone and everyone loved her so she'd never been able to fully grasp the magnitude of rivalry between their families. But Hattie was pushing it. And enjoying it.

"No." Mabel sighed. Her getting all moony-eyed and tongue-tied and conflicted over Jensen would be *interesting*? Maybe for Hattie. "You recall incorrectly." Mabel wasn't just a good pool player—she was a *very* good pool player. Growing up in a house full of men, learning to play pool had been a survival skill. Tonight, avoiding pool and Jensen was a far more important survival skill.

"No, I'm not. I remember watching you trounce RJ Malloy once. He deserved it, too, after sassing you and acting like you couldn't play because you were a girl." Hattie laughed.

It had been highly gratifying to watch RJ's condescending smile give way to pure astonishment. "That was a long time ago—"

Hattie snorted and waved her hand. "Fine, if you've gotten rusty. I get it. Don't want to make a fool of yourself."

Mabel was all too familiar with this tactic. Pick and goad and prod until she gave in. *Not tonight, Hattie Carmichael.* Not where Jensen Crawley is concerned.

"Daddy'd like it." Samantha swayed back

and forth, grinning up at her. "He says nice things about you all the time, Mabel."

Mabel's heart slammed into her rib cage. *He did?* She swallowed the question. "I can't imagine your daddy being anything but nice." She regretted the words as soon as they were out. Kitty was listening—and so was Hattie. Hattie, who was grinning like a Cheshire cat. She glanced at Samantha and was struck by an idea. "But you know, princesses need to go to bed to get all their beauty rest." She winked.

Samantha was all smiles.

"Good point." Kitty held out her hand. "This little princess needs to get home. Tell Mabel thank you for the book."

Mabel crouched in time for Samantha to launch herself into her arms. "Thank you," she whispered, her little arms tight around her. "I think I'll like Junior Rangers if you're here."

Mabel hugged her back. She didn't have it in her to mention her time in Garrison was wrapping up. One more week and she was supposed to head back to Wyoming. "You give the best hugs, you know that?" Nobody hugged like Samantha. Nobody. She released the little girl to tap her on the nose.

"Daddy says that, too." Samantha rocked back on her heels.

Of course he did. She stood, hugging herself.

"Do you think Daddy will read this to me tonight, Auntie Kitty?" She glanced over her shoulder at Kitty, the book pressed tightly to her chest.

Kitty took her hand. "I don't think so, sweetie. I doubt he'll be home from Buck's for a while. But I'll read it to you." She led Samantha to the door. "Thanks for tonight, Hattie."

"We'll see you next time. Don't forget your hiking clothes." Hattie waved.

"I can wear a hat for shade." Samantha nodded. "No tiaras."

Mabel laughed and waved goodbye. As soon as the door closed, Mabel started cleaning up.

"What was that?" Hattie went along the tables, spraying them with cleaner. "You were practically tripping over yourself for a minute." She paused, glancing at her. "Did you think Jensen was on a date? Is that why you were all out of sorts?"

"I was not," Mabel argued, refusing to admit the truth.

"Okay." Hattie used paper towel to clean. "Then what was it?"

"The horse." Mabel took some paper towels from Hattie. "The paint horse? Samantha still doesn't know about it." And now that she was thinking about it, she was irritated all over again. "I mentioned it and Kitty shook her head, all panicked."

"Maybe he sold it?" Hattie asked, frowning.

"He knew how much I wanted her." Mabel pushed back, rolling up all of her conflicting emotions and focusing all her energy on her anger. "If he sold her, you'd have thought he'd let me buy her."

Hattie tossed the paper towels into the trash can. "You don't know for certain he sold her. There's only one way to know for certain."

Mabel stopped and glared up at Hattie. "No."

Hattie held out her hands in mock surrender. "I'm just saying."

"No." Mabel repeated. There was no way she'd go over to Buck's to confront Jensen over the horse. It would be foolish and reckless and… She *could* find out where the horse was and what happened. "No," she repeated, for herself this time.

JENSEN LAID HIS domino down. "That's ten." He nodded at the two ends lined up perfectly.

Tyson shot him a look. "Five plus five is ten?" Tyson got grumpier with each game he lost.

"We can play something else," Jensen offered again.

"Nope." Tyson studied his dominoes, then turned his narrow-eyed gaze upon the domino configuration on the tabletop. "I've got this."

Jensen beat him three moves later, but he bought a round of beer to take the edge off. "Anything new?" he asked.

"Nope." Tyson took a sip. "Nothing with me. I'm not the one everyone's talking about these days. That'd be you."

It was Jensen's turn to give him a look. "I hear the fairgrounds got broken into." Tyson Ellis was the city parks manager as well as manager of the county fairgrounds. If he got the man talking shop, he wouldn't have to worry about all the nonsense and gossip being spread about him and Mabel.

"They were. We can come back to that." Tyson chuckled. "Come on, now. You can't expect me not to ask some questions." He leaned forward, resting his elbows on the table. "Mabel Briscoe and Jensen Crawley? Lifelong enemies exchanging lingering glances—Miss Patsy's description, not mine."

"Glad you cleared that up." Jensen grinned.

Tyson shrugged. "It seems to me you are part of Garrison's very own Romeo and Juliet story."

Jensen almost choked on his beer. It took a while for the coughing to stop and even then, all he could do was stare at Tyson.

"What?" Tyson chuckled. "Mabel Briscoe is a beautiful woman. You can't tell me you haven't noticed."

He pressed his lips together.

"And she's kind. From what I hear, Samantha thinks she hung the moon and the stars so..." Tyson shrugged again.

"So?" Jensen knew she was beautiful. And kind? He'd seen it, firsthand, time and time again. Tyson was right about Samantha, too. But that didn't change things. "I'm not sure I get what you're hinting at."

Tyson scratched the stubble along the side of his jaw. "You don't?" He shook his head. "Fine, I'll get right to it. If you like this woman, you should court her. Briscoe or not."

Jensen was laughing then. "Just like that, huh?"

"Just like that." Tyson wasn't laughing. "No need to make it complicated."

That was a question Jensen had asked himself on more than one occasion. "I'm not disagreeing with you. But that's not possible with me and Mabel. You can thank the last generation of Crawleys and Briscoes for that." He sighed, staring into his beer.

"That's it?" Tyson asked. "Koch was at that horse auction over in Holsom and he said it looked like you two were having an awful intense conversation. And that Mabel was crying."

Jensen sighed, not bothering to hide his impatience. "People talk too much."

"You made her cry?" he asked.

"No, I... She—" He didn't remember a whole lot about that conversation—only her blue eyes full of tears and her heartfelt plea to take care of the mare. Even now, it knocked the air from his lungs a little, picturing her like that. She had huge eyes—bottomless. The sort of eyes he'd have let himself get lost in, if she were anyone else. He took a sip of his drink, willing those eyes and that face from his mind. "She was upset about a horse." A horse that wanted nothing to do with him or anyone else on the ranch. That was a whole other problem that needed tending to.

"But... You *do* like her." Tyson wasn't gloating. He sounded more...thoughtful than anything.

"It doesn't matter." That much was true. His feelings for Mabel, whatever they were, didn't factor into things. They couldn't. He shot Tyson a look. "Moving on. What about you?"

"What about me?" Tyson rolled his eyes. "I'm too tired for dating. I work, I sleep, and I—"

"Binge-watch some TV show about state troopers?" Jensen cut him off. "I'm sure the Garrison Ladies Guild would be happy to help you find the right woman."

"Don't even think it." He shuddered. "They kept throwing me and Brooke together like we'd eventually stick." He spun his beer. "We're friends and all, but she's where she's meant to be—with Audy." He lifted his glass beer mug in a toast. "And I'm here, with you."

Jensen chuckled. In the two years since Casey had been gone, he'd gotten used to being alone. There were times he was lonely—so lonely he could barely breathe—but Samantha needed him and that gave him the purpose and drive to keep it together. But he couldn't keep lying to himself. Watching Mabel and Samantha had sort of woken something up inside him. A warmth. And an ache.

"This break-in." Tyson leaned forward, tipped his hat farther back and started in on his tale. "You know RJ?"

"Who doesn't?" Jensen asked. RJ Malloy was loud and opinionated and that was before he got drunk. Drunken RJ was downright unbearable. "He did it?"

Tyson nodded. "We were getting ready for the preliminary youth rodeo. The grounds were pretty crowded, trailers and trucks and campers from all over, and RJ takes one look at a horse trailer and gets it into his head that it's his."

Jensen sat back in his chair, spreading his legs out in front of him. "It wasn't."

"No. It wasn't. But he was past the point of thinking clearly—or walking in a straight line, for that matter. He didn't even bother hiding when he tripped the floodlights. He just stood there, with his arm up, yelling at me to turn off the lights." Tyson started laughing.

"By then, he was fumbling with the hitch on the trailer. He didn't seem all that troubled by the fact that the trailer was hitched to someone else's truck or that the gates were locked and there was no getting in or out." But Tyson stopped then, his gaze locking on something or someone over Jensen's shoulder.

"What a surprise." Hattie Carmichael clapped him on the back. "You two look like you're in deep conversation. Didn't mean to interrupt, but figured saying hi was the neighborly thing to do."

"Glad to see you." Tyson stood, his tone changing entirely when he said, "You, too, Mabel."

Mabel? Here? Jensen set his beer on the table and took a deep breath. Just when he was starting to relax. He stood, bracing himself as he turned. "Evening."

"Hey, Jensen." Hattie eyed the table. "Dominoes, huh?"

He wasn't sure whom she was asking but, for the moment, he wasn't answering. As much as he'd like to think that his last interaction with Mabel had hardened his heart toward her…it hadn't. Seeing her now made his insides go soft and warm. There was no denying she looked as pretty as a picture in her button-down blue shirt covered in stitched white flowers, jeans that only accentuated her femininity, and boots, but it was those eyes that disintegrated any walls he tried to build between the two of them. Those big blue eyes had him pinned in place, whether he liked it or not.

What threw him further off guard? From the looks of it, Mabel Briscoe was angry. With him.

"Jensen beat me, oh, four times, at least." Tyson didn't sound nearly as upset as he'd been when Jensen was actually beating him. "Course, that's because I let him win."

Why is she *mad?* Jensen had tried to offer an olive branch at the Buttermilk Café. He'd wanted to clear the air between them. She hadn't.

"Of course," Hattie agreed.

Jensen ran a hand along the back of his neck, tension rising up. She had no right to show up, looking like that, only to glare at him for no reason.

"Since he doesn't get out much and all," Tyson added.

Jensen wished he could read what was going on behind those blue eyes so he could figure out what had happened. *No.*

He sighed. *Whatever is eating at her is her problem. Not mine.*

And yet, he found himself searching her gaze. He didn't know what he was looking for or what he expected. Quite simply, he was caught up in this strange hold she had on him. A magnet. A homing beacon. It was irritating and frustrating and irresistible. He couldn't shake it—couldn't shake her.

Mabel drew in a wavering breath. "Jensen." Her gaze shifted from him to the dominoes on the table.

Just like that, there was air in the room again. Finally. He took a deep breath, his lungs struggling. "Mabel," he murmured, more rattled than ever. He ignored the silence that descended and the inquisitive looks on Hattie's and Tyson's faces.

"Well, we'll let you two get back to your conversation. We're going to get some barbecue and might play a little pool later on." If Hattie picked up on the tension between him and Mabel, she didn't let on. "You two feel like playing, come on over."

Like that was going to happen. If he was smart, he'd wrap this up with Tyson and head home to avoid further…whatever this was. But Mabel reached up to smooth her hair from her shoulder and a splash of red caught his eye. "You hurt yourself?" he asked, catching himself before he reached for her.

"What?" she asked, looking confused.

"Your hand." He nodded, tucking his hands into his pockets.

Mabel held her hand out. "Oh." She shook her head. "That's paint. Levi's pirate rock."

"Is that code for something?" Tyson asked.

"Junior Rangers." Hattie laughed. "We painted rocks we can put along the nature trail."

"You're helping out with that?" Tyson asked Mabel, who nodded. "Why would you sign up for such torture?"

"Because I love Hattie." Mabel smiled at the other woman. "And I loved Junior Rangers growing up so…" She shrugged.

"Sounds like fun." But Tyson's expression said otherwise.

"It was. I think?" Hattie glanced over at Mabel. "Well, everyone got out unscathed."

He had to laugh at that. They all did.

"Samantha had fun," Mabel said. "She painted a beautiful butterfly rock." Her gaze darted his way, then back to the dominoes on the table.

"She'd been looking forward to it." He

didn't add that she'd been looking forward to
it because she'd been hoping Mabel would be
there. For two weeks, Samantha had seemed
to be on the lookout for Mabel. Every place
they went, she'd take her time making a men-
tal inventory of whom she saw. And every
time she didn't see Mabel, her disappointment gutted him. He'd hoped, in time, Samantha would get over her affection for
Mabel but… No such luck.

Kitty had probably loved that. He ran a
hand along the back of his neck. He'd likely
hear all about it when he got home.

"You want to join us?" Tyson asked.

"No." Mabel blurted out the word. "We…
We don't want to intrude."

Jensen couldn't decide if he was more irritated by Tyson's invitation or Mabel's response. Either way, he needed to wrap things
up. And fast. "I'll be heading out soon, so
you two could keep Tyson company."

Which earned him an eye roll from Tyson.
He might have been wrong, but he was pretty
sure Tyson mouthed, "Chicken," too.

"Well, in that case." Hattie sat in one of
the four chairs, all smiles.

Unlike Mabel, who looked as uncomfortable as he felt as they all took their seats.

Initially, it seemed like Hattie and Tyson were working together. Like the two of them had some sort of plan to break him and Mabel down with work anecdotes and harmless gossip that made them all laugh. And it worked. It didn't take long for Jensen to relax. Was he aware of Mabel's every move? Yes. But was he able to keep up with conversation without turning into a staring fool? Mostly.

"What's the total menagerie up to now?" Hattie was asking Mabel.

"Let's see." One of Mabel's eyebrows cocked up as she stared up at the ceiling. "My Alpine dairy goats, of course. Tulip, the mini-horse, who is best friends with Harvey and Juniper—our donkey. Uncle Felix has formed a singular attachment to my wily little Chihuahua mix, Roscoe. And Harvey, of course, who has decided Audy is his person. Really, I can't claim them as my menagerie anymore." She sighed. "Since JC passed away, right before I left—"

"JC?" Hattie asked.

JC? Jensen stopped turning his empty glass mug to look Mabel's way. A million thoughts flitted through his brain, overlapping and rapid-fire. He knew… Somehow he *knew* who JC was. It was the only animal she hadn't mentioned. The kitten he'd left for her. She'd named it JC? For her to have pulled the name out of thin air seemed like too big a coincidence, which meant… *All this time, she knew?* He wasn't sure what caused warmth to roll over him, but there was no fighting it. Was it her knowing and keeping the kitten a secret, her knowing and loving it anyway, or her knowing and loving it *and* naming it after him? Any way he looked at it, he knew it meant something. All of it—all of this—meant something. He was pretty sure it was something good, too.

Mabel must have felt him staring at her because her cheeks went pink.

"Oh, you mean that mean, one-eyed cat of yours? The one that followed you around like a dog?" Hattie shook her head. "Mangiest thing. And it lived forever."

"He wasn't mean." Mabel shook her head, sounding forlorn as she said, "He was my boy. And I miss him."

"How is it being home?" Tyson asked Mabel. "I've watched a few episodes of that video blog diary thing you did with the horses. Looks like you were going nonstop."

This was the first Jensen had heard of it.

Then again, most folk tended not to bring up anything Briscoe related when he was around.

Mabel covered her face with both hands and groaned a little. "I had no idea people were watching it. It was meant for the sponsors as a way to see where their money was going."

It wasn't the first time Jensen had thought the word *adorable* fit Mabel perfectly.

"Fritz Koch had the kids in his classes watch them. Good idea, I think. Seeing folk out working in support of something they believe in is inspiring." Tyson nodded at Mabel. "You're doing good, Mabel. And setting an example kids can learn from."

Her cheeks were scarlet now. "I'll be heading back soon."

Her words were a gut punch. She was leaving. He took a deep breath, willing himself to stay calm. But he couldn't stop staring at her. *Again.* For all the grief he'd received since her homecoming, the idea of her leaving made him sad. *For Samantha.* He tore his eyes from her and focused on his empty mug again. The neon beer light on the wall. The big-screen TV playing game highlights—anything but Mabel.

"When will that be?" Tyson asked.

Jensen ran a hand along the back of his neck. *This is good.* It was. For him, anyway. With her gone, he'd be able to wipe her from his mind—to stop looking for her when they were out, just like Samantha. When she left, this ache in his chest would stop and things would go back to the way they were before she'd come back into his life.

"I'm not sure, exactly." Mabel shifted from one foot to the next. "A week or so. The foundation is pretty flexible—thankfully—and I've got a few things to take care of here first."

"I guess I was hoping you'd stick around." Hattie didn't look happy. "Who will be there to help me stop Levi Williams when he starts making up stories and scaring the others?"

The waitress finally made it to the table so Hattie and Mabel could order, putting their conversation on pause. While Tyson was asking about the special, Jensen glanced at his watch. It was early yet. If he left, Tyson would know why. He'd called it. When it came to Mabel, Jensen was a chicken. He glanced her way, wishing the sight of her didn't get to him. But it did.

Mabel turned and their eyes locked, doing

a number on his heart rate. Not that she seemed happy. If anything, there was a hint of accusation on her face. "Did you sell her?" she whispered.

So soft that Jensen leaned closer to hear. *Bad idea.* Up close, she was prettier than ever. *If that's possible?* He shook his head. He had to admit it—Tyson was right about a lot of things when it came to Mabel.

She blinked, a furrow forming between her brows as she studied him.

A series of emotions played over her features, leaving his insides all twisted up. What was she looking for? And why did he have to be so drawn to *this* woman?

"Jensen…" Her voice shook. "Did you sell her?"

He forced himself to focus on her words, struggling to regain his balance. "Sell who?" Her frown returned and it clicked. The paint horse. "No. I didn't." Did she really think he'd sell the animal to anyone without giving her the option first? He knew how much she'd wanted the horse and how much it'd grieved her to let it go. He gripped the arms of his chair. Mabel Briscoe had him on a seesaw. One minute, she said or did something that warmed him through. The next, she was looking at him like he was lower than dirt. Like now. And it rubbed him all the wrong way.

Mabel's gaze swept over his face. "I don't understand. Samantha said she didn't have a horse."

"That made you think I sold it?" Jensen ignored every reaction she caused except one: anger. Here she thought the worst of him and, yet, she expected him to answer her questions? He didn't owe her an explanation about Samantha or the horse—or anything, for that matter.

If you like this woman, you should court her. Briscoe or not. Tyson's simple statement seemed almost comical now. Not in a funny way, but in a sharp, jagged way that cut deep. "While I appreciate your interest, Miss Briscoe, I have things well under control." He saw her flinch, saw her lean away from him in surprise, those big blue eyes blinking rapidly. Even though he had every right to his anger, he hated the effect it had on her. *Enough.* "I'm heading out." He stood quickly, touching the brim of his hat. "Y'all enjoy the rest of your evening." He didn't look any of them in the eye or wait for a response. Instead, he turned on one booted heel and tried not to bolt from the place.

He didn't need or want to feel this torn over a person who held such a low opinion of him. He couldn't get away from Mabel fast enough. This time, he'd stay away.

CHAPTER NINE

Mabel poured herself a cup of coffee and peered at the near-black liquid. "Uncle Felix make the coffee this morning?"

"Yup," Forrest said from behind his morning newspaper. "It'll put hair on your chest."

"Great. Just what I wanted." Mabel normally didn't doctor her coffee, but this was no average cup of coffee. With a spoonful of sugar and a splash of cream, it looked almost palatable. She carried her cup to the large kitchen table and sank into a chair opposite her big brother. "Anything new?" She blew on her coffee, then carefully took a sip. It sent a shudder down her spine, but she swallowed it all the same. After tossing and turning most of the night, she was going to need help to get through the day.

"Morning." Audy pushed through the kitchen door and made a beeline for the coffee. "What's wrong with Sleeping Beauty over there? You're looking a little rough."

"Has anyone ever told you you know how to make a gal's morning?" Mabel shot him a fake smile as he sat beside Forrest on the other side of the table.

"Seriously?" Audy took a sip of coffee, without reacting, and cocked an eyebrow her way. "You okay? Feeling all right?"

Forrest set aside his newspaper to really look at her. "Oh."

"Really?" Mabel glared at her brothers. "Isn't there another way you could have worded that?"

"What? It was one word. All I said was 'Oh.'" Forrest looked at Audy for support. "Can't a brother show concern for his little sister?"

"Of course." Mabel ran a hand over her face and slumped forward over the table. "I didn't sleep well last night."

"Well, that's obvious." Audy pointed in her direction. "Why? Feeling bad? Or something weighing on your mind?"

Mabel knew better than to tell the truth. To admit that Jensen Crawley was the reason she had tossed and turned the whole night would likely enrage both of her brothers. Not that she had been tossing and turning all night worrying about a man. No, that would be too easy. Rather, that she was tossing and turning over a Crawley. "I guess I was just feeling restless."

"You should go for a ride," Forrest said, again looking to Audy for support.

Audy nodded. "Sounds like a plan."

Mabel perked up a bit. It had been a while since she'd taken a ride across the ranch. There were places on the property that seemed to help ease her when she needed it most. Like now.

Audy paused, his eyes searching hers. "You sure there's nothing bothering you? Sometimes just talking about something can help." He shrugged. "Or not."

Mabel couldn't help herself—she had to laugh. "While I appreciate the offer, I think a ride is more likely to help." She stood, eager to get out and clear her mind.

"You should go on and do what you need to do today, Mabel." Forrest was studying her, his eyes narrowed just a bit. "Maybe taking a ride will make you rethink leaving."

"Not that we don't get how important your work is to you, but… It'd be nice if you were…here." Audy looked down into his coffee mug. "Think about it, anyway."

Her stoic, dry, sarcastic brothers were

being emotional. For them, anyway. And it touched her heart more than she could put into words. "I'll think about it," she promised, giving them both a quick hug. "I'll take Firefly out on the trails. Like we used to. You're sure you don't want to come?" They both mumbled excuses, so with another hug, Mabel went to change.

When they were little, they would all ride into town. There was a winding deer path that led from their property to erste Baum park. And while it took the better part of the day to get there, it was a beautiful ride. A peaceful ride. *And boy could I use peace right now.*

Mabel was getting dressed when her phone rang. It was Hattie. She almost hit Mute and ignored it but... It was Hattie. "Good morning."

"It is morning." There was a smile in Hattie's voice. "What are you up to today?"

"I was thinking about taking a trail ride with Firefly." She brushed her hair back and braided it. "What about you?"

"I'd be happy to tag along. If you're okay with that? I know last night I kind of forced things when I shouldn't have. I am sorry— and I hope you're not mad at me." She took a deep breath. "And I promise, from now on I'll leave you and Jensen alone."

"Of course I'm not mad." She'd been irritated, maybe, but she was over it. "But I appreciate that—the apology and no more Jensen *stuff*." Mabel didn't want to think about the harshness of Jensen's tone or his abrupt words from last night. Worse, she didn't want to think about how she'd felt when he looked at her with such open scorn. Maybe she had overstepped. The horse wasn't hers and she really had no rights to ask about it... She sighed. "Come on out and you can ride one of our horses."

"I'll pack a picnic lunch and we can eat in the park." Hattie sounded excited.

"Good idea." As long as Hattie honored her word and there'd be no more talk of Jensen or Samantha or any of that, today would be the restful, fun sort of day she needed.

About an hour later she and Hattie set out. Firefly seemed just as excited as she was to be on the trails. And while Hattie wasn't exactly quiet, she did keep up an entertaining line of conversation.

"Looks like somebody is celebrating something," Hattie said as they headed into the park, shielding her gaze as she stared at the group of people gathered beneath the first tree.

It wasn't unusual. The park was beautiful and the shade of the tree kept temperatures at a comfortable level. She smiled at the children milling around, some holding on to balloons as they ran, chasing each other, around the wide trunk of the tree.

"Well, it looks like they're having fun." Mabel smiled, steering Firefly with the slightest touch of her knee. "I guess we'll set up on the far side." They skirted the large group of people and headed around to the other side of the tree, but before they reached their destination, Mabel heard a little voice that instantly caught her attention.

"It's Mabel, see?" Samantha Crawley. Mabel would know that voice anywhere. "Right there. On that horse."

Hattie rode Marmaduke alongside Firefly. "I know today was about having some peace and quiet. If it helps, I don't see him… Oh. No. There he is." Hattie sighed. "I'm sorry, Mabel."

"Why are you apologizing? It's not like you knew they were going to be here." She turned in her saddle, her eyes narrowing. "Did you, Hattie?"

Hattie burst out laughing. "You really think I didn't learn my lesson after last night?"

Which wasn't exactly an answer, but Mabel let it go. They were here. No point turning back when they had a picnic to share—even if Jensen Crawley did decide to darken her day with his presence.

"Mabel, Mabel." Samantha came running, tugging Kitty behind her. "Is that your horse? He's so big."

"It is. This is Firefly." Mabel patted the horse's neck. "It was too perfect a day not to take a ride. What are you up to?"

"It's Miss Gretta's birthday." Samantha announced this with great glee.

Kitty agreed. "And we should probably get back to the party now."

"But… Mabel…" Samantha was staring at her with wide eyes.

Don't say a word. It wasn't her place. Kitty was eager to steer them back to the party, and Mabel understood why, *but* Samantha had asked about Firefly. She and Kitty weren't exactly friends, but they'd worked together for Samantha's sake at the Junior Rangers meeting. Maybe Kitty would do the same now? "Would you like to meet Firefly, Samantha?"

Samantha shook her head, then paused. "Really?"

"If you want, you could come closer or give him a pat." Mabel offered up what she hoped was her most encouraging smile.

Samantha was still hiding behind Kitty's legs as she asked, "Does he want to be my friend?"

"Definitely." Mabel swung down from the saddle, adjusted her hat and took Firefly's reins. "But you don't have to. I know he is a lot bigger than Harvey. And—" she bent forward and whispered "—Firefly doesn't have as soft a tummy as Harvey does. But don't tell him. I don't want to hurt his feelings."

"I won't tell him." Samantha nodded sagely. "Should I, Auntie Kitty?"

For the first time, Mabel looked at Kitty. The woman was watching their exchange closely. Just like she had the night before at the Junior Rangers meeting. It was almost like Kitty Crawley couldn't make up her mind about Mabel. *I know the feeling.* There wasn't much she could do except… Mabel smiled at Kitty. A real smile. Nervous, maybe, but a sort of olive branch. *Now it's up to you, Kitty.*

"Well, I'm sure he wants to be your friend."

Kitty looked at Mabel cautiously. "But we should probably ask your dad."

"That's a good idea, Samantha. Hattie and I are going to set up a picnic right over there." She pointed out the shady patch. "If you want to come meet Firefly, he will be there, too."

"You won't leave without saying goodbye, will you?" Samantha asked, taking a few steps forward.

"Nope." Mabel crouched, eager for one of the little girl's fierce hugs.

Samantha didn't disappoint. She ran forward and gave Mabel a sweet, hard hug. "Okay. I'll go ask Daddy." Just as quickly as she'd hugged her, her little arms slipped free and she turned to run back to the party and her father, with Kitty trailing after her.

While Marmaduke and Firefly nibbled at the green grass, Hattie spread out their picnic blanket, and Mabel took the basket from the back of Firefly's saddle. She'd like to think that she and Kitty Crawley had made some sort of progress. Maybe?

"Forrest said you woke up rough this morning?" Hattie said between bites.

"He said that?" It wasn't the first time Hattie had mentioned Forrest—or vice versa. "When was this?"

"He texted this morning." Hattie shrugged. "He was worried about you."

Texting to pick up milk was one thing. Texting just to text was another. Mabel couldn't help being a little stunned. "Forrest texted? *My* brother?" She shook her head when Hattie nodded. "Oh? Is that why you called? To keep an eye on me?" Mabel was only partly teasing.

"No." Hattie tossed the apple core to the horses. "I feel really bad about last night. *Really.* I do."

"You don't need to. I don't hold you accountable for any of that Jensen *stuff.*" If Jensen Crawley wanted to be a jerk, he could be a jerk. *I no longer care what he thinks or says.* Mabel *almost* believed that. "You and Tyson seemed to get along well last night."

"Uh-huh." Hattie rummaged through the canvas bag for a sandwich. "He's a nice guy."

Mabel smiled. "Yes. And he's handsome—"

"You think so?" Hattie glanced at her. "You're interested in *Tyson*?"

"No." She waved her hands in front of her face. "I am not. But if you were—"

"Me?" Hattie looked at her like she was growing a second head. "Me? And Tyson?" She was laughing then.

Long ago, Mabel had come to realize that Hattie didn't see herself as she was. She didn't see her big green eyes or her strawberry blond curls or the sprinkling of freckles across her nose that made her so pretty. Hattie was too no-nonsense for that. But Mabel saw her for the gem she was. Hattie was bighearted and funny and deserving of someone who'd love her. Just not Tyson Ellis, apparently. "So that's a no?" Mabel asked when Hattie was done snorting and laughing.

"That's a big no." Hattie sighed, still smiling. "I don't think I could ever date a man from Garrison, Mabel. I know them all too well. They're all like…like…brothers, more or less."

"Speaking of, how is your brother, Billy?" Mabel asked.

"Oh, he's good." Hattie adored her brother and hated the fact that he'd moved away from Garrison for work. Hattie wrinkled up her nose. "He says he'll be home for the Founders Day Festival this fall. I was hoping he'd be here for LAT Day." Love a Tree Day was a big deal in Garrison. But this year, with the threat to the beloved First Tree, the day would likely be the biggest one yet.

"Founders Day will be here before you

know it." Mabel tossed an apple toward the horses and lay on her back, staring up at the sky overhead. "Look at that fluffy cloud."

Hattie flopped down beside her. "That one looks like a rabbit."

Mabel tilted her head and stared at the lone cloud. "A rabbit?" She tilted her head in the other direction. "Um, more like an octopus."

"An octopus or a rabbit. Close enough."

They both laughed.

"Whatcha laughin' at?" Samantha asked, leaning over them.

"The clouds. Come look." Mabel patted the blanket between her and Hattie. "What does that cloud look like, Samantha? I said an octopus and Hattie says it's a rabbit."

Samantha lay between them and peered up at the fluffy cloud moving slowly across the bright blue sky. "I think it looks like a… mushroom."

That had Hattie and Mabel laughing all over again—Samantha, too.

"I'm not sure I want to know." Jensen's voice reached them before he was standing at the blanket's edge.

"Cloud shapes, Daddy," Samantha explained.

Jensen shielded his eyes and looked up.

"That one? Looks like a… It looks like an octopus." He looked down at them. Correction, Samantha. "Close?"

"You match with Mabel, Daddy." Samantha sat up.

Hattie made something that sounded an awful lot like a laugh-cough, but since she'd rolled away, there was no way Mabel could confirm it. Instead, she sat up, put her straw cowboy hat on and risked a quick glance at Jensen.

No man should look this good. Ever. And yet, he did. Tall and strong and oh-so-handsome. He wore a dark blue button-down the same color of his eyes. Not that she cared what color his eyes were. Or how broad his chest was or how gentle his smile was when he looked at his little girl. He was either going to let Samantha meet Firefly or he was here to give Mabel a talking-to about minding her own business… *Like he'd done last night.*

He helped pull Hattie up, but Mabel ignored his hand and stood on her own, avoiding those beautiful haunted eyes of his. She had to if she wasn't going to like him anymore. "What can I do for you, Mr. Crawley?" She managed to sound calm—that was something.

"Samantha said something about meeting your horse." He sounded detached. No, not detached. *Strained is more like it.* "If the offer still stands, Miss Briscoe?"

"Can I meet him, Mabel?" Samantha wasn't exactly standing behind Jensen, but she was definitely within arm's reach of her father.

"Of course you can." Mabel decided it would be easier to ignore Jensen altogether. "Firefly is a very special horse."

"Because he hugs and he's nice and he lets you ride on him?" Samantha asked.

"Yes, all that is true." Mabel nodded. "But he helps other horses when they come to the ranch. It's a new place and they're not sure what's what and who's who and if my brothers and uncle and I are nice, so I let Firefly go into the corral with them." She clicked her tongue, and Firefly headed toward her, his ears perked forward. "I don't know what it is about him, but he makes those horses feel right at home."

"I bet he tells them you're nice, too." Samantha watched Firefly, reaching out and taking Mabel's hand. "I bet he tells them how lucky they are, too, to live with you and your family."

Firefly stopped directly in front of them, allowing Mabel to run a hand along his neck. "See? He's just like Harvey. Big but gentle." She kept running her hand down his neck.

"He's a lot bigger than Harvey." Samantha's voice had dropped to a whisper.

"Firefly, this is Samantha." She spoke gently, right next to Firefly's ear. "She is a very special little girl so you be extra gentle."

Firefly snorted.

"What did he say?" Samantha whispered, her hold tightening on Mabel's hand.

"I think I offended him." Mabel chuckled. "He's always extra gentle. Aren't you?"

Firefly snorted again, earning another tiny smile from Samantha. The little girl was a mix of nerves and excitement—one wrong move and the whole thing could fall apart. Mabel didn't push. Jensen stood by, silent as a statue. Firefly was curious about the little person holding on to Mabel, but he seemed to sense that patience was needed. The horse waited until Samantha slowly put out her hand before he lowered his head to whiffle and blow around her hair and head.

Samantha closed her eyes, giggling. "What's he doing?"

The sound of Samantha's giggle filled

Mabel with happiness. She couldn't stop her smile any more than she could stop the sun from rising. Her gaze darted from Hattie to Jensen, overjoyed by Samantha's reaction to Firefly. Jensen looked the same. Happy and smiling and relieved and blindingly beautiful. The moment his eyes locked with hers, Mabel realized her heart was in danger. It didn't matter how many times she told herself not to like Jensen or how many times she told herself she'd gotten over her childhood crush or how often she reminded herself that the two of them could never be—not ever— it was time to face facts. Feuds and enemies and insurmountable obstacles couldn't sway her heart. The fool thing seemed convinced it belonged with Jensen, and there was nothing Mabel could do to change that.

JENSEN HAD BEEN prepared to be civil. Neighborly, even. Last night he'd driven home, wishing he could wipe the evening away. He'd snapped so hard at her, Mabel had physically recoiled from him. Had that made him any less angry? No. It'd made things ten times worse. Not with her, with himself. This thing with Mabel was a problem but as long as they steered clear of one another, it'd pass. He had to believe that. But that was last night, when he was home and Mabel was miles away and he'd been able to convince himself that what he was thinking could somehow actually happen.

Here, now, was another story. There was no way he could have prepared himself for Mabel, with the sun on her face and a smile full of joy. The tug in his chest he'd been trying so hard to ignore went from gentle to fierce. There was no ignoring it. And no ignoring her, either. She was…beautiful.

"Daddy." Samantha was still giggling.

"I see you, little miss. And I see you've made a new friend, too." He shook his head, once again stunned by the trust Samantha had in Mabel.

"Just like Mabel said." Samantha reached up, running her hand along Firefly's chest. "He's soft, too. Aren't you, boy?"

Firefly lowered his head, gently nudging Mabel in the chest.

"He wants to hug you." Mabel crouched beside Samantha. "But you don't have to. I know he's big—"

"It's okay." Samantha let go of Mabel's hand. "I like hugs."

The horse rested its chin on Samantha's

back and tucked the little girl close. "I'll be." Jensen chuckled. He also saw Mabel watching closely—taking extra care with his little girl.

"I told ya." Hattie's voice was low. "He's something."

Jensen nodded. "I see that."

"Daddy, Daddy, did you see?" Samantha stared up at him. "I hugged Firefly."

"And he hugged you right back." He winked. "I've never seen anything like it."

"Firefly's special, Daddy. He'd have to be." She stood on tiptoe to whisper, "Not every horse is good enough for a princess."

Ah, yes. The princess thing. He really should sit her down and explain that, as unique as Mabel was, there were no real princesses in Texas. But there was a tiny part of him that worried about how telling her that might change things. In next to no time, Mabel had his skittish little girl petting a dog and hugging a horse. There was time enough to clear up the whole princess thing later. For the moment, he'd leave it alone.

Mabel swung up onto Firefly's back. "If you want, you can ride with me. I'll walk him real slow, in a circle, right around your dad."

Jensen put his hands on his hips and stared

at the woman. He admired her determination and Samantha had made huge progress, but that didn't mean—

"Can I?" Samantha asked.

"Ride?" Jensen knelt in front of her. "You sure?"

She smiled at him. "Yep."

Jensen wasn't going to argue. Mabel would keep her safe; he didn't doubt that for a minute. If Samantha wanted to ride, he was willing to give it a try. He scooped her up and helped Samantha drape her leg over the saddle to sit in front of Mabel.

Jensen stepped back. "You look good." Samantha was smiling, but there was no denying she was nervous. He was a little nervous, too.

"We can just stand here for a bit," Mabel said, her arms coming around Samantha to hold the reins. "Let you get comfy. I'm right here."

"I'm okay." Samantha took a deep breath. "Slow?"

"Slow." Mabel clicked her tongue and Firefly took a step.

Jensen wasn't sure what to do. His instinct was to cheer, but he didn't want to startle Samantha or the horse. Same thing with clapping. So, he stood there, marveling at the sight of Samantha riding a horse. She smiled and waved as they made a slow circle around him.

"Maybe she is magic," Hattie said, shielding her eyes to watch them take another lap. "Last night... Sorry about that. I guess it was obvious Tyson and I were sort of egging the two of you on. I know better but..."

He knew better than to ask, but he asked anyway. "But?"

"I guess I thought I saw something between the two of you." Hattie shoved her hands into her pockets. "But I must have been seeing things."

"Must have." He'd be a fool to let himself believe anything differently. Better to enjoy Samantha's expression—her nerves and fear giving way to wonder. He knew his father would give him an earful for not coming straight back to the ranch after dropping off the girls at the party, but he couldn't leave now.

The two rode for a while. The circle got bigger and bigger, but Samantha was having too good a time to notice. Whatever else he may or may not feel for Mabel, he was grateful. He couldn't count the number of times he'd tried to get Samantha near a horse, let alone ride one. And yet, here she was, about as carefree as a little girl could be—*riding* a horse. He might not understand the bond she and Samantha had formed, but it was real. Seeing them together proved that.

Kitty joined him and Hattie, looking pensive. "Is this a good idea?"

Jensen couldn't remember seeing Samantha happier. "You tell me," he murmured.

"That's some smile, all right. Then again, she is riding on a horse with her favorite real-life princess." Kitty nudged him. "You should ask her to help with the paint mare."

"I don't think so." That had disaster written all over it.

"Well, I do." Kitty shot back. "Hattie, and a good portion of Garrison, seems to think Mabel has a way with animals. That little paint needs…something. Maybe Mabel can help with that."

Jensen agreed with everything his sister was saying but… "How would that work, Kitty? It's not like she can just stop by our place." He could picture his father shouting and shooing Mabel off.

"Twyla's not a problem. You just wait until she's at work," Kitty suggested, returning Samantha's wave as they rode past.

"And Dad?" He glanced at his sister. She

and Hattie were wearing identical expressions, like they were working through a puzzle in their mind. "Besides, even if we could get him out of the house, there's no guarantee Mabel will figure out what's wrong with the horse." Which was a lie. She would and he knew it. He remembered the look on Mabel's face that day in the barn—saying goodbye to the horse. She'd know—and she'd fix it.

Hattie shot him a disbelieving look. Kitty did the same.

"Now you're on her side?" Jensen asked, nodding at Mabel.

"I'm on Samantha's side." Kitty stared up at him. "And that poor horse, too. As far as Daddy goes... I'll tell him I can't take Samantha to dance practice tomorrow afternoon. If he takes her, he'll stay to watch and that would give you and Mabel at least an hour. It's something."

"Assuming she'll say yes," he murmured. Once again, the image of her teary-eyed in the horse barn after the auction surfaced. *She'll say yes.* Now all he had to do was get up the courage to ask her.

Ten minutes later, the party was wrapping up and Kitty called a reluctant Samantha down from Firefly.

"You stay put and talk to her about tomorrow," Kitty whispered, taking Samantha's hand in hers. "Tell Mabel thank you."

"Thank you, thank you." Samantha was her usual bouncy self. "And thank you, too, Firefly."

Mabel waved. "Maybe we can do it again someday." She patted Firefly's neck. "He'd like that."

"Me, too." Samantha waved, skipping along beside Kitty as they made their way back to the party. He heard Samantha chattering away, bursting with pride over her ride and making friends with Mabel's horse.

Making friends with Firefly wasn't the problem. It was the paint horse he was worried about. And that was why he was walking toward Mabel, that was why he'd ask her for help and hope she didn't immediately say no.

"Thank you," he said, tipping his hat forward to keep the sun from his eyes.

"You're welcome." But she wasn't looking at him; she was fiddling with something on the saddle.

"No, Mabel. Really, thank you." He cleared his throat. "I mean it."

Her gaze darted his way, almost wary. But she must have seen something that convinced her he was being sincere because there was a ghost of a smile on her lips as she said, "You're welcome."

Since there was no point in beating around the bush, he jumped right in. "I've no right to ask you to help me with something else, but I'm out of options." He took a deep breath. "The paint. She's…" He shook his head. "For two weeks, I've tried to get to know her— to draw her out. But she's not interested. In me or Kitty or any of the ranch hands. I get too close and she backs up, on edge. Now she's not eating much and she's…depressed. I guess. Can a horse get depressed?"

Mabel slid off Firefly to stand in front of him, one hand resting on the horse's shoulder. "They can." She nibbled on the inside of her lip, her eyes fixed on some distant point. "I couldn't pinpoint it, but I think she's been through something. Maybe lost someone?" She blinked, focusing in on him. "Do you know anything about her? Did the seller give you any information?"

He shook his head.

Her expression became pensive, and she went back to staring into space.

He'd never seen her so absorbed. Whatever she was pondering, she was doing so with great intensity. And she was so pretty, she took his breath away.

"Jensen…" His name slipped from her lips, more a whisper than anything.

And hearing it sent a shiver down his spine.

She was still working through things in her mind. Her eyes narrowed a little and she sighed. "I can't really talk to them… Animals, I mean. Not with words." She shrugged. "I wish I could, that'd be easier. It's more a…feeling." Her blue eyes locked with his. She paused, then cleared her throat. "If you can dig a little? Anything you can find out about her might help."

"I'll do my best." He nodded. "Could I ask you to come out and take a look at her?"

"To Crawley Ranch?" She frowned. "But… how… Is that a good idea?"

For the horse, yes. For him? *I don't know.* Like it or not, she was his only hope. "Dad's taking Samantha to her dance class and Twyla will be at the shop. All told, we should have an hour before you'll need to run for the hills." He was teasing—sort of. "If you can come tomorrow, around four?"

A gust of wind caught her hat and carried it a few feet. He took off after it and didn't realize she'd chased it until their hands collided, both reaching for her hat on the grass. The longer he stared into her blue eyes, the more he wanted to stay like this. Behind Firefly, out of view, staring at her to his heart's content.

He smoothed the hair from her shoulder, the shock of contact nearly singeing his fingertips. "If you're free?" He sounded gruff because his throat was tight. He put her hat on her head.

Mabel hadn't moved. She'd stood, silent and staring, since their hands brushed. He didn't know what to make of it. Now, she was pink cheeked and looking at him in open confusion. "Okay." She opened her mouth, then closed it, shaking her head.

"What?" Did he want to know? *Yes.* Yes, he did.

"No. Nothing." She pressed her lips together, still looking at him.

He ran a hand along the back of his neck, beyond frustrated. "I know I'm asking a lot, Mabel." She drew in a deep breath, her eyes fluttering closed. "I know this has disaster written all over it, but…" He broke off when her eyes opened and she smiled. He'd been working toward a point… One he couldn't remember. But she was smiling—that had to be a good sign. He started again. "I appreciate it. I'm sure the horse will appreciate it, too."

She nodded. "What if I can't help? What if she'll never be a good fit for Samantha?"

He didn't even have to think about it. "Then I'll sell her to you." Which was probably what he should go on and do now—if it wouldn't likely send his father's blood pressure through the roof.

He didn't know how long they stood there, trying to get a read on one another. At least, that was what he was trying to do. Mabel's eyes gave so much away, but she was being careful and keeping her guard up.

It was time to lay it all out there. "I've got no hidden agenda, Mabel. I'm not looking to add further offense or insult to the feud or hoping to lure you in for…for vengeance or some despicable purpose…" He sighed. "I get it, I do. There's no reason to trust what I'm saying. I'm me and you're you and—"

"That's the thing. I've don't think of you as the enemy, Jensen." She swallowed. "You're a Crawley and I'm a Briscoe, but you've been nothing but kind to me—for as long as I can remember. Maybe, for now, we can put all that aside and do this together?" Her eyes searched his. "If that's possible?" She made an odd sound, a hard laugh and sigh, garbled and thick. "I guess that's asking too much—"

"No," he cut in. "It's not." *It's what I want.* "It's possible." He swallowed against the tightness in his throat.

"Okay." She held her hand out. "Shake on it?"

Jensen smiled and took her hand in his. In the time it took to shake her hand, his nerves were firing off all sorts of signals. How his hand dwarfed hers. How his hands were rough while hers were silk. How when she smiled, a real smile—like now—he could see it in her eyes. How her hand fit, right here, in his. And worse, he realized he didn't want to let her go.

CHAPTER TEN

MABEL WALKED INTO the kitchen the following morning with a spring in her step. She poured herself a cup of sludge-like coffee, gave Uncle Felix a quick kiss on the cheek and decided to make some cinnamon rolls. Today she'd finally get some time with the paint horse. Ever since the day of the auction, the horse had been there at the back of her brain. She wasn't one to let go of a puzzle. She'd worry over it and try it from all angles until she'd figured it out. Letting that horse go without understanding what was troubling it had been as irritating and persistent as an itch she couldn't quite reach. Knowing the poor horse had been struggling since Jensen had taken it home only made it that much worse.

But today would fix that. Hopefully. No, it would. Mabel was determined. And, as Uncle Felix said, "Once Mabel made up her mind to do something, you'd best get out of the way and let her do it." Her mind was definitely made up.

She was putting the tray of cinnamon rolls into the oven when she turned and found all eyes on her. "What?" she asked, frowning.

"You had to drag yourself in here yesterday and today you're all chipper." Forrest held his coffee cup between both hands, studying her.

"You do seem extra peppy this morning." One of Uncle Felix's salt-and-pepper brows arched high.

"I have to agree with Forrest." Audy held his hand up. "I know, I know, that's unheard of, but… In this case, I'm a little surprised."

"You've always been a morning person." Beau shrugged, the corner of his lip cocking up. "It's just nice to see you here—for all of us to be together."

Mabel smiled. "It is nice, Beau."

Her other brothers made a range of dismissive sounds followed by eye rolling and head shaking.

"Too touchy-feely for you all this morning?" She laughed. "At least one of you can emote." She turned toward Webb, who'd propped himself up on the table. "Go on. What about you?"

"I'm just excited about the cinnamon rolls." Webb pointed at the oven.

Mabel was laughing all over again.

"I emote." Audy's brow was furrowed.

"We know." Forrest shot him a glance. "We were all at the picnic. All of Garrison knows."

And that opened the floodgates on poor Audy and his very public, very sweet confession to Brooke Young.

Mabel shook her head, listening as they bickered and poked at one another. She'd missed this, missed them. This was one of those times when going back to Wyoming didn't seem all that pressing. It wasn't like there weren't others to carry on the work of the foundation. Taking a little more time to enjoy mornings like this wouldn't hurt. Either way, she needed to make up her mind.

"I heard you were spotted at Buck's night before last?" Audy piped up.

Stay calm. "Yes."

"And that Tyson Ellis was there, too?" Audy asked, smiling as her other brothers and uncle all turned to look her way.

She waited, silently dreading the minute Audy mentioned Jensen's presence. Maybe whoever had ratted her out to begin with decided to give her a break? *Please, please, let that be the case.* "So?"

"Tyson's decent," Forrest murmured, uncomfortable.

"No arguing that," Uncle Felix agreed. "You two a-courtin'?"

Mabel blinked. "What? No." Was that really all there was to talk about? Who *might* be dating whom? First Jensen. Now Tyson.

"There's nothing wrong with Tyson," Webb said. "Are they almost ready now?"

"Not yet." Mabel didn't bother looking at the timer. "Hattie was with me. Did whoever-it-was tell you that?"

Audy nodded, his smile tightening. "And that Crawley was there, too."

"Yes. He's friends with Tyson and Hattie," Mabel pointed out, turning to check on the cinnamon rolls—even though they were fine. "It was me and Hattie having a bite. Nothing more. Nothing less." She closed the oven and turned to find all eyes once more on her.

"I think there was more to it than that." Audy sat back, enjoying himself. He'd always had a flare for the dramatic. "I heard Crawley stormed out—after he said something to you."

Mabel got all fired up then. It didn't matter

that her brother was telling the truth, it was that someone—there was always someone—had been taking notes over the whole thing. "That sounds like a good tale to tell, doesn't it?" She crossed her arms over her chest and stared Audy down. "Nobody would care or believe that he said good-night and left. That would be boring." She sighed, tossing the kitchen towel onto the counter. "I forgot how everyone tries to get into everyone else's business in Garrison. And if there is nothing to tell, someone will make something up that sounds good."

An uncomfortable silence fell. At least her brothers and uncle had the decency to look a little shame-faced now. Granted, this time it was all true, but they didn't need to know that.

"If you want to know something, how about you ask *me* instead of taking the word of someone who is *not* me?" She took a deep breath and the timer dinged. "Now they're ready, Webb." She turned and pulled the pan of golden-brown cinnamon rolls from the oven and slid it onto the marble countertop. "Just remember they're hot."

Webb was already up. He grabbed a roll

and started tossing it back and forth between his hands like a hot potato.

"Webb." She stared at him.

"I know, I know." He dropped the roll onto his plate. "But I learned a long time ago that if I don't want to go hungry, I gotta get while the getting is good." He grabbed another one and added it to his plate, then slathered them both with her homemade cream cheese glaze.

Luckily, no one brought up any more gossip while they enjoyed their breakfast. Mabel began to think she'd gotten off scot-free until Forrest stuck around to help her clean up the kitchen.

"Mabel." He grabbed a towel and dried the now-empty pan. "Don't bite my head off here, but…you're sure there's no truth to this talk about you and…well, you know who."

Jensen Crawley? He couldn't even say Jensen's name. She didn't want to think about how Forrest would react to her going out to Crawley Ranch. After all these years, how could she honestly expect her brother—her family—to consider Jensen as an individual, apart from the Crawley name? *Because I want them to?* Because she couldn't get over this…whatever *this* was. If she could get her fool heart to let go, she would.

"Mabel?" Forrest pushed.

She didn't look at him, she couldn't. Forrest was her big brother—he always saw right through her. If she tried to argue with him, chances were he'd hear the uncertainty in her voice. And then he'd scent blood in the water and he'd know... *He'd know what?* She swallowed, hard. The truth: Jensen was in her heart.

"I know you think I don't have emotions..." His face flushed red. "But I don't want you getting hurt, is all."

Mabel turned to her brother and hugged him tight. "You don't need to worry about me," she murmured against his chest. "But I love you all the more for it."

He patted her awkwardly on the back. "I worry. You think I don't, but I do." His voice was gruff.

It was the first time she felt bad for teasing him. He might not be the most demonstrative man, but she'd never doubted he loved her. "You're a good big brother, you know that?"

He made a noncommittal sound, stepping away. "Hattie said you were helping her out at Junior Rangers?"

Interesting how much you and Hattie talk, big brother. Instead, she said, "She needed extra hands. I can tell you with one hundred percent certainty that I am nowhere near ready to be a parent."

"No rush." Forrest chuckled. "Not until you've found the right person."

Mabel glanced at her brother, the question pushing and pushing until it spilled from her lips. "What about you, Forrest?" And Hattie? Was that a thing? Yes, they were friends, but she didn't even talk and text with Hattie as much as Forrest did.

"Me?" Forrest looked confused. "Like I have time for that nonsense."

But Mabel didn't have time to pursue the conversation any further. The kitchen door swung open and Uncle Felix walked in, fiddling with a tie. "Mabel. I need a hand."

"What are you doing all spruced up?" Forrest asked.

Uncle Felix cleared his throat. "I thought I'd go on to the Veterans Hall. There's a fish fry and bingo tonight—to raise money for this summer's Fourth of July fireworks. I figure I'll help set up and...all."

Her uncle was nervous. "There." Mabel fixed his tie and patted his chest.

"Since when did they expect you to wear a

tie to a fish fry and bingo?" Forrest grabbed an orange off the top of the fruit bowl.

"I think you look nice, Uncle Felix." Was her uncle going courting? *I think he is.* She smiled. "You have fun."

He nodded, running a hand over his thick salt-and-pepper hair. "Mmm-hmm." He turned, walking quickly from the kitchen. "I'll be late," he called back over his shoulder.

"What in the Sam Hill was that about?" Forrest stared at the now-closed kitchen door.

"The fish fry is being hosted by the Ladies Guild, Forrest." Mabel shot her brother a look, exasperated when that wasn't explanation enough. "Barbara Eldridge will be there."

Forrest's brows went up. "Huh." He carried his orange from the kitchen.

Huh? Yep. Her brother. A man of few words. She finished wiping down the kitchen counter and glanced at the clock. She still had hours before she was supposed to head to the Crawley place. And, unless she found something to do, she'd wind up cleaning and organizing the pantry to pass the time. Instead, she flipped off the kitchen light and headed into the large home office. She sat, turned on one of the computers and typed in "Holsom auction." There were pictures of all the animals that had been auctioned off— including Samantha's little blue-gray mare.

There wasn't much in the way of information. The horse had a name. "Stardust," Mabel murmured. *Samantha will love that.* Other than that, not much information. She sighed, scrolled down to the contact information for the auction itself and scribbled it down on a piece of paper. Knowing what happened to Stardust didn't guarantee Mabel could help, but it would definitely cut down on the guesswork. Since she had only one hour, she needed to make every second at Crawley Ranch count.

As long as Jensen didn't act too dreamy or look too good and her heart behaved and she didn't get rubbery knees, she could get a lot done in an hour. Like that was going to happen. All he had to do was stand there and she'd get muddled. There wasn't time for that today. Maybe it would be best for her to shoo Jensen out of the barn—that way there would be no time-wasting distractions.

JENSEN HAD BEEN pacing the gravel drive leading to the barn for ten minutes. The closer it got to four, the more agitated he'd become. So far, so good. Samantha and his father were en route to dance practice and Twyla and Kitty were at work. His father had been in an unusually good mood—all excited to take Samantha to a fish fry and bingo over at the Veterans Hall—and Kitty had promised to give Jensen a heads-up when they headed home. Technically, he and Mabel should be able to pull this off. As long as they stayed focused on the horse and he didn't get side-tracked by Mabel, that is.

He hadn't expected to see a beaten-up blue pickup truck rattling down the road. *A truck in need of a tune-up.*

It parked, the grind of the parking brake alarming. Mabel jumped out of the driver's seat. "Hi."

She wore an oversize plaid shirt tucked into too-big jeans with her hair braided and tucked under a cowboy hat that didn't come close to fitting her. "I figured driving out here in a Briscoe Ranch truck might draw attention so I drove one of the work trucks." She patted the hood of the jalopy. "And, just in case anyone did do a double take, I came incognito, too."

He bit back a smile. "I see that." She resembled a scarecrow—all thrown together. And yet, somehow, she managed to still look oh-so-pretty.

She pushed the hat back enough to see him, those big blue eyes of hers sweeping over his face before falling to the gravel at their feet. "Why don't you show me the way and then you can go about your business."

As far as dismissals went, it was pretty cut-and-dried. He'd hoped to watch her in action—maybe pick up some pointers. But she was doing him a favor and they were too short on time for any further delay. "Follow me." *It's better this way.* If he wasn't with her, there was no chance he'd make a fool of himself or say or do something he'd regret.

Mabel pulled up the waist of her jeans a good three inches and tucked her hands into the pockets to hold them up.

"Maybe you should steal some suspenders next time." He shot her a grin.

"I tried to find some." Her hat slipped forward. "But Uncle Felix is the only one that wears them and they're *way* too big for me."

Unlike the rest of her outfit? He didn't say it, but his face must have given him away.

"I know." She shrugged. "I feel like I'm

playing dress-up." She pushed her fists out, tugging her pants up a bit.

He chuckled.

She smiled up at him, the sort of impulsive smile she'd normally give Samantha or Hattie. It was sweet and free, with just a hint of mischievousness. But she seemed to catch herself and that smile was gone too soon and her gaze fell from his.

It was fine. They were keeping it about the horse. That was the only reason she was here. "The mare was so jumpy and agitated that I moved her over here. It's a backup barn— mostly used when we bring in extra riders to wrangle the herd or vaccinate cattle. But the corral is big. Half covered, half outside. And she's got the place to herself." Which would also make it less likely for any of the ranch hands to come strolling in today. If he and Mabel were caught? Well, he didn't want to think about it.

While they walked along the path to the horse barn, he noticed her staring around her.

"Scouting out the enemy territory?" he asked, teasing. He held the barn door open for her.

"Thank you," she said, stepping inside. "You know me. Up to no good."

He chuckled, shaking his head. "We don't really know each other, though. Other than the gossip the Ladies Guild has been circulating, that is." He cocked an eyebrow. "So that means you're a no-good Briscoe—"

"And you're a lying Crawley?" she cut in, those blue eyes of hers meeting his. "What do you want to know?"

Where did he start? The air between them grew heavy, heavier the longer they stared at one another. He had so many questions, but the one that came out surprised them both. "Rumor has it, you've set your cap for Tyson. Is that true?"

She blinked rapidly, then wrinkled up her nose and started walking. "First, I don't own a cap. Second, ew and no. Third, I'm assuming the rumor came from the Ladies Guild? Those women need a hobby." She sighed. "Tyson's nice and all but…no."

"Kitty will be relieved—" He stopped walking. "I shouldn't have said that." Why had he said that?

"It's okay." She rested her hand on his arm. "I won't say a thing, I promise."

He stared down at her hand, remembering the feel of it—all warm and soft—in his. "I appreciate it."

"The last thing I'd want to do is throw your sister under the Ladies Guild's bus. They mean well, I know they do, but…" She shrugged. "Tyson's so private, he wouldn't thank me for it, either. But I'll be rooting for them."

Jensen was keenly aware of her touch. He believed what she'd said, too, and a sudden warmth filled his chest. It was a soft whinny that had her turning from him. Once she saw the horse, her hand slipped from his arm and she hurried to the fence.

"Stardust," she whispered.

"I did a little digging on her, but I'm not sure it'll be much help," he said, watching her.

"Oh?" she asked, her gaze fixed on the horse.

Jensen rested one booted foot on the bottom rung of the pipe fence. "About a year ago, she was a 4-H horse. I don't know how she got from there to the auction in Holsom, but I'll keep tryin' to find out."

"4-H?" Her gaze flitted his way, considering. "Interesting. Thank you, Jensen," she murmured, standing on the bottom rung of the fence. "Hey there, girl." She pushed the hat far back on her head. If she realized it fell to the ground, she didn't acknowledge it. "You remember me?"

The horse looked her way, raising its head high and flicking its ears forward.

Looks like she remembers Mabel all right. Jensen sighed. She *was* pretty unforgettable. A fact he was becoming aware of.

Mabel bent and slid through the fence rails. "Hey, Stardust, pretty girl." She clicked her tongue, but didn't advance.

The horse's tail swished, but that was about it. He didn't want Mabel to come out here, to risk all she'd risked, to get the cold shoulder, but he was a little relieved it wasn't just him.

Mabel was talking, low and soft. "I remember you. And Jensen, here—" she pointed back at him as if the horse understood everything she was saying "—thought it'd be a good idea for us to have a visit."

Stardust bobbed her head, snorting once.

Mabel smiled.

Jensen watched the two of them in absolute silence. There were things he could be doing, there was always work to be done on the ranch, but he had to admit he was curious to see how this worked. With extreme care, he slipped his boot from the fence and stepped back, sitting on a box of mineral blocks and vitamins against the wall.

Mabel had fallen silent now, but there was no tension in her posture. It was like she spent every day standing in the middle of a corral, talking and staring at skittish horses. *Who knows? Maybe she does?* But he hadn't just dug into Stardust's past last night; he'd found himself searching for Mabel's vlog. He got so caught up in her posts that he didn't realize it was almost three in the morning. It wasn't that she was working in harsh conditions to keep the animals healthy and on public lands, it was the passion with which she lobbied on the animals' behalf. Who else could speak for the mustangs with such love and eloquence? Listening to her, he could almost believe she could communicate with them. How else could she describe their plight so well?

No, sitting in the shadows, Jensen was pretty sure some sort of communication was taking place. The horse hadn't moved—it was as if Mabel had mesmerized the animal. But the way Mabel stood there, with her head cocked to one side, and the way Stardust studied Mabel, he got the impression they were sorting things out. *Somehow.*

He held his breath when Stardust took a tentative step toward Mabel. Then another.

Mabel stayed as she was, her hands shoved deep into her pockets. He couldn't decide whether she was trying to keep her pants up or if she was trying to come across as nonthreatening as possible. Surely, the horse could sense that? That she wanted nothing more than to bond with this animal and help the horse feel at ease. He could sense it.

Stardust stopped inches from Mabel, stretching out her neck just enough for her to get a good whiff of Mabel. That eased the horse enough to get her to take a few more steps.

"Okay?" Mabel's whisper was so low he barely heard it.

That was when, oh-so-slowly, Mabel pulled one hand from her pocket and lifted it.

Stardust stepped back, then stopped, inspecting the hand with her nose before allowing Mabel to rest it against the side of her neck.

I'll be. He'd tried carrots, apples and sugar cubes and the mare would have nothing to do with him. Kitty had clicked and cooed and done everything but beg the animal for attention, but Stardust had given her the cold shoulder, too.

After watching her videos last night, it shouldn't have been a surprise that Mabel was able to connect with the mare. Of course, he'd heard all sorts of things about Mabel and animals and accepted them as truths. But seeing it firsthand was… Well, it was something.

Mabel ran her hand along the horse's neck and walked slowly out from the shade of the tin roof into the uncovered part of the corral. The sun beamed down on her blue-black braid and, without her hat, she had to squint to see what Stardust was doing.

The horse followed.

In time, Stardust let Mabel brush her dusty coat and clean out her hooves. All the while, Mabel chatted on in a soft voice. The horse's muscles no longer jumped or twitched at Mabel's touch and her overall anxiety eased.

If Kitty hadn't texted him, he'd have continued to watch the two of them.

Dad wants us to meet him at the fish fry. Twyla and I are heading that way when we close up. Meet us there?

Jensen ran a hand along the back of his neck. At least he didn't need to worry about any of them coming home.

Another text rolled in. How's it going?

Jensen held up his phone and took a picture. Mabel had one arm draped over Stardust's shoulders and was working through the tangles in the horse's mane. Stardust was as content as a horse could be. Mabel was in her element. It was a sweet picture. And the sort of thing that'd cause all sorts of trouble if Samantha or his dad or his sisters ever got his phone... His thumb hovered over the delete button, but he couldn't do it.

I don't know whether to be jealous or grateful. Seconds later, Kitty added. What is she wearing?

She's incognito. He smiled and hit Send, turning his attention back to Mabel.

"I guess we're running out of time?" Mabel asked in that soft voice, continuing to work on the horse's mane.

"Almost." He stood. "Kitty said to meet them at the Veterans Hall for some fish fry my dad's taking Samantha to."

Mabel glanced his way. "Oh dear." She nibbled on her lower lip.

"Oh dear?" He walked slowly to the fence.

"Uncle Felix is there." She turned, resting her hand on the horse's back. "Bingo and a fish fry, courtesy of the Ladies Guild." She looked at him. "I'm thinking your father and my uncle are going for the same reason."

It took a second for Jensen to catch on. "Oh dear is right." He shook his head, resting his arms on the top bar of the fence. "They're both in their seventies. They'd never go and do something…" *Foolish? Like pick a fight?* He stopped himself right there. His father was one of the most pigheaded men he had ever met. He loved him, but when the man was out of sorts or riled up, his temper could get the best of him.

"Never say never. Until today, I didn't know Uncle Felix owned a tie, but he was wearing one when he left." She patted Stardust. "I think the last time he wore a tie was for Gene's funeral." A shadow crossed her face.

Jensen was struck by another memory of Mabel. He'd been in high school, leaving football practice early for some sort of appointment. That hadn't been the important part. He'd walked outside to find Mabel hiding behind the gym, hugging her legs tight with her face buried against her knees.

She was crying, softly, the sound muffled somewhat.

He'd almost walked on. Almost. But her grief stopped him. "You all right?" he'd asked.

She sniffed, peering up at him with those tear-filled sky blue eyes. "No," she'd whispered.

Jensen had eyed his bicycle and knew he'd get a talking-to for skipping his appointment but... He'd dropped his backpack and sat on the ground beside Mabel. If she noticed, she didn't say a thing. She'd sobbed like the world was ending. He'd patted her back and took one of her hands—like he'd have done for Kitty or Twyla. But Mabel had clung to him, letting him pull her close so she could soak the front of his jersey. He'd stayed there until practice had let out and he spied Forrest coming out of the gym.

"Forrest is here," he'd whispered. "I'll get him."

"No, no." She shook her head, holding on to his hand with both of hers. "He'll want a fight." Her breath wavered and she hiccupped, letting go of him. "Just go. Please." She wiped at the tears, but they kept on coming. "Th-thank you." Her gaze had held his as she'd added, "Jensen."

When he'd gotten home, he'd learned the news that Gene Briscoe had been killed on active duty. He'd been glad he'd stayed then. Even if Forrest had picked a fight, staying had been the right thing. The fight did happen—well, it wasn't much of a fight since Forrest pummeled him senseless. But Mabel hadn't been there to see it. Something else Jensen was thankful for.

He blinked away the vivid images, pulling himself from the past, to find Mabel staring at him. Her getup didn't alter the way he saw her. *She's beautiful.* Inside and out. He swallowed against the tightness in his throat. *Mabel.* Did she remember that day? Or the day with the fox in the woods? Had she named the kitten after him? They were questions he wanted answered, but knew better than to ask.

"I guess we should go?" Mabel cleared her throat, her gaze falling from his. "Run an intervention, if necessary?"

"I guess."

Mabel whispered something to Stardust, gave her another pat and slipped back through the fence. After picking up her hat and giving a final wave at Stardust, the two of them walked back to the barn doors.

"What were you thinking about? Just then?" she asked him.

He shook his head. "A memory, is all."

"What's next?" she asked. "Stardust is easy with me, but she'll need time and patience to trust you and Samantha."

"I was sort of hoping this wasn't a onetime deal." He shrugged. "I don't know what just happened here, but I'd feel better if you were with Samantha when she meets Stardust."

Mabel's smile was a thing of beauty. "I'd like that, Jensen. I think the two of them will be good friends. In time."

Time. Which reminded him. He stopped, staring down at her. "You… You still heading back to Wyoming?" *Don't go.* He swallowed, but couldn't look away.

"I don't know." She opened her mouth, shut it, then asked, "I know me leaving will make things easier on you. What with all the talk and all."

He frowned. "That's no reason to leave, Mabel." It took effort not to step closer. "I figured you were missing the horses or Wyoming or something."

"I'm…not." She swallowed. "And there are good people there. The work will go on."

"You're going back because of…" He

waited. Was she leaving because of him? Because of the talk? Or was it something else? His heart was like a jackhammer—pounding against his ribs. "Don't go."

"Why... Why would you care if I stayed or left?" she whispered.

Now that he started, he might as well see it all the way through. "I've asked myself that a lot." He ran his hand along the back of his neck, expecting her to bolt at any minute. "I keep coming back to the same answer, Mabel." He stepped forward then, relieved when she didn't move away.

"And what is...the answer?" Mabel hesitated, then stepped forward, tilting her head back to look at him.

He reached up, slowly, to press his hand against her cheek. His heart was tripping over itself now. "I care about you, Mabel." He'd said it. But he didn't stop there. "And, right now, I want to kiss you more than just about anything."

"You do?" she whispered, breathless.

He nodded. "If you're okay with that?"

She nodded, unsteady, her hands resting against his chest.

His arms wrapped around her waist and he held her close, pressing his lips against hers

and breathing her in. Mabel. In his arms.
In his heart. It was right, he could feel it
in his bones. Her sweet kiss filled his heart
and gave him something he hadn't had in so
long: hope.

A bark of laughter, distant but audible, had
them jumping apart. Before he had time to
think, she was out of his arms, shoving her
hands into her pockets and hurrying to the
barn door. Like a startled deer.

Jensen hurried to catch up. "Mabel—

"I should go." She sucked in a deep breath.
"You should go. The fish fry…" She was
having a hard time looking at him."

After that kiss, this was not the response he
was hoping for. "Right." Had he just ruined
everything? Since she was all but running
away, he was pretty sure he had an answer.

"Maybe, next time, you and I can work
with her? And then, depending on how that
goes, we'll bring in Samantha. She can just
watch at first, if you like—until you're feeling comfortable about them meeting." She
glanced up at him. "She'll sense it if you're
not."

There would be a next time. He could
breathe. "Samantha or the horse?" He loved
the way she rolled her eyes.

"Both." She smiled. "It might be easiest to text me when you know what time would work best."

He loved her smile even more. "This isn't easy and, well, keeping things from family is hard. I know I'm asking a lot—"

"You are." She nodded. "But I seem to remember a time or two you've helped me out so I guess you could say I owe you."

"A time or two?" he asked, clearing his throat.

She paused. "You know." Her gaze met his. "Gene? The fox? And more. Or maybe you've forgotten—"

"No." He shook his head, touched that she remembered. "I haven't."

They stood that way, staring at one another, until Jensen had to know. "JC?"

"Was my cat." She wouldn't look at him as she pulled her phone from her pocket. "Your number?"

He frowned but let it go. Once they'd exchanged phone numbers, they headed outside. He had a hard time not smiling when he saw her holding the waist of her pants up. Her pace had quickened and, if she didn't hold them up, she ran the risk of tripping.

When they reached her rattletrap blue

truck, he found himself looking for something to say to delay her leaving. It was foolish. They'd taken enough chances as it was. He'd taken a few himself. His heart was on the line here and he didn't want to say goodbye to Mabel.

"I guess I'll see you at the fish fry?" she asked. At his nod, she climbed into the truck and turned on the engine. A roar and a squeak erupted from the hood, making her wince and him laugh. But he wasn't laughing when her taillights disappeared in a cloud of dust. Tyson and his Romeo and Juliet joke wasn't so funny anymore. He wasn't sure when or how this had happened but he, Jensen Crawley, had fallen for his *enemy*, Mabel Briscoe, with his whole heart.

CHAPTER ELEVEN

MABEL DIDN'T HAVE time to change. She wanted to, she did, but she'd pulled up at the same time her brothers were all piling into the ranch SUV.

"What are you wearing?" Webb asked, his horror-stricken expression genuine.

"We don't have time," Forrest said, waving them into the vehicle. "Hattie said we need to get there. Something about Barbara Eldridge and Crawley and Uncle Felix all bent out of shape."

Mabel's heart sank as she climbed into the vehicle.

"Where have you been?" Beau asked.

With Jensen Crawley. *Kissing.* She fanned herself, instantly flushed by the memory. "I was taking in the truck." She shrugged. "If I stay, I figured I should have some wheels of my own while I'm here."

Forrest's gaze met hers in the rearview mirror. "You could take one of the ranch trucks. I'm not sure that work truck is street-worthy. What'd Chris say?"

"It'd be better off staying a work truck." It wasn't exactly a lie. That was what he'd said before she'd left for Wyoming.

"I'm pretty sure you didn't have to take it to a mechanic for that." Beau grinned.

"Where's Audy?" Mabel asked, eager to change the subject.

"Where do you think?" Webb sighed.

Mabel grinned. "Oh no, is he with Brooke again? Whatever is he thinking?"

Beau and Forrest chuckled. Webb did not.

"Might as well get used to it," Forrest said. "The two of them'll be gettin' hitched in no time. But for now, let's concentrate on keeping things calm and peaceful between Uncle Felix and that…that…"

"Mr. Crawley?" Mabel filled in, worried his brother might launch into a tirade of all-too-colorful insults. Considering she'd been blissfully wrapped up in Mr. Crawley's son's arms not thirty minutes ago, it didn't seem right. Her lips still tingled from Jensen's kiss.

"Uh-huh." Forrest glanced at her again. "We'll go with that."

"Just so I get this." Webb held up a hand.

"Uncle Felix is courting Barbara Eldridge?" He seemed confused by the question.

"It would seem so." Mabel thought about how nervous he'd been this morning. "He did wear a tie."

That earned her looks from all of them.

"It's a tie. Not a crown." She rolled her eyes. "What we're concerned with, other than the fact that he's wearing a tie apparently, is that Mr. Crawley is also interested in Barbara Eldridge."

"Well, isn't that a pickle." Webb scratched his head. "How can she? Talk about apples to oranges. It doesn't make any sense."

Mabel held her tongue, but she'd come to accept that love rarely made sense. Today, when Jensen had been lost in a daze, she'd found herself getting lost in *him*. To look at him made her breathless. His voice sent a warm buzz along every nerve ending. When he smiled, she was helpless not to smile back. How she thought she'd ever outgrow him, she didn't know. This was no passing fancy or adolescent crush. Her heart had been lassoed by Jensen long ago and hadn't bothered to come back to her—not really. And when he'd kissed her... She was fanning herself again.

From the scrawny teenager who'd helped

her with the fox to the boy who calmed her when Gene had died to the young man who had snuck onto her land to leave her the kitten she'd hand-raised, he'd always been there when she needed him.

The question was, how could she *not* love him?

I care about you, Mabel.

She stared out the window, processing this realization. Accepting the fact that he was the moon and the stars and she loved him only made things more complicated than ever. *And he cares about me.*

Which made everything better. And worse. For both of them. If she told him she cared, then what? What kind of future could they have? Would they have to sneak around? Risk discovery, adding to the whole feud? No. She wouldn't do that to Jensen or Samantha or her family. Once Stardust and Jensen and Samantha were all settled, she'd head back to Wyoming. Her days were spent working so hard that she slept like the dead every night. There'd be no room to get caught up in ridiculous what-ifs that could never come true.

Don't go. His voice echoed in her ears and tore at her heart.

When they entered the city limits, she

found herself noting all the things that made Garrison special. From the green awning that shaded the front door of Old Towne Hardware and Appliances to the old-fashioned red-and-white barber's pole in front of Brooke's salon. The familiar Hill Country Veterinary Clinic and Grooming Salon with their whimsical multicolored animal-shaped decals running across the large windows that took up most of one block. The old clock tower that sat atop Garrison Bank and Trust and the bench with the statue of a reading mother and child that greeted all the Garrison Library visitors. The painted patchwork pig sign over the Crawley sisters' Calico Pig shop. The planters out front of Garrison Gardens and, normally, old Mr. Green could be found whittling little figures he gave away to customers when they bought a plant or flowers. The Buttermilk Pie Café. Cowboy Outfitters. Der Restaurant Von Ludwig that served the best—if overpriced—schnitzel in the world. There were so many things to love about her hometown.

And yet, she and her brothers weren't turning off Main Street and taking the twisty Chapel Street to the Veterans Hall for the food and companionship. No. She and her brothers had hurried into town to prevent their uncle from doing something he'd later regret. Oh, she'd heard the battle stories from their youth. How he and Dwight Crawley had squared off on more than one occasion. But that had been years ago, when they were kids. One wrong twist now could result in a broken hip or worse.

"You don't really think it'll get physical, do you?" She met Forrest's gaze in the rear-view mirror.

"I don't know, Mabel. I've never seen him light up like that—not ever." Forrest didn't sound very hopeful—*resigned* was more like it.

"He's eighty-what?" Webb snorted. "He's in no shape to fight."

"He is seventy-two." Mabel gave each of her brothers a look. "In shape or not, if his pride is on the line there's no telling what could happen." Isn't that what this was all about? Pride. She sighed.

The rest of the drive was made in silence. When Forrest parked, the parking lot of the Veterans Hall was packed.

"You're here." Hattie was standing just inside the door, selling tickets. "You're all here." Her eyes widened.

"Best be prepared." Forrest sighed. "What'd you do?" He was staring at Hattie.

"What?" Hattie ran a hand over her beige uniform.

"No." He made a few circles with his pointer finger at her head.

"Oh." She reached up. "Brooke. She did some straightening thing to it." She shrugged. "I don't know."

But Mabel was still in shock. Her brother had recognized the change in Hattie's hair. Yes, she normally had a mass of strawberry blond curls versus the sleek waves resting on her shoulders but... *Forrest* noticed. Mabel had no idea what that meant, only that it meant something.

"I see Tess," Beau said to no one in particular, grabbed his ticket from Forrest and headed inside.

"Young love." Hattie shook her head, then seemed to really see Mabel. "What *are* you wearing?" Hattie asked, counting out change for Forrest. "You look like you're trying out for the Scarecrow in *The Wizard of Oz*."

"Ha!" Webb clapped his hands. "That's it. Nailed it, Hattie." He laughed.

Mabel smoothed her hands over the too-big chambray shirt. "I was...working." She shot Hattie a look—hoping her friend would get the message.

"Oh?" Hattie blinked. *"Oh."* She nodded. "Well, then, you're dressed fine, aren't you?"

Mabel didn't miss Forrest watching the two of them.

"What are you two up to?" he asked.

"Up to?" Hattie sputtered, going wide-eyed. "Nothing. I'm selling tickets is all. Doing my job. Now shoo." Forrest went, her other brothers in tow, but Hattie put a hand on Mabel. "So, how'd it go?"

"Stardust will be fine. She's got something bothering her, but we'll get past it." Mabel would make sure of that. For Samantha. And for Jensen. Just thinking of his name had her heart in her throat. And the memory of his lips against hers. "Oh, Hattie." She groaned, shaking her head. "I... I... You were right." She took a deep breath. "I do care about him, too much, and I don't know what to do."

It was Hattie's expression that tipped Mabel off. Someone was behind her. Someone Mabel probably wouldn't want to hear what she'd just said.

"Kitty. Twyla," Hattie said. "How are you two?"

Twyla gave Mabel a scathing head-to-toe

glare, paid Hattie and headed inside without a word.

"Hi." Kitty's smile was small. "Nice to see you…both." She glanced at Mabel. "Thanks for today. Jensen sent me a picture of the two of you that looks promising." And she walked into the hall.

"The two of you?" Hattie's eyes went round. "You two took pictures together? I want to see. Not here, of course. But if those get out—"

"I didn't know he took a picture of me and Stardust!" Why would he take a picture? Surely, that was exactly the sort of evidence neither one of them wanted to exist. "I should go in. In case."

"I'm sure it'll be fine." But Hattie didn't look convinced. "So far, it's been a lot of staring and glaring and barely restrained hostility. I'll catch up with you in a bit?"

Mabel nodded, running a hand over her braid. She couldn't do much about her outfit, but at least she'd left the hat in the car. Not that people inside the Veterans Hall weren't noticing her attire. They were, but she didn't let it get to her. Okay, her clothes were a little odd, but if that was the only Briscoe gossip that came from tonight, she'd be just fine with it.

Big band music was being piped through speakers while people were talking and eating and generally enjoying themselves. She saw her brothers in line for food and decided to wait until her uncle and brothers were seated to get her food.

A quick search and she found Uncle Felix sitting at a round table with Audy and Brooke. He was holding baby Joy and smiling. Dickie and Kelly Schneider sat on the opposite side of the table. From all appearances, their hurried rescue mission was for naught. From her chair, there was no sign of the Crawleys—though she tried to keep her search as subtle as possible.

"You don't say?" Uncle Felix said, smiling at Joy.

"Hey," she said, sitting between Audy and Kelly.

"Hey, yourself." Kelly didn't bat an eye at her outfit.

"I never thought I'd see the old man so smitten with a baby—" Audy broke off. "Mabel? Out of clean clothes or something?"

Mabel ignored him, preferring to watch her uncle dote on little Joy.

Kelly pointed at the food line. "You better get yourself some food before it's gone."

"I'm fine." If she got in line now, she'd have to stand behind Twyla Crawley. If anything could kill her appetite, it would be one of Twyla's withering glares.

The rest of her brothers arrived shortly thereafter, their plates stacked high with fish and sides, making the table cramped. No one said a thing. Folding chairs were rearranged and trash was cleared away.

"Not eating?" Forrest asked.

"You better hurry." Webb nodded at the line. "They were almost out of...well, everything."

"It didn't help that you took two servings." Audy eyed the food tray.

"I'm a growing boy." Webb winked.

"If you're not careful, you'll start growing out instead of up." Forrest took a sip of his iced tea. "You really should eat something, Mabel. I paid for it."

With a sigh, Mabel stood. "Fine."

"No, now, you don't have to—" Uncle Felix said, glaring at Forrest.

"No, I really do," she argued.

Forrest's gaze bounced from their uncle,

to something behind her, to Mabel. "It can wait," he agreed, frowning at her.

"And then there will be no food and you'll have wasted your money." With a narrow-eyed grin, she headed for the food line. As much as she appreciated their worrying over her, sometimes it was a little much. Like now. She concentrated on not stepping on the hem of her jeans or falling as she navigated the zigzag ropes that had been set up to keep a longer line more orderly. A weird outfit was one thing. Wiping out in the food line of the Veterans Hall was another. She tightened her hold on the waist.

What was that all about? She looked up, and everything made sense. *That would do it.* Jensen was in front of her.

She closed her eyes and took a slow, calming breath before looking at her table. Every eye was on her. *Great.* She waved, fluttering her fingers and smiling. Brooke, Kelly and Dickie waved back. No one else was amused.

She turned, pretending to be considering the meager remains to choose from. "Don't turn around, please. We're being watched."

Jensen stiffened. "Got it."

"Well, if it isn't Mabel and Jensen. Again?" Dorris Kaye stood, wearing a brightly colored hairnet that looked suspiciously like a shower cap. She turned toward the other women working in the kitchen, pointing at the two of them with her large serving spoon.

"This just gets better and better," Jensen murmured.

Mabel pressed her lips together to keep from laughing.

Miss Patsy, her flaming-red hair peeking out from the bright orange kerchief she had tied on her head, clucked her tongue at them. "You two do make a striking couple. Too bad." She sighed, feigning disappointment.

"What is going on between the two of you?" Martha Zeigler eyed her and Jensen. "I know what *they* are saying." She pointed at Dorris and Patsy. "But I want to hear it straight from the horse's mouth, if you will."

"What's going on? Well, I'm hungry," Jensen said. "So...I'm here for food. I'm guessing Miss Briscoe is as well, since she's here. I guess you'd say hunger? Since we're both hungry. That's about it."

Mabel was having a very hard time controlling her laughter now.

"Ha ha." Martha's eyes narrowed. "Dorris, go get those fries. Patsy, get the cobbler out of the oven." Her tone left no room for argument. As soon as the two women scampered off, Martha said, "My husband was from the wrong side of the tracks. No one wanted me to marry him. He was dirt-poor and everyone thought he was after my money. I knew better and I didn't listen. I had him for thirty years and I never once regretted it. People still talked, of course, but it didn't get to either one of us. *We* knew the truth." She glanced back and forth between the two of them. "If Dorris and Patsy aren't prattling on and making up nonsense and the two of you *do* fancy each other, you think about that. This is your life, not theirs. Your happiness. Not theirs. There's a choice to be made here. And it's *your* choice, not your father's or uncle's or brothers' or sisters'. You take time to make the right choice and you won't regret it, either."

Mabel blinked, shell-shocked by the older woman's rapid-fire delivery of what was a rather insightful and emotional speech. She glanced at Jensen.

His jaw was clenched tight and his hold on his dinner tray had all but collapsed the flimsy thing.

Martha noticed, too, one steely brow arching high. "And another thing. If I see any mischief from your father—" she looked at Jensen "—or your uncle—" she turned to Mabel "—I will go out of my way to make their lives miserable. And I can do it, too, don't think I can't." She shook her head, staring beyond them into the Veterans Hall. "This nonsense over Barbara. Like they're back in grade school again. She's kind to everyone. Kind. And yet those two get gussied up thinking she's sweet on them." Her dismissive snort said it all.

Dorris practically tiptoed back over, a large tray of fresh french fries in her hands.

"That's all?" Martha looked at her. "You are slower than molasses on a cold morning, you know that, Dorris?"

Dorris bristled. "Well, I—"

"And full of excuses, too." Martha walked to the kitchen and returned, balancing trays of macaroni and cheese, green beans with bacon and another of coleslaw. "Go get the fish, Dorris." She sighed. "I can only carry so much." She ignored Dorris, and the scowl the woman sent her way, and turned back to them. "What do you two want?"

Jensen insisted Mabel go first, much to Martha Zeigler's approval. Once her tray was full, she had to wait on Jensen. She didn't mind, especially when he shot a quick smile her way. That smile. Those eyes. That kiss. She took a deep breath. Now was not the time. She was beginning to worry about how long this was taking and the likelihood that one of her brothers would turn up—

"Mabel?" Forrest asked.

Right on time. "Forrest?" she asked, imitating his tone.

"There a problem?" There was no mistaking that look. Or his tone. Or the overall tension rolling off him.

"No." Mabel shook her head. "They were restocking the trays and Jensen had them serve me first."

"You couldn't have turned around and come back the way you went in?" Forrest asked.

She could have done that very thing, but there was Martha's talk and Jensen's smile and Martha's warning for Uncle Felix. "Miss Martha was sharing."

"Humph." Martha stared down Forrest. "Don't you come over here looking to pick a fight, Forrest Briscoe. You're too old for that, you hear? Jensen has behaved like a true gentleman this evening and I expect the same out of you."

Mabel waited, slightly in awe of the woman.

"I've no intention of doing otherwise, Miss Martha." He touched the brim of his hat. "Come on, Mabel."

"You remember what I said," Martha said. "You hear?"

Mabel nodded before turning to walk back through the zigzag maze of ropes, more confused than ever.

JENSEN POKED AT his fish, the crisp corn bread batter flaking off onto the plate.

Samantha stopped eating her french fries long enough to ask, "Don't like it, Daddy?"

"It's good, little miss." He winked at her and forced himself to take a bite.

"What's eating you *now*?" his father asked, an unmistakable emphasis on the *now*. They were talking, sort of. When his father felt like talking to him, he would. When he didn't feel like listening to Jensen, he wouldn't.

"Nothing." Jensen took another bite of fish. "How was your dance lesson? You still working on your dance for the Tree Festival?"

Samantha nodded. "We are going to dress up like trees." She lifted her hands over her head. "Swaying in the wind."

"And stomping away." His father chuckled. "Don't forget the stomping."

"It's clogging, Paw-Paw." Samantha grinned. "Auntie Kitty, do you think there's a way to make a sparkle-y tree? Miss Gretta said we could be sparkle-y trees. A whole forest of them."

"I don't see why not." Kitty smiled. "I'll get with Miss Gretta and see what she has in mind."

"Thank you." Samantha climbed down from her chair, ran around the table and threw her arms around Kitty's neck. "Thank you thank you."

"Well, I want some of that." Twyla reached over, tickling Samantha along the sides until his little girl was red-faced with laughter.

"You see that?" his father asked, staring across the open room. "Did they fall on hard times all of a sudden?" He shook his head. "I've heard that one's an odd duck and now I see why. Look at what that girl is wearing."

His father had been making colorful observations all evening so this one didn't especially stand out.

"What's an odd duck?" Samantha asked.

"One that doesn't fit in," Twyla explained. "Sort of like your story? The ugly duckling?"

"Oh." Samantha nodded. "When the duckling wasn't a duck? He is a beautiful swan?"

Twyla shrugged. "I guess it's a little like that."

"Who are we talking about?" Jensen asked, earning himself a hard kick to the shin under the table. He frowned, eyeing his sisters. Since Samantha was still in Twyla's lap, it had to have been Kitty.

Kitty made wide eyes at him, shaking her head.

"I guess it can't be helped. Growing up with all those hotheaded boys and no woman to guide her." His father sat back, shaking his head. "I almost feel sad for her."

The clothes, the comments, the kick. It made sense now. His father was talking about Mabel.

"Who her, Paw-Paw? Who is sad?" Samantha leaned forward to take his father's hand.

"Oh now, don't you worry your pretty little head over nothing, tater tot." His father winked. "No one worth wasting your energy on, that's for sure."

Jensen opened his mouth and Kitty kicked him again, harder this time. He managed to muffle his moan, for the most part.

"Ladies and gentlemen," a voice silenced the room. "We have done an amazing job tonight. So far, we have raised several thousand dollars for our fireworks show." The voice was Barbara Eldridge's. "We'll start clearing the room and setting up our bingo shortly. All the prizes have been donated by local businesses, so let's give them a round of applause."

His father not only clapped, he let out an ear-splitting whistle that caused several heads to turn. Barbara Eldridge included.

"Well, that's one way to get her attention." Twyla chuckled. "Real subtle, Daddy."

"What?" their father grumbled. "I'm just applauding, like everyone else."

He, his sisters and Samantha all turned to stare at him.

"You were way louder, Paw-Paw," Samantha said, giving him a thumbs-up.

His father chuckled.

"If you could lend a helping hand and clear off your tables, that would be a big help. We'll be starting bingo in about ten minutes." Barbara stepped back from the microphone, but his father never took his eyes off the woman.

"Everyone done?" Jensen asked, standing.

"I'll help," Samantha said, picking up her tray.

"Be careful," Twyla said, eyeing the large

pool of ketchup in one of the compartments. "Don't get any on your pretty dress."

Samantha nodded.

Jensen stacked up the rest of the trays. "You ready?" He carried the trays to the closest trash can and dumped them in. "Samantha—"

Samantha was being very careful. Step by step, she inched along at a snail's pace, her eyes glued on the ketchup. She had the tip of her tongue sticking out and her nose wrinkled up in concentration and she was just about the cutest thing he'd ever seen. "You good?" he asked.

"I've got it, Daddy." She nodded, in no hurry.

"I know it." He grinned.

And then it happened. Samantha stepped on a pat of butter someone had dropped on the floor. One little foot slipped out from under her and down she went. The tray went up and, even though he moved as fast as possible, he couldn't reach it in time. But Forrest Briscoe did.

He'd never been more surprised. Ever.

Samantha was on her feet and hugging the man around the knees. "Thank you, Mr. Forrest."

"It's all right." Forrest smiled down at her, patting her on the back.

"You're a real knight in shiny farmer. And a prince charmer, too." She stared up at him with such awe.

The whole room was watching, holding their breath, waiting for Jensen's reaction. *What choice do I have?* "Thank you, Forrest. Good reflexes."

Forrest nodded, hardly sparing him a look.

"Oh, Mr. Forrest." Samantha's head popped up. "Is Mabel here? I haven't seen her in a long forever."

Yesterday. But close.

"That's a long time." Forrest had no problem smiling at Samantha. "She's sitting over there."

"Daddy, come on." Samantha grabbed his hand. "Mabel is *here*. Right *now*." She was so excited that Jensen took her hand. A few steps later, Samantha let go and ran the rest of the distance.

"Samantha!" Mabel's voice was warm and rich and happy.

The tug of Jensen's heart was more like a yank. Hard and fast and demanding.

"Who is that?" Samantha asked, staring up at the toddler standing in Mabel's lap. "She looks like a doll."

"Doesn't she?" Mabel smiled. "This is Joy. Joy, this is Samantha."

Baby Joy clapped her hands, bouncing excitedly on Mabel's lap.

"Nice to meet you, too." Samantha imitated Mabel's baby voice, smiling up at Joy. "I read the story. Well, Auntie Kitty read it to me." She climbed up into the folding chair beside Mabel, oblivious to everyone else. "You're right about the horse. It's so pretty. I like how it looks blue and it was nice to Princess Lizzy-bett and how they rode all over to find the kingdom."

Mabel nodded.

"Just like you and Firefly. You rode all over your kingdom." Samantha grinned.

"I'd never thought about it that way, but you know what, you're right." Mabel bounced Joy. "We can all be Garrison princesses."

"Really?" Samantha was practically quivering with joy.

"I don't see why not." Mabel shrugged.

"Samantha, we should get back to Paw-Paw." He was getting a little fed up with the range of hostility the Briscoe brothers were sending him. Especially Webb.

"But Daddy, it's Mabel." Samantha's pleas were so earnest he didn't know what to do or say.

"I know." He ran a hand along the back of

his neck. "But Mabel is here with her family and we're here with ours."

"But I'm always with my family," Samantha countered.

"Tonight is a family night." He held out his hand.

She stared at his hand, but didn't take it. "Daddy… Mabel—"

"Samantha." He was rarely stern with his daughter. Mostly because he didn't like seeing her upset. Like now. With her little chin crumpling and her lips pressed flat and red flooding her cheeks. "Give Mabel a hug and let's go back to our table."

"Okay, Daddy." Her words wavered and her breath came out as a hiccup.

"It's okay." Mabel scooped Samantha into her lap and wrapped her up close. "It's okay, little miss."

"I just wanted to see you," Samantha whispered—loud enough that everyone at the table could hear. "You're my favorite, Mabel."

Her words had his heart twisting into knots. He knew his little girl was fond of Mabel—knew it and had done nothing to discourage it. *Because I'm in love with her.* And he liked spending time with Mabel, too.

That was the problem. Or was it a problem? Did it have to be? Miss Martha didn't seem to think so. Her unasked-for advice had struck a nerve. Everything she'd said rang true.

Mabel pressed a kiss against Samantha's forehead, but she stared up at him. And the moment their eyes locked, Jensen was doomed. He tried to shut her out and ignore the pull in those eyes. But try as he might, there was no breaking the hold she had on him. Every second of every minute they'd spent together today replayed in his mind. From him telling her he cared about her, to kissing her, to her leaving without a word about either.

It was plain to see Mabel loved his daughter. He thought, he hoped, there was something between them. *Or am I just seeing what I want to see?* Either way, if she kept looking at him that way, her friends and family and most of Garrison would realize that there was some truth to all the gossip.

"Are you coming to Junior Rangers?" Samantha asked. "Will you help me find a home for my rock?"

"Of course." Mabel gently clasped Samantha's shoulders and held her back. "No more tears, now. You'll have to help your Paw-Paw win some prizes." She tapped Samantha on the nose. "Okay?"

Samantha nodded, slid from Mabel's lap and took his hand.

Jensen wiggled her arm, but it didn't get him the smile he was hoping for. "Good evening," he murmured to the table at large, then led Samantha back to his table.

"We need to have a talk," his father mumbled. "This sort of thing isn't acceptable, Jensen. Now, you know that."

"We can talk, but I can tell you now, we're going to disagree on this." Jensen ignored the surprised expressions on his family's faces and looked down at Samantha. "Wanna go for some ice cream?"

"Paw-Paw, you don't need my help with bingo?" She patted her grandfather's arm.

"No, I'll manage. You go on, sugar plum, and have some ice cream for me." His father was all smiles for his granddaughter.

He walked from the Veterans Hall, swinging Samantha's arm and humming the tune to one of her favorite princess movies.

She was skipping before they reached the truck. He lifted her up and spun her around before buckling her into her booster seat.

"Jensen?" Kitty hurried across the parking

lot. "What about Daddy? And Mr. Briscoe? What do we do if they do something stupid?"

He stared up at the twilight sky. "You just answered that question, Kitty. I'm tired of being Daddy's keeper. He is making these choices. You don't have to own them. I'm tired of seeing the Briscoes as my enemies. They're not."

"Forrest did sort of beat you to a bloody pulp," Kitty reminded him, frowning at the memory.

He couldn't argue; it was true.

"But I get what you're saying." She took a deep breath. "Does this have anything to do with Mabel?"

He didn't say a thing.

"Fair enough." Kitty hugged herself. "You two have fun." She waved at Samantha through the window, then blew her a kiss.

Samantha waved.

Jensen climbed into his truck. "You ready, little miss? I say we get a sundae piled high with cookie dough and cherries and whipped cream and chocolate sauce."

Samantha's face squinched up. "Gross, Daddy. Icky."

Jensen laughed. "Is it? What do you want?"

"Vanilla." She bounced her legs in her seat. "Please."

"Coming up." He put the truck in gear and headed to the Buttermilk Pie Café, listening to Samantha sing—at the top of her lungs—her favorite princess movie song.

Why was it so hard for his father to accept he wasn't the only one who felt affection for Samantha? He understood that family came first; he'd grown up hearing those words over and over. But the older he got, the more he began to question what that really meant. Did it mean making sure they were healthy and safe or did it mean carrying on a tradition of hate that had no place in the here and now? As far as he was concerned, he had an obligation to his daughter not to instill blind hate over something that happened so long ago the details were all circumspect.

The fact of the matter was, the details didn't matter. Whether or not Hannah Monroe picked a Crawley or a Briscoe generations back shouldn't decide whether a Crawley could pick a Briscoe today.

Does this have anything to do with Mabel? *It has everything to do with Mabel.* There was nothing he'd have liked more than to sit down beside her tonight. His father might think Miss Martha needed to "hush her mouth" but Jensen was glad the woman had spoken up tonight. There was no easy answer here. Next time he had the chance, he'd find out exactly what Mabel wanted. After he told her what he wanted. Her. He wanted her. A life with her. There was nothing he wanted more. If Mabel gave them a chance, he'd be asking her to face all sorts of ridicule and disappointment from her family. If she rejected him, it'd hurt something fierce, but he'd understand.

The worst thing he could do was stay silent. He didn't want to live with that sort of regret.

"Daddy, what's wrong?" Samantha's voice reached him.

"Nothin, little miss." He winked at her in the rearview mirror. "Nothing at all."

CHAPTER TWELVE

"THANKS FOR DOING THIS," Mabel said, climbing into Hattie's big half-ton game warden truck and pulling the door closed behind her.

"It's no skin off my nose." Hattie grinned. "Besides, it's sort of romantic." She put the truck in gear and drove out onto the county road. "Sneaking around."

"I should never have said anything." Mabel closed her eyes. "It's not romantic, Hattie. It's…pathetic."

"Hush now." Hattie wagged her finger back and forth in denial. "This thing will take some figuring out, that's for sure. But you know he cares about you."

I do. Mabel folded her hands on her lap and stared at them. *But he has no idea how I feel.* After Miss Martha's speech, she'd been pondering her options. Tell Jensen how she felt, risk it all or leave and let things go back to the way they were.

"Mabel." Hattie blew out a slow breath. "All you can do is try, right?"

At lunchtime, Jensen had texted her. He'd kept it short. We have a window from three to four today, if you're free?

Mabel hadn't hesitated to send a response. I'm free. See you and Stardust soon.

But this time, she knew she couldn't borrow clothes and the work truck without raising eyebrows and facing a whole slew of questions when she got home. It was Hattie who had come up with the idea. They'd been planning on meeting up for dinner so Hattie offered to come pick her up. She'd drop her with Jensen, come back and pick her up, and they'd have their dinner as planned.

Now Mabel was cruising down the road toward the Crawley Ranch with a stomach full of nerves and clammy hands. She rubbed them on her skirt, wishing she knew what the right thing to do was.

"You look nice." Hattie smiled. "Much better than the last getup. But if we're being honest, it wasn't all that hard to top."

Mabel managed a smile.

It'd been two days since she and Jensen had kissed and the fish fry, two days since Jensen and Samantha had left the senior Crawley openmouthed and staring after them. But Dwight Crawley wasn't the only one staring after them. The Ladies Guild would likely have a field day interpreting what had taken place. As much as she didn't want to think that she was the cause of whatever obvious disagreement father and son had had, the odds were against her.

Forrest had watched the exchange with narrowed eyes—before shifting his attention her way. He had questions, but she wasn't ready to give answers.

Hattie chattered on about some baby raccoons she'd be taking custody of in the morning. "I might be calling you."

Mabel nodded. "Raccoons, huh? I've never worked with raccoons before."

"I have a feeling Princess Mabel can make any animal feel better." Hattie smiled. "That little girl sure adores you. And the whole princess thing? That's adorable."

"Princess thing? Doesn't every little girl like princesses?"

"I guess so. I didn't… But that's just me." Hattie glanced her way. "You do know she thinks you are a real live bona fide princess. Right?"

"What? What are you talking about, Hattie?" Yes, Samantha was all about the princesses, but she couldn't think Mabel was one.

"Well, I'm pretty sure you're the only one that doesn't know that. She waltzed into The Calico Pig the other day, proudly announcing that she had met the royalty of Garrison, Texas. Twyla Crawley looked like she'd swallowed a fly." Hattie chuckled. "I know that's mean of me. But sometimes that Twyla can be so high and mighty."

Mabel was lost in her own thoughts the remainder of the ride. From the princess thing to Miss Martha's advice to the shock on Mr. Crawley's face when his son and granddaughter had left the fish fry. It was a lot. A whole lot. And every time she went over it again, she was more divided. When Hattie turned on her blinker, then pulled into the longer gravel drive leading toward Crawley Ranch, Mabel's case of nerves quadrupled.

Just like last time, Jensen was waiting for her. Unlike last time, she felt a little more prepared. Maybe it was because she had taken a little more time with her appearance. And the fact that she was wearing clothes that actually fit her. Maybe wearing a skirt wasn't the most practical attire, but her family thought she was going for a girls' night with Hattie so...

"Hattie." Jensen nodded. "Good to see you."

"I can't stay. I'm still on the clock." Hattie slid her aviator sunglasses in place. "I'll be back in an hour. Y'all have fun."

When Jensen turned to face her, Mabel blurted out, "Samantha thinks I'm a real princess?"

"Ah. About that." He ran his hand along the back of his neck. "She does."

Mabel crossed her arms over her chest and stared at him. "How? Why?"

Jensen shrugged. "She came up with it all on her own. It seemed harmless enough at the time. And it makes her happy." His dark blue eyes traveled over her face. "I thought she'd figure it out eventually. Then again, I hadn't expected her to curtsy for your uncle and brother." He shook his head, but there was a smile on his face.

"It all makes so much sense now." She laughed. "As far as that goes, she's won them all over." The problem with Jensen smiling was how ridiculously off-balance it made her feel. At the moment, she was having a hard time not staring at his lips. Or thinking about that kiss. Or all the things she wanted to say to him. *If only I knew if I should.*

It didn't help that he was looking at her like he'd looked at her before he'd kissed her. She took a deep breath.

He did, too. "So… I'll see if I can't get her interested in something else. Dinosaurs. I liked dinosaurs growing up. Maybe then she won't be so stuck on the whole princess thing." He shook his head. "I get the feeling Stardust has been waiting for you so we might as well head inside."

Mabel didn't say anything; she just followed along behind him. Since she'd gotten his text earlier, she'd sort of imagined a variety of scenarios for this afternoon. She had things that she wanted to say to him, but she got tongue-tied and overwhelmed at the idea of saying such words to Jensen, the real Jensen walking ahead of her—not the Jensen in her head. This Jensen was loyal to his family and daughter and she didn't want to get in the way of that. It was one of the things she loved most about him.

He opened the barn door and the two of them walked inside, the temperature dropping a good fifteen degrees. "It's awful hot out today."

"And seasonably so." *Now we're talking about the weather?* "Jensen…"

Jensen turned, coming to a complete stop.

Her planned "I'd like to talk to you" would not come out. Instead, she said, "What do you think Samantha is going to say when she meets Stardust?"

A smile formed on Jensen's mouth. "Well, she has this new favorite bedtime story about a horse that looks an awful lot like Stardust." Had he taken a step closer? Or was it her imagination? "Her favorite person, a real-life princess, gave it to her."

Mabel was frozen. Her lungs emptied and her heart picked up speed. Waiting. Hoping.

"She loves you, you know. You walk into a room and she lights up and gets an extra spring in her step." He was definitely closer now.

"I love her, too." If she reached out, she could put her hand on his chest. She was having a hard time breathing normally.

Jensen seemed to be weighing his words. He was being cautious, she could tell. Part of her wanted him to…go for it and let it all out. "I've been thinking a lot about what Miss Martha said." He swallowed, the muscles of his neck working. "About us."

Us. She pushed the hair from her shoulder, holding one strand and twining it around her finger, fidgeting. "I guess I have to."

He nodded. "I was hoping we were on the same page." His hand rested against her cheek, warm and solid.

"I don't know, Jensen." Her eyes searched his, an ache filling her chest. "Miss Martha is a brave woman. I've never been brave."

Jensen stared at her, looking confused. "You? Mabel, I don't know of a single person that would leave the comfort of their home to camp out in tents in horrible weather. You put up with miserable conditions with no guarantee that the animals you are working so hard to protect will be safe. Maybe that's not bravery in your book, but it is in mine. I'd say it's fearless. You're fearless." His hand brushed against hers as he let the strand of her hair slide between his fingers.

He thought she was fearless? She was terrified to tell him she loved him—terrified of how this would impact the lives of everyone she loved. And yet, she had to tell him. She had to. Here and now. "Jensen… I'm not fearless… I… You…"

Jensen dropped her hair and took a step back. "I understand, Mabel." There was a sadness to his smile that tore at her heart. "I do. It's not what I want for us but—"

She stepped forward, pressing one finger over his lips. "I'm scared to death, but I'll try to get it out." She took a deep breath.

The resounding slam of the door at the far end of the barn jolted them both.

"Where, Paw-Paw?" Samantha's voice reached them.

"Your daddy wants to keep it a surprise, but I couldn't wait a moment longer." Mr. Crawley chuckled. "But don't tell on me, or your daddy will be spittin' fire."

Mabel watched as understanding rolled over Jensen. His jaw locked tight and he braced himself for what was to come.

"You've got to be kidding me." He ran a hand over his face. "Stubborn old fool." He swallowed hard. "Mabel, I hate to ask, but can you come with me? Please. My dad? That horse? I don't want things getting out of hand. Well…more out of hand."

If he wanted her here, she'd stay. "Okay." But Jensen was already walking away so she hurried to catch up.

Everything seemed to happen in slow motion. Samantha, seeing the horse. Mr. Crawley, all smiles—until he saw Jensen… And her. Stardust, snorting and wary with so many people staring at her. When Jensen reached his father, the two of them started in on each other. Luckily, Samantha was too entranced by Stardust to notice. So entranced that she slid between the rungs of the pipe fence and into the corral with the horse. That was what set Mabel in motion.

Samantha went running across the corral toward the horse. Mabel went running after her.

"Samantha! Stop. You don't want to spook her." Mabel tried to keep her voice calm, but the closer Samantha got the more fearful Mabel became.

Samantha heard her, though, and did as she was told. She turned into a little statue and waited for Mabel. "I'm sorry. I got excited. She's so beautiful. She looks just like the horse from my bedtime story."

"This is Stardust, Samantha. You remember how you used to be before you rode on Firefly?" She waited for Samantha to nod before going on. "Well, that's kind of how Stardust feels about people."

"Oh." Samantha stared up at the horse. "I'm sorry, Stardust. I didn't mean to scare you."

Mabel squeezed Samantha's shoulder gently. "She knows that. And I think, in time, she will follow you around just like the horse in your bedtime story that follows the princess around."

"I have to be patient?" Samantha hadn't taken her eyes off the horse. "Is there anything I can do to let her know I'm a friend?"

Mabel held her hand out to Stardust. "It's okay now. Everything is okay. Samantha is yours. And she will take good care of you from now on."

Stardust snorted, her ears swiveling forward and her tail swishing as she stared down at Samantha.

"Hi." Samantha waved at the horse. "That's me, I'm Samantha."

Mabel smiled. "Why don't you and I go find her an apple?" She took Samantha's hand and started to lead her back across the corral. Neither one of them noticed Mr. Crawley until he was face-to-face with Mabel.

"Samantha, get yourself in the main house." Mr. Crawley was red-faced with a vein popping out on his forehead—struggling to keep his anger under control.

"Do what your grandfather says, Samantha." The last thing Mabel wanted for this little girl was to see her grandfather go from somebody loving to somebody mean. "You can find the perfect apple."

"Okay, are you sure?" Samantha looked back and forth between the two of them, fully aware of the tension between the two adults. "Are you mad, Paw-Paw? I know I shouldn't have run at the horse—"

"*You* didn't do a thing, sweetie pie." His tone had lost its snap. "I just need a moment with Miss Briscoe here."

"No, you don't." Jensen came striding across the corral. "I asked Mabel to come here. We need her help."

Mabel wasn't sure whether to escort Samantha out of the barn or to send the little girl on her way alone. But seeing the worry on Samantha's face helped Mabel make up her mind. "Let's go find that apple."

"You are not taking her anywhere." Mr. Crawley grabbed Samantha's arm. "You need to leave."

"Dad, let Samantha go." Jensen's tone was gruff, but he managed to keep control.

"I don't understand you, son. Why would you have her here? Why would you trust her?" He started across the corral, dragging a shocked and wide-eyed Samantha with him.

Stardust went on the defensive. The horse pawed the dirt with one hoof and shook her head. A few sidesteps and a sharp snort warned Mabel. Mr. Crawley's voice and posture had upset the animal, and this time, Mabel feared the horse wasn't going to stop. Mabel managed to push the old man and Samantha out of the way, but in the process, the sharp-hooved blow Stardust had intended for Mr. Crawley slammed into Mabel's shoulder.

Mabel wasn't sure who was more upset, Samantha or Stardust. It hurt, to be sure, but she knew now wasn't the moment to fall apart. Both of them needed reassurance. Both of them needed to understand that she knew this was an accident. Stardust wasn't trying to hurt Samantha or Mabel; she was trying to defend them from a strange man making lots of noise and jerky movements.

Stardust came up to Mabel, pressing her nose against Mabel's chest.

"I'm fine." She rested the hand of her uninjured arm on Stardust's neck. "I'm fine."

Samantha wrapped her little arms around Mabel's legs and held on tight.

But it was Jensen's soft touch that almost broke her. "Are you okay? Anything broken?" She shook her head, but he didn't quite believe her. "Mabel, now is not the time to be brave."

"This is exactly the time to be brave."

He sighed, nodding an understanding. "Fine. Just tell me where it hurts." He was careful, feeling her shoulder for any break. Once it was clear she didn't need immediate medical attention, his hands stayed warm and strong against the middle of her back.

"I won't have an animal with that kind of temperament on my property, you hear me?" Mr. Crawley had the good sense to keep his voice down this time. But there was no denying the man was outraged.

"I'll give her to Mabel."

"Oh no, you will not." Mr. Crawley bowed up. "Don't you think that was the plan all along? Her getting all close to you and Samantha, just so she could get a hold of that horse. To spite you. To spite me."

Mabel was horrified to realize the man truly believed what he was saying. "Mr. Crawley, I give you my word that was never my intention."

"The word of a Briscoe?" Mr. Crawley snorted. "I've already told you to leave once. You best get now. Before I call the authorities."

"Dad, you need to calm down. I can't take care of Samantha and Mabel with you tossing out threats and getting your blood pressure in an uproar. Take Samantha inside. I'll be there in a minute." It wasn't a suggestion.

"Family comes before all else, you know that. This woman isn't family, son." His father looked so disappointed it was like a slap to the face. Mabel hurt for Jensen.

"I want her to be, Dad. I want Mabel to be part of my family." Jensen's hand stayed firm against her back. "I love this woman and no matter how much you rail at me, you can't change that."

The shock and contempt on Mr. Crawley's face stole the comfort of Jensen's touch. "Well, that's your choice. Her? Or me? Because if you're with her, you're no longer a Crawley."

Right then and there, no matter how much it was going to hurt, Mabel knew what she had to do.

JENSEN FELT LIKE he'd been punched in the gut. Over and over. Pretty much the way he'd felt when Forrest Briscoe had used him like a punching bag. But it wasn't just his body being battered. It was his heart. He knew his father could be stubborn. And opinionated. And yet, the idea that his father would turn his back on him had never crossed his mind. Not seriously. Sure, his father had his moments and his fits, but he got over it. This was different. He could see it on his father's face and hear it in his voice. It might be that the hate he bore the Briscoes was stronger than the love he had for his son.

"Mr. Crawley." Mabel took a deep breath, supporting her injured arm with the other. "That's not necessary. I know tempers are high and this is a...highly stressful situation, but I was here to help with the horse. As fond as I am of Samantha, I'd never considered a future with Jensen. I know that could never work."

No. It could work. They could be wonderful. *And you know that.* He'd seen it in her face moments before they were interrupted. She felt this thing between them, yet she was throwing it away. Why was she saying this?

"If I said or did something to make you believe differently, I'm sorry." She took another deep breath and turned those tear-filled sky blue eyes upon him. "Your dad's right. Family comes first. I've lost enough of mine to be able to appreciate that."

He'd lost people, too. But his father's argument was flawed. Blood didn't make you family, love did.

"Samantha." Mabel reached down to pat his daughter on the back. "Everything is okay. I'll help you find a good home for your rock at the next Junior Rangers meeting. Sound good?" She smiled down at Samantha's upturned face. "Dry your tears, everything is fine."

Nothing was fine. Jensen felt hollowed out. Raw and bleeding on the inside.

"Well, then." His father regarded Mabel closely. "If you want to buy that horse, I'll sell her to you. For what I paid for her at auction."

"It's a deal." Mabel went to hold her hand out for a handshake, but wound up wincing and cradling her arm against her chest. "I'm gonna call and see if I can get a ride home."

"I think you should go to the clinic. And I'll take you." Jensen wasn't ready to say goodbye, not this way. Not with so much left unsaid.

"No, I already texted Hattie. I'll be fine." Her eyes locked with his. "I'm not your problem, Jensen. And just so you *both* know, I would never use what happened here today against your family."

"Well, I have witnesses, but let's hope it doesn't come to that." His father grunted, dismissing her. "You go on and get checked out. You can pick up the horse later. As soon as I get my money, that is." He turned, stalking back across the corral and out to the gate he'd left open.

Jensen could hardly breathe. He had to fix this. He had to make it right—so she'd understand how much he needed her in his life. She had to know. She had to see they were meant to be. No matter what their families—his father—might say. He turned, committing her every feature to memory. "Mabel—"

"No." She shook her head. "I'm not Miss Martha. I am not brave. Not brave enough to face *this* every day." She nodded in the direction his father had gone. "You are a good man, Jensen. You'll find the right woman." She patted Stardust's back and smiled at Samantha. "I'll send one of the ranch hands over with the trailer later. And the check." She didn't sound happy. She sounded sad—but she was trying, so hard, for Samantha. "How about you walk me out, Samantha?

You can keep me company until Miss Hattie gets here."

"Okay." Samantha sniffed, frowning at the way Mabel was holding her arm. "Need a Band-Aid or ice or something?"

"I'll make sure to get ice and a Band-Aid when I get home, I promise." Mabel ran her hand over Samantha's curls.

Jensen could tell it pained her to smile, but she did so, for his little girl. He stood beside Stardust, racking his brain for something to say to make her stay. She had to know how he felt—he'd said he wanted her to be his family. *And she said no.* If she meant that, there was no point going after her.

Stardust nudged him between the shoulders, nibbling at his shirt and blowing hard.

Jensen turned, running a hand along the horse's back. He hadn't told Mabel what he found out. "I guess I should tell her? Before she goes?" He patted Stardust on the neck and followed Mabel and Samantha from the barn. "I wanted to tell you… I found something else out about Stardust." He had a hard time looking at her. He had a hard time not looking at her.

Mabel looked surprised. "Oh?"

"She'd been a one-family horse. But the

girl's family fell on hard times and they had
to sell her—which was hard on the horse
and the girl that owned her." He lowered
his voice, not wanting Samantha to hear the
rest. "Stardust was being transported when
the truck pulling the trailer was in a multi-
car pileup. It was bad. They found her on
the side of the road with her leg and haunch
tangled up in barbed wire." He shielded his
eyes, Hattie's truck already coming down the
drive. Panic rose up and his heart lodged itself in his throat.

"Poor Stardust." Mabel shook her head.
"It makes sense. All the sudden changes—
then that trauma and pain without the person she'd had her whole life. It's no wonder
Stardust's so skittish." She glanced his way,
then stooped to Samantha's level to say, "I'll
see you at Junior Rangers."

"Okay. Don't forget the ice and the Band-
Aid." Samantha gave Mabel a quick hug. "I
love you."

He caught Mabel's wince when she hugged
Samantha back. "I love you, too." She didn't
look his way as she said, "Thank you… For
everything. I'm sorry, about today. About…
everything." Her voice broke, but she set off
for Hattie's truck before he could stop her.

Hattie's truck had barely come to a stop before Mabel was climbing into the passenger seat and slamming the door. She said something, but she was too far away for Jensen to hear. Whatever it was, Hattie gave him a little salute, turned her truck around and drove off.

"Is Mabel going to be okay?" Samantha reached up and took his hand. "Is Paw-Paw still mad?" She paused, tugging on his hand. "What's wrong, Daddy?"

"Everything will be fine, little miss, don't you fret." At least, he hoped it would. *How?* He had no idea. As much as he wanted to soothe Samantha's worries, he was too heartsick to say more.

As he and Samantha headed across the lawn to the house, Kitty and Twyla got home. They must have passed Hattie and Mabel, because the two of them started asking questions right away.

"Paw-Paw got angry and Stardust got scared and Miss Mabel saved Paw-Paw and got her shoulder hurt. And then Paw-Paw told her she had to leave and that she could buy Stardust and then Miss Hattie picked her up…" All of a sudden, Samantha started to cry. "She got hurt real bad, didn't she?"

Kitty and Twyla both looked to him for an answer.

A vise clamped tightly around his heart as he scooped his daughter up. "Miss Mabel is stronger than she looks, Samantha. Miss Hattie will see that she's taken care of. And she has a whole bunch of brothers and an uncle that will take real good care of her when she gets home." It gave him some comfort to know she had so many people looking after her; he just wished he could be one of them.

"Goodness, what a day." Twyla was frowning. "Where is Daddy now?"

"I told him to go inside and calm down. To say he was in a temper is putting it mildly." Even now, Jensen struggled to control the anger his father's words had stirred.

"I guess I'll go check on him." Twyla headed inside. "Come on, Samantha, let's get you a cupcake and some apple juice and one of your princess movies going. Sound good?"

"Can I, Daddy?" Samantha wiped at her tears.

"Of course. That sounds good to me. Just save me a cupcake." He gave her a wink as she walked off with Twyla.

"Are you okay? You don't look okay."

Kitty rubbed his arm. "Did something happen? Beyond the whole horse-attack, Daddy-yelling, Mabel-fleeing stuff you already mentioned?"

"No." He had no doubt his father would share all with his sister soon enough. He didn't think Kitty would give him any grief. Twyla was another story. "I just…humiliated myself, is all."

Kitty rubbed his arm again. "I doubt that."

He stared down at her. "I guess not. I just…told her how I felt. In front of Dad." He shook his head, trying not to get angry all over again. "I tried. That's more than some people can say." He forced himself to smile.

"Is that some kind of dig?" She lifted her hand. "Are you saying *I* haven't tried?"

"I don't recall saying your name." He shrugged. "Though it might not hurt if you let Tyson know you're interested. The man seems to keep his eyes focused on whatever is directly in front of him. So, unless you stand directly in front of him 24/7, you're going to have to give him a little help."

Kitty did not look pleased with this announcement, but she took his hand and led him back into the house.

"We need to finish what we started." His

father was sitting in his favorite leather recliner, a large glass of iced tea in his hand.

A quick scan of the room revealed that Samantha and Twyla were gone. "You did enough talking. It's your turn to listen. You are my father. I have always given you respect. It's time you did the same for me. The things you just said to the woman I love makes my blood boil." He took a deep breath, flexing his hands. "Mabel couldn't help that she was born into her family any more than I could pick being born into this one. She is a good woman. A strong woman. Selfless and kind. She came here, knowing she was hated, to help Samantha and that horse. Without a single thought for herself." He had his father's full attention now. Kitty's, too. "I have to ask myself, Dad, how am I going to raise my daughter in this house and preserve her free spirit and loving nature? Whether or not Mabel loves me, my little girl isn't going to grow up hating Briscoes just because they are Briscoes. What Kitty and Twyla decide to do is their choice. This is mine. I won't hold any person living under the Briscoe roof accountable for the things their great-great-grandparents did."

"I'm supposed to forget that that Forrest

boy broke your nose and beat you senseless?" His father spat out the words.

"If I can forgive him, then so can you. Honestly, I understand why he did what he did. He was out of his head with grief. It was like that for me when Casey died. But I didn't lash out. I couldn't, I had Samantha to think of. Forrest had lost his parents and the big brother he idolized... Of course he was angry. That wasn't about me or him or our history. I know it. He knows it. Now it's up to you to come to terms with that."

His father stared at him for a long time. So long that the ice in his tea glass shifted and clanked against the sides. "You'd have picked her, wouldn't you?"

Jensen wasn't prepared for the sting in his eyes. "It doesn't matter now, does it?"

"You really think that girl could make you happy?" His father couldn't seem to grasp the concept.

"She did make me happy, she does." He knew if he didn't get out of there soon, he'd start lashing out, too. Today he'd lost the only future he'd looked forward to in a long time. Losing Casey had taught him how to go through the motions, no matter how hard he was grieving or hurting on the inside. But he wasn't sure he could do that, go on like nothing had happened, when he saw Mabel around town. How was he supposed to smile and act normal when he looked at her? If she went back to Wyoming, he'd miss seeing her, and the hollow ache in his chest would still be there. Either way, his heart was broken and hurting something fierce and there wasn't anything he could do to change it.

CHAPTER THIRTEEN

IN THE WEEK and a half since the ordeal at Crawley Ranch, Mabel had done her best to lie low. Her shoulder was bruised something fierce, but was otherwise okay. She'd mumbled something about falling off a horse to her brothers and, even though it was an obvious lie, they'd left her alone. Maybe they could tell she was broken inside and were too scared to trigger tears and having to deal with them to push her for more. Whatever the reason, she was grateful.

Even though she knew she'd done the right thing, Mabel couldn't stop the ache in her chest. It was there all the time. While she was making breakfast, working with Stardust, hanging out with Hattie and Kelly and Brooke, or lying in bed hearing Jensen telling his father he loved her.

I want Mabel to be part of my family. Those were the words that triggered her tears every time. A family, with Jensen and Samantha. She wanted that—with every fiber of her being. *Jensen wouldn't think I'm brave if he knew I was crying myself to sleep every night.* Every night since she'd climbed into Hattie's truck and away from Crawley Ranch.

As happy as they were that she'd decided to stay in Garrison for a few weeks longer to care for Stardust, her uncle and brothers were worried about her, she could tell. That was why she'd forced herself to be extra chipper this morning and gush on about how exciting the day's Junior Ranger expedition to erste Baum park was.

She was looking forward to it—to seeing Samantha. But she'd almost canceled on Hattie for fear of her reaction if Jensen showed up. She'd sent him a quick text, asking him not to come. He'd responded in seconds. One word. Okay. She'd felt ten times better and twenty times worse.

"You good?" Hattie asked, looking up from her clipboard. "You look tuckered out."

"I'm good." Mabel's smile felt tight. "I am." She sighed. "Stop looking at me like that, Hattie. I'm here—I'm trying."

"Okay, okay." Hattie patted her arm.

"But I am tired so maybe don't give me a

group with Levi?" she added, smiling more naturally now.

"I'll do my best." Hattie shook her head, then started laughing. Then stopped, her eyes going wide.

"What?" Mabel asked, panicking. Was he here? Jensen? She hesitated, then turned to see what had Hattie so shaken.

The last person Mabel had expected to see at the Junior Rangers meeting was Dwight Crawley. She blinked, squinting. It was him all right. The man who'd made his opinion of her crystal clear and stolen any chance at her happiness was walking toward her, holding Samantha's hand. He was smiling, talking to his granddaughter, acting like nothing out of the usual was taking place. Before Mabel could react, Samantha was running straight at her.

"Mabel, Mabel!" Samantha launched herself at Mabel's legs, twining her little arms around them and squeezing her oh-so-tight.

"It's good to see you, too, little miss." It was. She'd missed Samantha's smiles and laughter and her hugs most of all. Since they had an audience, she managed what she hoped was a civil smile for Mr. Crawley. "Mr. Crawley."

"Miss Briscoe," he said.

Mabel blinked, surprised by the older man's tone. Where was the sarcasm? The bite? Or hostility? He sounded almost... pleasant.

"Are we going to find a home for my rock?" Samantha reached into her pocket, then into her other pocket. "Paw-Paw, I think I left my rock in the truck." She pointed at the truck sitting in the parking lot.

"Well, go on and get it, then." Mr. Crawley nodded, patting Samantha on the head. "I can see you."

He might be a horrible person to *her*, but there was no denying he loved his granddaughter.

"Okay, Paw-Paw, I'll run fast like a velocee-rapatar," Samantha said, dashing off.

"Velociraptor?" Hattie asked.

"It's a dinosaur. Couldn't tell you which one. Looks like it's a fast one. Jensen's idea." He frowned, shaking his head.

Mabel was torn between laughing and crying.

"Here we go." Hattie winced as the shrieks of little Abigail Koch reached them. "I better go put out that fire." She gave a little wave as she ran toward the kids.

"Good luck," Mabel said. Then she turned, intending to help Samantha search for her rock, when Mr. Crawley stopped her.

"Hold on, Miss Briscoe, I'd like a word," Mr. Crawley said. "I want to know why you lied to my boy."

Mabel blinked, completely thrown off guard. "I'm not sure I understand what you're talking about." Her heart started thumping.

His raised eyebrows and crooked grin told her he wasn't buying it. "My boy says he loves you. And you're telling me you don't love him?"

"That's what I said." Mabel glanced toward the truck, willing Samantha to hurry back. "That's all settled and done now so—"

"I know that's what you *said*, I was standing right there. I just can't figure out why." He scratched his head, giving her a hard look. "But then, I thought about what my boy said after you left. How he came in, all puffed up and self-righteous, to let me know how things were going to be from now on. I have to say, it's been a long time since I'd seen my boy so determined. So...alive." He sighed. "He was going on about you, good and kind and all that nonsense, and all I could think about was you lying."

Mabel had never been so enraged. "I didn't lie, Mr. Crawley." She had a hard time getting the words out. She was lying now and it didn't come easy to her. "Besides, I plan to go back to Wyoming soon." *It would just be easier for all of us if I disappeared.*

"Is that so?" He wasn't even pretending to look at Samantha anymore. He was full-on staring at her, and he was angry. "Turning tail and running, eh? The Briscoe way."

"If you're here to get a rise out of me, Mr. Crawley, I'm sorry to disappoint you. I don't buy into this feud or the wasted energy and missed opportunities it's cost both our families." She forced a smile. "I'll let you and Samantha enjoy the hike—"

"I'm not staying. I have no interest in any of this. I came here to see *you*." He scratched his head again, looking frustrated. "I have to say, Miss Briscoe, I was expecting a different reaction."

"To what?" Mabel's patience was beginning to wear thin. "I don't understand why you're here or what you're after, Mr. Crawley. Maybe you could give me a hint."

"Come on now, girl, don't make me say it." He let out a long, slow breath, part groan of exasperation. "I might be old and stuck in my ways, but there are a few exceptions. Those would be my children. And my grandchildren—I'm expecting to have a whole passel of them by the time everyone's married off and settled." He seemed pleased by this announcement, so pleased Mabel had a hard time not smiling. "So, what I'm saying is, if he wants you, then he should have you."

Everything came to a screeching halt. "I'm sorry?" What had he just said? She hadn't heard right. She hadn't. If she had… She must have stepped into some sort of alternate universe. *Something.* "You're speaking to Mabel Briscoe. You realize that?" *What's happening?* "That I'm a Briscoe. And you are a Crawley. And that Jensen and I—"

"Love each other." He waited, his hands on his hips and his eyebrows high. "You might as well admit it, Mabel, because I've seen the way you look at my boy. It's the same way he looks at you." He seemed to be studying her, really seeing her. "I want my son to be happy. You make him happy. That's all I want for him. Even if I have to suffer having a Briscoe for family."

Mabel stared up at the older man, in shock. "Mr. Crawley…" She shook her head.

"Weren't expecting that, now, were ya?" He grinned.

"Are you…" She broke off. "This isn't some sort of joke?"

"I wish." He chuckled. "But no. I'm serious, Mabel. You have my word on that."

She waited, staring at him until she believed him. She did. "I… I can't decide whether to hug you or never speak to you again."

"I wouldn't mind a hug. If you're staying here, and not running off to Wyoming, I'm thinking you'll be staying for my boy. And Samantha." He nodded. "Not talking to me ever again isn't really an option."

"I found it. I found my rock." Samantha came running, her little painted rock held high.

Mabel had never felt so torn. Part of her wanted to stay and have fun with Samantha. The other part of her wanted to run as fast as she could to Jensen.

"Samantha, honey, Mabel got called on some official princess business." Mr. Crawley stooped, whispering, "It's a secret. But I told her I'd stay with you so she could go do it."

He was going along with the princess thing? He was the last person Mabel had ex-

pected to... After this morning, Mabel suspected getting to know Dwight Crawley was
going to be an adventure.

Samantha stared up at her. "Oh, Mabel,
hurry. Paw-Paw will help me. You go to your
princess duties."

"And tell the prince he's got my blessing.
Get a move on." Mr. Crawley took her hand
and gave it a gentle squeeze. "You go on."

Mabel ran down the path, climbed into
the Briscoe Ranch truck and threw it into
gear. There was no rush; she knew that. No,
that wasn't true. She didn't want to waste
one more minute. She'd take as much time
as she could, savor every precious minute,
with him at her side.

En route, she called the Mustang Foundation and explained she wasn't coming back.
They were sad to see her go, but wished her
happiness.

I'm working on it.

The drive to the Crawleys' ranch had never
seemed so long. *And I never imagined driving a Briscoe ranch truck down the drive
of Crawley Ranch.* But Mabel was smiling
all the same. She parked, climbed down and
paused. Normally, Jensen was here waiting
for her. As it was, she didn't know where to

look for him. For all she knew, he was out riding somewhere.

She pulled her phone from her pocket and sent a quick text. At the barn. Need a minute. She pressed Send and leaned against the hood of the truck. But five minutes turned into ten, and ten turned into fifteen, and Mabel's impatience got the better of her.

She headed along the path, exploring things with new eyes. This was Crawley land. Jensen's home. A place she was no longer banished from. She stood atop the hill, taking in the primary barns, livestock pens, chutes and exercise wheel, and several small outbuildings and what appeared to be a bunkhouse or two. It was an impressive setup, busy, but orderly. She paused long enough to appreciate the view.

Where are you, Jensen?

"Mabel?"

She spun at the sound of Jensen's voice, her smile wavering when she caught sight of him. "What's wrong?"

He ran a hand along the back of his neck and shrugged. "Nothing. You said you needed a minute?"

Mabel had never seen him this way. He had dark stubble on his jaw, his eyes were bloodshot, and he had a general rumpled appearance. A far cry from the normally well-put-together man she'd come to expect. Not that this Jensen was any less beautiful than the well-put-together one. He was still Jensen, after all. And he needed to know she loved him. So much. She took a deep breath. "Your dad came to the Junior Rangers meeting tonight. Did you know that?"

Jensen closed his eyes and shook his head. "Whatever he said, Mabel, I'm sorry. I was hoping we'd hashed everything out the other night."

The other night when Jensen had said whatever he'd said to make his father come around. "What happened?"

"Nothing." He avoided her gaze. "I'll talk to him when he gets home. He has no right to keep pestering you. You've made your feelings known. You're no longer a threat to his precious family... He's just a stubborn old fool."

She stepped forward. "You look tired."

The muscle in his jaw clenched. "I haven't been sleeping. It'll pass."

"Why haven't you been sleeping?" She frowned.

"Mabel." His gaze met hers, and fell away. "Is there a reason you're here?"

"I'm here to apologize." She swallowed when his eyes found hers. He was doing his best to keep his distance, she could tell, and it tore at her heart. She'd done this to him. *I have to fix it. I have to be brave.*

JENSEN HAD NEVER been so happy to see someone—and so desperate for them to go. He'd done his part, left her alone, but now she was here. Those sky blue eyes of hers were staring at him, too full of warmth. And asking him why he was tired? Like she cared about him. *You don't.* "I think we've said everything that needs saying, Mabel."

"No, you're wrong." She took a deep breath and then exhaled loudly. "You said I was brave. I want to be. If you'll give me another chance, I promise I won't let you down."

He shook his head, his fool heart so happy she was here. Like always, she had a hold on him. Even if he wanted to walk away, he couldn't. But she wasn't making sense. "I don't understand—"

"I'm sorry," she murmured. "I love you."

She loved him? He froze.

"I have always loved you." She stepped

forward, resting her hands on his chest as she stared up at him. "Always."

He didn't think when he pulled her into his arms. If he had, he would've remembered her shoulder injury. And once he did, he let her go. "I'm sorry. I'm so sorry. Your shoulder."

"It's fine." Mabel kept her arms tightly around him and buried her face against his chest. "I'm fine. More than fine." Her breath was warm through the fabric of his shirt. "Just tell me I'm not the reason you had a hard time sleeping."

"If I said that, I'd be lying." His hands cradled her face, tilting it back so he could see her. As happy as he was, a lingering doubt remained. "What about Wyoming? Hattie said you were all fired up and raring to go."

"I was." She gazed up at him. "But—"

"Because Mabel, I can't stand in your way." Watching her vlog had made it clear that looking after the wild mustangs was what she was meant to do. "I've seen what you do. I get how important that is. If that's truly where your heart lies—"

"Jensen Crawley, you have held my heart since the day you saved that horny toad on the school playground from RJ. You probably don't remember. RJ said he was going to step on it… Just to make me cry, I think. You were older. All knees and Adam's apple. And you were the most beautiful thing I had ever seen. Especially when you pushed RJ over, picked up the horny toad and carried him over to a big bunch of rocks. You said he'd be safe there."

Jensen didn't remember. "That's a long time ago, Mabel Briscoe." He shook his head. "Too long. I hope you won't be disappointed."

"I don't think that's possible." She shook her head. "I guess admitting I've had feelings for you since grade school might seem a little…pathetic." Her cheeks went red.

"No." *Pathetic* was the last word he'd use for Mabel. "Incredible, maybe." She'd cared about him all this time? How had he not known? "How did I get so lucky?"

Her smile was so bright, it warmed him through.

He smoothed her silky-soft hair from her forehead. "I've got some time to make up." There was no resisting her. "What I was going to say was, if your heart lies in Wyoming, we'll go with you. Me and Samantha, I mean." She blinked, going so still Jensen worried he'd gone too far too fast. "Or we… We can come visit you, whenever you want."

She stood on tiptoe and pressed a soft kiss against his lips. "You... You would do that? Go to Wyoming?"

"Yes." Her kiss had left him a little dazed, but oh-so-hopeful. "If it would make you happy? Yes."

"Your father surprised me today." He wasn't really in the mood to talk about his father at the moment, but she went on. "He came to the Junior Ranger event to give me a talking-to. The long and the short of it was he knew I'd said what I said so you wouldn't have to choose. He wants you to be happy and if I make you feel that way then I need to stop lying and be happy with you."

He'd never expected his father to come around, not ever. But Jensen would do anything to make Samantha happy. His father loved him that way, too, he supposed. And knowing that, knowing he didn't have to choose, that he had everything he could ever want, filled every hole and fracture in his heart with love. "He's as crusty and stubborn and hotheaded as they come, but he loves with his whole heart." He rested his forehead against hers. "The way I love you."

Her eyes fluttered shut. "Jensen." She whispered his name on a sigh. Sweet and soft and pure bliss. "We might need to rescue him."

"My father?" he asked, in no hurry to let her out of his arms.

"He stayed at Junior Rangers." She looked up at him, grinning. "He told Samantha I'd been called to do important princess duties and he was going to fill in for me at Junior Rangers."

"My father?" He couldn't picture it. "At Junior Rangers?"

"Who knows, maybe he'll teach Levi Williams some manners." Mabel rested her head against his chest. "He told me to tell the prince we have his blessing."

"I'm the prince?" He buried his nose in her hair.

"My prince." She nodded against his chest. "Or would you rather be a velociraptor? I'm fine either way."

"Something else to love about you—your willingness to adapt." Jensen chuckled. "Does this mean we have to have a theme wedding? Not dinosaurs, of course," he murmured against the top of her head.

Mabel pulled away and stared up at him.

He wasn't sure what to make of her expression. "What did I say?"

"I'm not sure," Mabel whispered. "Something about a wedding?"

He pressed a kiss to her forehead. "I want us to be a family, Mabel. I love you and, if you'll have me, I promise to save horny toads and one-eyed cats for you and love you every day for the rest of my life."

"I knew it was you. JC. I knew it." She laughed, but there were tears in her eyes. "Jensen..."

"Will you marry me, Mabel?" He laughed. "Even though your uncle and brothers are likely to argue and might not give us their blessing—"

"Yes, I will marry you." She stood on tiptoe and pressed her lips to his.

Kissing Mabel was beyond imagining. Kissing her wrapped him up, his heart, in all the exuberance and joy that made her Mabel—a mix of sweetness and passion. *And she's mine.* "I love you," he murmured against her lips.

"I've been wanting to say that for a long time," she said, breathless.

"You know, now that we're engaged, you can say it anytime you want." He wrapped a long dark strand of her hair around his fingers. "Or kiss me whenever you feel like it."

"Really?" she asked, smiling broadly. "Like…now?"

"Now works." He pressed a featherlight kiss against her lips and stared straight into those sky blue eyes, marveling that the love he saw there was for him. "I love you, Mabel Briscoe. Even though Tyson is likely to laugh and bring up the whole Romeo and Juliet of Garrison thing, I can't wait to tell the world you're mine."

"Romeo and Juliet?" She shook her head. "Us? No. Not us. We have a very happy ending."

"Like Samantha's fairy tales? And they lived happily ever after?" He grinned. "I like the sound of that."

"Exactly." She nodded.

"Happily ever after—starting now." It was a promise he'd keep. And to make it official, he drew her close and sealed it with a kiss.

* * * * *

Look for the next book in
Sasha Summers's
The Cowboys of Garrison, Texas, series—
coming soon!

HARLEQUIN SELECTS COLLECTION

19 FREE BOOKS IN ALL!

From Robyn Carr to RaeAnne Thayne to Linda Lael Miller and Sherryl Woods we promise (actually, GUARANTEE!) each author in the Harlequin Selects collection has seen their name on the *New York Times* or *USA TODAY* bestseller lists!